Nyteria Rising

Three planets, two wars, one union...

THE THIRD BOOK
IN
THE THIRTEENTH
SERIES

by

This book is published by
Grosvenor House Publishing Ltd
28-30 High Street, Guildford, Surrey, GU1 3EL.
www.grosvenorhousepublishing.co.uk

A CIP record for this book
is available from the British Library

ISBN 978-1-78148-761-7

Dedication

In loving memory

of

Jamie R - forever a teenager.

Deeply loved & missed.

*

And in recognition

of

Variety, the children's charity - improving

young lives every day.

*

Thank You

*

Visit: www.variety.org.uk

The Thirteenth Series in order:
The Thirteenth
The Turncoats
Nyteria Rising

Never, never, never believe any war will be smooth
and easy, or that anyone who embarks on the strange
voyage can measure the tides and hurricanes they
will encounter. The statesman who yields to war fever
must realise that once the signal is given, they are
no longer the master of policy but the slave of
unforeseeable and uncontrollable events.

Sir Winston Churchill

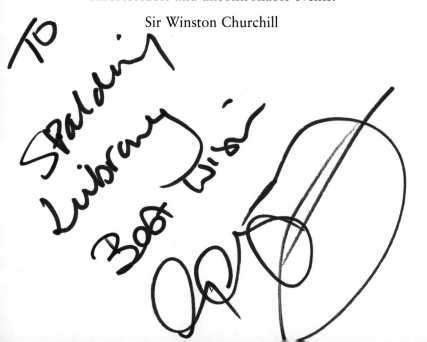

CHAPTER 1

The Prison Calls

The horrible grate and clunk of grinding gears sent shockwaves of noise over the otherwise peaceful roadway. Seconds later, Wendy's Morris traveller swerved erratically around the corner, arriving at far too swift a pace onto Sam's driveway. It jerked violently to a halt and then stalled, shuddering as if grateful to have survived.

In the driver's seat, Val Saunders grasped the steering wheel, her knuckles blue from the lack of circulation and gulped in oxygen, sweat droplets clinging for dear life on her forehead. "I can't do this!"

Her dad calmly undid his seatbelt. "Hunny, take a deep breath. You know it's fine, we just have to keep trying." Mike proceeded to peel his daughter's fingers off the wheel. "Val it's over now, please let go. Look at the positive side: you *didn't* set yourself on fire today." He chuckled quietly and took the keys from the ignition.

"Why can't I do this, Dad? I can catch a prisoner from another galaxy, but I can't reverse a car!" She slumped her head onto the wheel. They had been doing this for days and she felt no further advanced in skills or confidence.

"Sometimes we're better at some things than others, it doesn't mean you get to give up. Come on, your Mum's waiting for us."

1

It was so frustrating! She didn't want to drive; she had no interest in driving, but Zac had insisted that she learned after her little run-in with the Warden over her illegal teleports. He had pointed out that, on Earth, driving was a good way to travel. Plus, three trips in Sandy, the TVR with Jason had gone to his head. She climbed out of the car, flicking the L-plate next to the dent as she passed. "I'm not telling her about the bump, you can do that. It was your idea to go down that narrow street."

"It could have been worse," he replied, a hint of angst in his tone.

"In what way?" she groaned.

Mike shrugged his shoulders as he opened the door. "Susan we're back."

"How did it go?" she called from the kitchen.

"Better," Mike replied, placing his finger to his lips as Val rolled her eyes.

"Lovely. Lunch will be ready in fifteen."

"What are we hav..." Val grimaced as a shooting pain suddenly shot through her arm, sending all thoughts of food out of her head. She pulled her t-shirt sleeve up to reveal the tattoo on her arm; it was glowing and throbbing. That was odd; this tattoo had never given her any trouble before.

"Dad," she said. As she turned to him, her dad, who was standing next to her, changed rapidly from a solid form to a translucent ripple and then completely faded from sight. Screaming she reached out, "DAD!" But he was gone. What was happening to her? Her body felt like it was breaking into a million pieces. The pain was so intense. Then everything went dark.

*

Val's head was pounding as her vision started to return. Instinct warned her to protect herself. Was this Lailah attacking? Her stomach was churning and her legs were unstable. It was the most intense teleport she had ever experienced. She tried to stand, but found herself involuntarily dropping to her knees. Then she felt someone grabbing her arms. Glancing up she was met with an expression of intense annoyance.

"Stand up." The young Guard hauled her onto her feet. He released her quickly and stepped away, clearly uncomfortable.

"Thanks," she mumbled. As she regained her balance and control of her intestines, she took a moment to survey her surroundings. She recognised the corridors instantly. She was on Alchany. But it felt different: quiet and solemn Guards. She realised that the Guards were walking at a quickened pace, their heads hung low as if all in deep concentration. "How and why have you brought me here?" she demanded, straightening her t-shirt and reaching into her back pocket to check her sword was there.

"I didn't!" he grunted at her. "However..." he made a point of inspecting the tattoo which was still glowing on her arm. "Looks like a single journey loop extraction. It's used in emergencies to get specific Guards out of extreme situations quickly. And why? Because there's been a lock-down." he nudged her to start moving as she was causing congestion.

"What do you mean lock-down?"

"It means there's a serious problem and we need specific Guards to return, then they lock-down the portals, letting no-one on or off the Prison."

Suddenly a loud siren rang out, making Val physically jump and for a moment she couldn't hear what he was saying. "Why me? What's specific about me?" she bellowed as the siren stopped. She felt foolish as several Guards turned to glare at her.

"I really can't imagine," he replied, looking her up and down. "However, it may have something to do with the fact that the Warden has been taken."

Val's mouth gaped. "The Warden! What do you mean taken? Did someone come here and kidnap him?" She now understood why the others looked the way they did. The Warden was, apart from the Judges, the most important person on the Prison.

"Kidnap?" The Guard was clearly unfamiliar with the meaning of the word.

"Yeah - you know someone sneaked onto the planet whilst he was sleeping..." She stopped realising from the way his head was tilting to one side like a dog that he had no idea what she was talking about. "Forget it. I just can't imagine why they would need me." Surely they could see she still had enough to deal with back on Earth. Although Lailah hadn't made any significant moves since she'd arrived, that was probably only because she had no portal and no Dellatrax. In some ways Val wished she had attacked; waiting for something that never seemed to happen was worse. "So what exactly happened?" Val sympathised.

"He was off the Prison at the time of the attack. We believe this was the first phase of a full-scale assault. He relayed information warning us that we were to be attacked in the coming weeks and the next thing we heard, he had gone," the Guard told her as he pushed her along in front of him. "Why would the Warden have to go on an assault? Surely there are enough of you to do things like that?"

Val saw a visible penny dropping as he looked at her with even more distaste. "I recognise you now! You're the reject Guard. You clearly have no idea of the power that the Warden holds, or the battles we must fight here day-to-day. It shames me to say you are one of us. As a Guard, you stand shoulder to shoulder in an assault, irrelevant of rank."

Val came to a standstill, placing her hand onto his chest. "Stop right there. I think *shame* is a little over the top. And just so you know the facts, I'm not one of you; I'm half witch, so a little less of the reject."

"I find it hard to believe you are the one who arrested Excariot."

"Well I did, with help from my friends." She plumped her invisible feathers. Who did this Guard think he was?

"A lot of help I imagine. Now move!" he snapped.

"Where should I go?" she asked. The Guard wasn't going to help her and seeing a gap, he pushed past her. "You know, you could be nicer. I haven't been a Guard for very long." Val was starting to feel uneasy. "And my day's not going so well either. I just crashed my best friend's very old and crazily slow car into a wall," she called out to the back of the Guard's head as he mingled into the crowd.

"Did you just say you crashed my car!" a familiar voice chirped up.

"Wendy!" Val spun around to find a smiling face greeting her. "I've missed you so much."

They embraced. "Tell me my Mum's ok," Wendy whispered in Val's ear, a tremor of emotion in her voice.

"She's great, don't worry." Val stepped back and looked her up and down. Wendy was dressed all in dark green, in a military-style roll neck top and trousers. "Nice uniform, matches your eyes," she joked.

"Thanks. Have you heard about the Warden?" she asked.

"Yes, but I still don't know why I'm here? Is there somewhere I should go to check in or passport control?"

Wendy linked arms with Val to keep her moving. "Not just yet. We need to talk first."

"Why don't I like the sound of that?"

Wendy pulled her in close and whispered into her ear. "We're in trouble. I've had a vision," she continued in a hushed voice, her eyes darting as if she was being observed in the centre of organised chaos.

"That's good isn't it? You're the best at what you do; you've got everything right so far. I can give them a reference."

Wendy squeezed her arm affectionately. "The Judges want to see if my vision is correct."

"And what was this amazing vision? Did you see me going home in time for lunch? Or maybe I was going home full-stop?" She followed her friend down the corridor, pleased to have a face she recognised with her.

"No, sorry. I saw that you would save the Warden." Val stopped walking, but Wendy dug her heels in to keep her moving.

A new emotion started to fill Val's body now – panic. "I take the reference offer back. You're as insane as that obnoxious Guard I just met."

"Like it or not, it's what I saw and I believe it's true. My training has been so intense. There are things I've seen since I've been here that have scared the life out of me, Val, and made me want to go home. But in the midst of the confusion there you were, leading the Magrafe to glory. You were the Prison's saviour, just like Joan of Arc."

Val choked. "Please forgive me if I forget the ins-and-outs of our history test, but didn't she get burnt at the stake as a witch? And what's the Magrafe?"

"Yes, she did, but that's in the past. I just wanted to remind you that an eighteen year old girl saved her country in battle. The Magrafe are the Prison's secret bodyguards, they are the chosen elite. No one really knows who's a member. After the vision I told the High Judges and they were interested, but didn't see a need to take any action. Then the next day the Warden gets kidnapped. So all of a sudden it went from pretty vision to prophecy."

"I take back missing you. Honestly, Wendy." Val pulled her arm free as a Guard bumped into her. "Sorry," he called.

Wendy's expression became soulful, "Val, if I could turn back time I would, but I can't. Did I tell you Sam's here?"

Val objected, "No, you can't use Sam against me. Look, just tell them you got it wrong, that it was a dream and that it was a mistake." They had no choice but to start moving again, standing still while everyone else was moving so quickly was a mistake. She was getting knocked from every angle. Yet annoyingly, no one seemed to even come close to Wendy.

"I can't, they trust me and I'm not wrong, you'll see."

Another siren rang out. Wendy moved Val along even quicker. "Just let me get you to your quarters. I promise it's not as bad as you think."

✳

As Val walked the corridors with Wendy the gravity of the Prison's situation was visibly growing. More sirens rang and they could sense the pressure rising. They arrived shortly at a doorway. Guards were moving in and out all around, so Val could only guess that this area was the general quarters. Wendy walked through a door and Val followed, silently hoping Sam would be there. But instead there was just some young Hunter. Val could tell by his bracelet.

"Welcome Twenty-three thirteen. I am Thirty-three twenty-nine. It is my duty to be your Hunter whilst you are here." His gentle yet formal speech was so different to Zac's bark.

"Well, that won't be necessary." She circled him gradually pushing him towards the exit. "I'm not stopping and I have a Hunter on Earth. We're connected." She flashed him her bracelet.

"Yes, I have heard of Zac. I will wait outside until you are ready for me, and if you wish to give me a name then that would be acceptable."

"I really don't think I can think of anything, thanks. You can wait outside." Closing the door she glared at Wendy. "What's going on?" she demanded, her annoyance oozing out. The door began opening, "GO AWAY!" she shouted.

Sam popped his head around the door. "Nice welcome. I see you've managed to get yourself into trouble again."

"Seriously," she threw her arms into the air, "I went for my driving lesson and came back to this. How can it be my fault?"

"You could find trouble in an empty cardboard box." His voice was smooth and rich - just the way Val remembered.

"Sam." Wendy lowered her head in respect as he entered.

Val didn't follow her example. "Yes, it's nice to see you, now get me home please," she requested.

"Not just yet." He walked across the room and placed his hand on the wall. To Val's surprise the wall started to glow and palpitate. It was as if it were feeding off his touch, the intensity growing with every beat of his heart. "See this Val?" She nodded, mesmerised by its glow. "This is the problem we have."

"Sorry, you've lost me. Your lighting's not working?"

"We have an endless resource of power on Alchany. We never need what you call fuel. We could power several planets without any trouble."

"Still lost." Val shook her head.

"Imagine if you could supply power to Earth forever and it wouldn't cost anything and would have no negative repercussion on the planet. A clean source of energy. What would it be worth?"

"Priceless I guess. So how do you do it?"

"Prisoners. You see we're all energy in different states of vibration. When the Judges extracted the very first prisoner, they discovered that they were left with pure energy. With the help of a friendly planet called Nyteria, we managed to harness the power and use it. The more prisoners we got, the more power we had."

"So where's the problem?"

"We suspect Nyteria wants it back."

"But if they showed you how to create the energy, surely they can do the same thing?"

"They have the technology that's true; they just don't have the prisoners or the ability to capture and hold that many people quickly enough."

"So why now?"

"The problems started when they recently voted in a new leader who clearly saw the potential to use the power for negative outcomes. He made comments that caused murmurs amongst the Judges. We have information he took the Warden. It was a risky move, but a clever one. He knows how important the Warden is, and how much the Guards will risk to get him back. It's a little bit like someone taking your Queen. Now I know this isn't your fight, Val, and I promise you a ticket home as soon as it's all over, but right now we can't take any risks. If Wendy's vision is right and you are the one who saves the Warden, then you need to be here where we can keep an eye on you. Plus, the Magrafe want to see you."

"So what you're saying is that just in case Wendy's vision is correct, I have to hang out here on the Prison while my family and friends on Earth are at risk of being killed and mutilated by Lailah and her gang of merry murderers? That includes your Mum," she said, pointing at Wendy. "Please forgive me if I turn your kind offer down. I wish you the best of luck and when this is all over you must visit."

"Lailah's on Earth?" Sam's brow broke into deep furrows of thought. "We need to deal with her."

"Stating the obvious, although she's done nothing yet." Val replied. "Well, that was until you teleported me here. They could all be her little puppets by now." She marched past him out into the corridor of siren filled chaos. To her left the young Hunter looked as if he was ready to attach himself to her again. She held a warning hand up to him. She looked right, trying to get her bearings. She was sure she'd seen that red headed Guard loitering on her way in. She started to walk. How could the pair of them have thought up such a stupid scheme? Let's get Val and keep her prisoner on the Prison that's under attack.

"Val!" It was Sam; he clearly wasn't going to give up.

"What?"

"Please listen to me. These are dangerous times; if we lose, then no-one will be safe. Not Earth, not the Prison, and the Nyterians will have the power to destroy anything they choose."

"Why would you create something that powerful? It's your fault this is happening, you created the weapon. Plus you only *suspect* they want that, you don't even know what's really going on!" She felt so frustrated.

"Please stay. There is more at risk than you see on the surface."

"Sam, what about my family? They're in danger."

He closed in on her. "Come here." Taking her arm he pulled her to one side. He touched the wall and a doorway opened. "There is a lot more at risk than just Earth and your family. Yes, they are important to me as well, but I need you to just do as I ask for now."

"What else is at risk?"

"This." Sam placed his hand around her waist and they teleported out.

CHAPTER 2

The Space

Val's landing was relaxed, compared to her earlier
uninvited 'single-journey loop-extraction'. She hated
technical descriptions for things. Her dad did it
when talking houses and so did Jason when he
explained fencing moves. She looked about; there
was no one else around. She and Sam seemed to be
inside some sort of huge cave. It reminded her of her
time underground saving Max and the others from
the rock-fall in Devon. Sam beckoned her to follow,
offering his hand as they climbed up a steep rocky
path.

"Where exactly are we going?"

"To a very special place. We're almost there."

As promised, over the next rise Val saw something
very odd. In the wall of the massive cave was a rusty,
heavy-looking metal door. Sam walked up to it and
knocked, glancing back to smile at her then pointed at
camouflaged cameras. Well, if nothing else he seemed
happy to be there. First there was the cranking of bolts
and clanking of locks, then the heavy metal door was
pulled ajar creaking and moaning.

Through the gap that had opened appeared a tiny,
pale face. This couldn't possibly belong to the person
who had opened the door; it was a child.

"Sam!" the boy squealed delighted to see him. "It's Sam!" he called back.

"Didn't you see me on the screen?" Sam asked, concerned at the fact the boy hadn't known who was on the other side of the door.

The boy seemed almost unable to contain his excitement at seeing him. "They're down again, awaiting repair."

"Ok, are you going to let us in Alsom?" Sam quizzed jokingly.

"Sorry." Alsom blushed and disappeared.

"They let children open the front door?" Val raised her eyebrows.

"He's the fastest person here. If there was a problem, he would be the best to escape. Never doubt children's abilities. I think it's one of Earth's biggest flaws."

In that moment Val heard a sound she recognised: wheels, spinning faster and faster. Maybe the door had a pulley system. She waited with Sam for it to slowly allow them access.

"All done," Alsom called as he came around the entrance at full speed and braked directly in front of Val.

"Oh my God!" she exclaimed grabbing Sam's arm tightly. The boy had shiny looking wheels instead of legs. Val couldn't take her eyes off them; she'd never seen anything like it. They weren't like wheels on a bicycle. They were polished and solid, letting him glide smoothly over the surface like he was on ice.

"Is she alright?" Alsom spun around her several times, changing direction with grace and agility. His blond mop of hair fell over his eyes as he huffed a breath up into his face, which controlled it for a millisecond.

"Yes, she'll get used to you." Sam reached out playfully to push him, but Alsom escaped into the distance. "Val this is The Space." She peered into the distant expanse. To her earthly knowledge, doors usually led to rooms. Big metal doors led to bigger rooms. But as she looked around her, nothing could have prepared her for what she was seeing.

"He has wheels! This is another civilization. Where is this? What are they? How did they…"

She was still looking around in awe, hanging tightly to Sam's arm as Alsom returned, now accompanied by another boy. Alsom took great pride in skidding to a halt. The other one was clearly not as confident in his skills and stopped gently next to Val.

This boy was different, he had one leg and one wheel, there was a bar jutting out of the side of his wheel on which, he now rested his foot. Although he was on what she would describe as a unicycle, and stationary, he was completely balanced.

"Welcome," he greeted her, face beaming, taking her hand. Val realised that wheel or no wheel this was a child. "Can you move a little faster?" He pulled her with all his strength. Val glanced at Sam who nodded, so she finally let go of his arm and followed her new found acquaintance.

They were still inside a cave, but there were people of all ages, shapes, sizes and colours living there. There were blankets made of a thick dark cloth hanging over various sized openings in the cave walls. Steps carved into the walls allowed access, even at the highest points.

"This is mine." the young boy stopped in front of one of these openings and pulled aside the cloth.

Val peeked in. So these openings were where the people lived! There was a bed carved out of the cave wall and a simple stool and table. On his table he had paper which surprised Val. "Come in." he beckoned her.

Once she was inside she had no choice but to sit on the bed as there wasn't enough standing room for someone of her height. The stone was cold on her bottom and it made her catch her breath. The boy giggled at her reaction. As her eyes grew accustomed to the lack of light, she started to see pictures all over the walls. "Wow, your drawings are amazing."

"Yes, I love to draw." His face beamed. "Do you draw?"

"Well I can do stick people, but that's about it I'm afraid. How do you make the colours?" Each picture was a rainbow of different shades. Yet the cave was extremely grey.

"These." He wheeled over to her, nudging her gently to move to one side. He lifted a simple grey piece of material to reveal a box of crayons and several copies of the National Geographic magazine.

"You have... crayons and magazines?" Now she was confused. Unless UPS delivered across the galaxy, how did he get them?

"Yes, Shane gave them to me." the boy said.

A voice called her from the doorway, "Val, come on." Sam had caught up.

"Coming. Thank you for inviting me in," she said as she made her way out of the boy's cave.

"Will you come back?" the boy stood in the entrance, his voice was inquisitive, as if testing her.

"Absolutely," she replied waving goodbye.

She and Sam made their way through the crowds that were assembled in the main area, who were busy chatting, sharing food and checking out pieces of equipment. A variety of metal tools and what looked to her like the boys' wheels, were being handed out. Val observed that the people here greeted Sam in a completely different manner than those at the Prison. There was warmth and gratitude from everyone. They all made Val feel welcome.

"You need to tell me about this place, Sam. Where are we? Why has that little boy got crayons and magazines from Shane, and a wheel for a leg? What's going on?" She knew Sam and Shane had a history, but Shane had been extremely cagey about discussing his past, saying it was safer to keep it a secret. 'Blooming big secret,' she thought to herself.

Sam smiled acknowledging her, but didn't respond until they had made their way to what seemed to be the largest and highest cave. "We're here. Everything will become clearer now." He took her hand again. "Enoch," Sam called. Val stood at his side patiently waiting to see how many wheels this one had.

A young man exited the cave. He was not what Val had expected. He looked strong, clean-cut, with a square jaw: perfect Guard material. His face lifted at the sight of his friend. "Sam." He trotted down to them and embraced him. They looked each other up and down. "You look well. Tell me what brings you here. You're not due for a few more weeks? And who is your friend?" He took Val's hand from Sam, which for some reason made her blush uncontrollably.

"This is Val. Enoch, we have a serious problem. We need to talk."

Enoch patted Sam on the shoulder. "Come."

They walked into the cave. This was a very different space to the one she had just visited with the little boy. It had a high ceiling and there was a ball of what looked like electricity flickering and skipping in the centre, giving off heat and light at the same time.

Enoch guided Val to a flat rock, "Please be seated." She thanked him and sat down.

"Tell me, Sam, what's wrong?"

"The Warden has been taken, we think by the Nyterians. We're expect an uprising anytime now."

A little blunt, Val thought watching as Enoch's expression changed. She could feel the tension rising.

"How will this affect us Sam? What's happening on the surface?"

"Sam, who's on the surface?" Val interrupted.

"The Space is directly underneath the Prison."

Val gasped, "No way!"

"Yes and all these people, the children included, were rejected and expelled from the planet for being imperfect. Rejects, like you."

She was deeply shocked. "Are you saying that these people were kicked off the Prison because they're not perfect?" Horror streaked across her face. "Those children I just saw, what was going to happen to them? Are their parents here?"

Enoch moved forward, placing his hand on Val's. His pained expression made her instantly feel sad. "No, they don't have parents; no-one does on the Prison. As for what was going to happen to them, well there's a very dark place on the Prison they call the Interspace. Some would have been sent there if it wasn't for Sam and his friends; some, like me, were near death; the Prison can't cure the dead, so we were abandoned." Val remembered how the Mechanic had left Zac on her bed when he was so ill, and she knew that they couldn't take Flo back to the Prison because she was dead. It was all starting to make sense, although not a sense she was comfortable with. "Is Shane one of those friends?" she asked.

Sam nodded. "And Elizabeth."

Val didn't instantly realise who he has talking about, then the penny dropped, "Jason's Mum? You knew Elizabeth."

He nodded again.

"Many have helped and many have been lost, but the other option is unspeakable," said Enoch. "Tell me what we must do now?"

"Wendy has delivered a vision to the Judges. She predicted that Val here, with the Magrafe, will save the Warden so they want to keep her safe inside the Prison for now."

Suddenly it dawned on her that he had a huge responsibility on his shoulders. He had been telling the truth when he said there was more at risk than her family, and though her family was still the most important thing to her, she now understood a little better what was at stake, and what was making him tick.

Enoch and Sam talked about the possibility of the Nyterians arrival and it seemed that as long as they could protect the entrance, they should be safe for now. Sam checked a list of new arrivals, organised for the cameras to be fixed and constantly praised Enoch for his hard work. He reinforced the danger they were facing and then it was time to leave.

"It's been good to meet you and I wish you safe passage to the surface. We'll ready ourselves and wait for news. Val if you need anything - you know where we are." Enoch waved farewell and they made their way down the rocks towards the larger congregation of people.

From this angle Val could see the extensive size of the area. "Now tell me what would have happened to all these people. Explain the place Enoch called the Interspace."

Sam ruffled the hair of a small boy and lifted a little girl who had fallen. "The Interspace was originally created to store an alien life form called the Novelia. They were the cruellest of all the criminals we have had the bad luck to encounter. We couldn't contain them on the Prison. Their energy was so vile and so negative that they killed anything that came in contact with them. So we imprisoned their essences in a containment field. Then, by chance, one of the Mechanics found that in their new environment the Novelia could sustain life indefinitely, but not in a way you or I could withstand. He discovered a place to hold a life essence forever, suspended in torturous pain. So on the odd occasion, the most dangerous of prisoners was sent there, as the ultimate punishment. It was our threat to the galaxy."

Val shuddered. "I find the power the Prison has scary. Who chooses who gets held in pain for all time? And that a child is dumped because they don't fit the mould? This would never happen on Earth. We love our children. And I know there are undesirables, but this is barbaric."

"How many of your humans have caused atrocities on the scale of destroying a whole civilisation?" Sam asked.

"A couple have tried," she retaliated. "We have evil masterminds as well."

"And do you not think they deserve a severe punishment?"

"Well, yes but… it's just not ok." Val had run out of steam. She knew from her short life that there had been people in history who had made wars, gassed millions and committed genocide, and she was sure if you had asked the families of the survivors they may have agreed with Sam, but something in her head still knew it was wrong.

Sam tried again. "Ok, let's go back in time. A long time ago, some very clever people found out how to travel from planet to planet in the blink of an eye, for the good of the galaxy. However, the technology also attracted all the wrong sorts of people: thieves, murderers and general scumbags. So, when it reached a point where no one could control the situation any longer, the Prison was created. It was formed by a group of leaders who felt the galaxy was falling apart. The Creators gathered the most talented and unique together and took action. These were the first official Judges and some still exist as High Judges. They appointed the Warden as the first Guard. They had to produce something that would make the galaxy sit up and listen. Something to make the criminals scared. The only way to do that was to demonstrate power that had no equal. The Novelia gave us a new opportunity to show our strengths."

"So you're all-powerful. I get it, but what do these innocent people have to do with the Interspace?"

"Through lack of understanding and fear, the Prison has no tolerance for imperfections. They found the easiest option was to get rid of it, and the Interspace was the perfect solution. No pollution, no questions."

"And you knew about this?" She stared at him in undisguised horror.

"No!" he defended himself fiercely. "I found out by chance when I overheard a Judge giving instructions to a Mechanic one night."

Val felt knots forming in her stomach, "You mean that Alsom and the other little boy would have been sent to this Interspace for no other reason than the Prison didn't see them as perfect." She felt sick and could barely look at him. "You're no better than the criminals."

"Why do you think I created the Space, Val?" he asked quietly. "The Warden and the Judges have no idea this place exits. Most of them don't know about the way the Interspace is being abused. I used only people who I could trust to not be influenced by the Judges' power. Then I started to pick up Guards who had been left for dead. Enoch was virtually on his last breath when I found him. Elizabeth looked after him for me and nursed him back to strength."

Val nodded, glad Sam was doing something to help, but she still felt sick. Her feelings for the Prison had never been great, but now she had hit rock bottom. They continued in silence. Alsom was waiting at the door. He reversed his wheels, digging deep into the ground, and pulled the door open wide enough for them to exit.

He was waving to them as the other boy appeared. He grinned and shoved a picture out through the gap. "Bye," he called as the door's heavy bolts engaged.

"Bye and thank you," Val responded, picking the picture off the ground. It was a drawing of the boy and her. He had replicated the Superman 'S' on her t-shirt to perfection. "Taran, that's his name." Val showed the picture to Sam who smiled. She folded it carefully putting it into her back pocket.

"Please tell me you understand now why I must keep you here. I know this is such a difficult situation, but I have to keep them safe and for that I need the Prison to be safe."

Val stepped in close to him, "Yes I do."

Sam wrapped his arm around her waist again and they left the Space behind.

*

Their arrival on the surface went undetected. Val and Sam exited the room and the mad bustling of Guards and Hunters outside was a perfect distraction. They slipped back into the stream of bodies and headed back to her quarters. The Hunter was still there waiting patiently with Wendy.

"Had a chat then?" Wendy's tone led Val to believe she knew exactly where they had been.

"Yes. I will be staying here for now, but I need to find a way to protect the others on Earth. Any ideas?" she asked them.

"If I may speak," the Hunter interrupted politely.

"Ok." Val was ready to listen now.

"When a special Guard such as yourself is extracted then you are automatically replaced. My Guard has taken your place."

Sam laughed out loud slapping the Hunter on the back, something he clearly wasn't comfortable about. "See Val, it's not every day you get to meet a Magrafe, and I had completely forgotten the Guard's code of replacement. Thank you for reminding me." The Hunter nodded stepping respectfully out of Sam's range.

"Ok, so who is your Guard? Will he know Zac? Is he trained in Earth customs? Will he be ready to fight Lailah?" Val shot questions at the Hunter.

"I feel certain he will do everything in his power to carry on your work," he responded to the barrage.

Wendy interrupted, "Val, we'll try and get some contact soon, but for now I have orders to follow and they state that I must get you a uniform," she said grinning as she pulled at her green roll neck. "You know I'm a pacifist, but revenge is going to be so sweet."

CHAPTER 3

The Magrafe

Wendy walked the corridors with a confidant stride. Val followed, her strange new Hunter trailing behind. He seemed extremely odd, saying nothing unless spoken to, and he didn't insult her. Was this how Hunters really acted or had Zac just been difficult? Knowing her luck it was the latter.

Wendy was grinning from ear to ear as they reached a blank wall. "We're here," she announced, placing her wrist against the wall. "This is where everyone comes to get their uniforms." A larger than normal door opened. Val couldn't believe her eyes. The area that stretched out in front of them was the size of St Pancras train station, where she had been recently with her mum on a day trip to London. Snaking on into the distance was a seemingly endless queue of Guards, Hunters, Collectors and Mechanics, plus a few oddities. She was sure that four armed aliens weren't going to be easy to accommodate. "Come on." Wendy coaxed Val through the door. "I promise it won't hurt."

"If it does I'll inflict the same pain on you, Whitmore," Val promised, joining the end of the snake.

A young Hunter, who had joined the queue behind her coughed, clearly seeking her attention. Val turned and smiled at him and he mirrored her expression.

"Excuse me," he whispered discreetly, "I don't mean to be rude, but aren't you '*the*' female Guard?"

"Yes - the very one." Val nodded politely.

"Is it true you captured the infamous Excariot?"

"Yes."

"Do you have a Hunter at the moment?" he asked eagerly.

"Yes, he's over there," she pointed towards Thirty-three twenty-nine who was checking out some new belts.

The Hunter's shoulders slumped just enough for Val to tell he was disappointed. "Oh. Well, if you ever need a new one please keep me in mind. I'm Forty-five twelve."

Val had no plan to use the one she had just been given, but didn't want to offend him. "Will do, Forty-five twelve." She turned back to follow the spiralling snake again.

As they shuffled along, she wondered what clothes size she would be? Something that was easy enough on Earth could potentially lead to a problem here. Fifteen minutes passed before she reached the front of the queue. A large man stood behind a counter, clearly not interested in his job or her presence. He reminded her of the cartoon character Desperate Dan, in a comic her dad had shown her when she was little. She smiled as she imagined this guy grabbing a cow pie and eating it.

"What are you?" He looked her up and down. "Ranswars don't come here."

Val remembered the Ranswars well enough. One had nearly got her extracted. "I'm a Guard." She flashed her bracelet at him.

He exploded in a loud fit of derisive laughter. "Little girl, Guards aren't female." He slapped the counter.

"Well, I hate to disappoint, but I am." This was embarrassing. The snake she had been a part of was glaring at her. "Look I'm the only one, so I understand your confusion, apart from the fact your chin is bigger than your forehead. I want you to understand right now that I don't want your stupid uniform, but if you don't give me one I will have to deal with you." She placed her hands firmly on her hips. She didn't want the damn thing and now she was being made to look a fool.

"I'm sorry, let me see what I can find for you." He tapped the side of his nose.

"Good." She felt a little happier.

He walked out of sight. She smiled at the Hunter behind her, pleased with her success.

"Here." The man returned and placed an item on the counter. Val picked it up. Raising the object with both hands she found it was a long silk-like dress. She could hear sniggers now coming from behind her.

She took a deep breath. "Get me my uniform now!" She was so angry that her voice trembled. Determined to show him that she wasn't someone he could mess with, she started a fire in the palms of her hands. She was astonished when the flames quickly devoured the dress, to gasps of horror from the queue. Her flames seemed much stronger and fuller here.

"Put it out," he grumbled reluctantly. She grinned and shrugged, enjoying the panic that filled his face. He dithered for a moment then grabbed a glass of blue fluid on the counter. Desperately he threw the liquid at the dress, extinguishing the flames.

"Well done," she teased him, enjoying the faint scent of incense that came from the liquid.

"Give me your bracelet," he grunted.

She offered him her arm and he scanned her wrist using a black circular device on the counter. His eyes examined the screen, looked up at Val, looked back down, his face scrunching in a bemused frown. He said nothing, but walked away again and returned in a timely manner with a pile of black clothes. "You will need to collect your weapons from the Magrafe," he said in a hushed tone, pushing the uniform at her, unable to make eye contact.

There was a hushed gasp from the people behind her in the queue as they recognised the uniform.

"Thanks." Val threw the sodden remains of the dress onto the counter and grabbed her pile. "Will they fit?" she wasn't queuing again today.

"Yes they all fit. Next."

"See you around," she said her goodbyes to the Hunter who seemed even more smitten with her after her show of power.

"Did you really need to do that?" Wendy asked.

"Yes, he needed to learn a lesson."

Wendy shook her head. "Come on, I can't wait to see you in your new clothes."

*

Back at Val's quarters Wendy waited patiently for her to emerge in her new uniform. As the door opened Wendy held her breath.

"Are you sure these are my boots?" Val called through the gap.

"Yes, they're what I was given for you. Come on," she said impatiently.

Val stepped forward feeling very self-conscious. "This is too hot, I can't breathe, the material itches and I can't reach my bracelet," she grumbled pulling at the neck.

"You look great! At least it fits. It's a little flimsy looking. Should it be that tight?" Wendy looked her up and down. Val was in black from head to toe. No geeky t-shirt, no jeans and no Converse.

"I feel dead inside; this is so not me. Why do I have these squidgy bits?" She poked at the legs. "They feel weird." She had what looked like gel pads in strategic places all over her uniform. She poked them, her finger marking the spot. The material quickly returned to its original state.

"I'm not sure, mine's not like that." Wendy also poked them now with interest.

They were both inspecting Val's bottom which had similar pads when Sam returned. "Am I interrupting?" he smiled.

"No, but you need to take me to the Magrafe for my weapons and why is my bum all soft?"

"I'm not sure about that one," Sam shrugged. "Let's go meet the others."

Wendy hugged Val. "See you later."

"Wendy," said Sam, "Please arrange for Val to eat with you tonight, and we can meet back here after your dinner."

As they headed out into the corridor, Val was determined to get a few answers about her predicament. "Sam, can I ask you something?"

"Yes of course. I'm not saying that I will be able to answer everything, but I'll try."

"I know the Magrafe are the special Guards for the Prison, but what's that got to do with me?"

"I'm not sure. They're extremely secretive about their missions. No one has contact with them unless it's completely necessary. They are selected at a very young age, normally because they've shown special talents or abilities, and are trained externally to their normal positions, so one could be a Guard, a Hunter or even a Collector. All we know right now is that you were with a group of Magrafe when Wendy saw you save the Warden. I'm sure they will protect you. Let's go and find out what's going on." He led her out. "By the way, you look very professional."

"Thanks." She pulled at her tight fitting collar.

*

As they walked she noticed how the Guards and Hunters were looking at her differently now. Her new uniform was clearly having an effect. As Sam moved confidently from one corridor to another, Val could feel butterflies building in her stomach. Who were these people she was going to be entrusting with her life and would they treat her with the disrespect everyone else seemed to show her?

Sam stopped in the middle of a quiet corridor. "I can't come any further with you; I'll see you later." He placed his hand on the wall and a door opened.

"So you're leaving the sinking ship?" she replied sarcastically, bending to peek through the gap.

"No, I'm making sure you arrive safely." He pulled her upright and placed a kiss on her cheek. "Pudding later - as promised."

"Ok," she replied watching him leave, then turned and walked towards her prophesised destiny.

*

Behind the door she couldn't see anyone or anything other than walls. She walked in and the door closed behind her, enclosing her in a large, empty room.

"Is this her?" a deep voice asked from behind her.

She turned but no one was there.

"Looks like it," another voice answered.

"Hello." Val said nervously.

A tall young man with mouse-brown hair stepped out of the wall in front of her. Val's instinct was to scream her head off, but she managed to keep it in her throat.

"I am Boden Ekwall, leader of this group and this…" he pointed at the other wall where another young man with white blonde hair and a very serious face shimmered into existence, "… is Hadwyn Houte, our partner."

"I'm Val Saunders and am not sure why I'm here or how I can help."

Boden smiled, "You, my friend, are one of us. I know you may be feeling confused so I will try to explain as much as I can."

"That would be good." She smiled.

"Your father, Gabriel, was the third member of our group. The last time we met he was leaving for Earth. As I'm sure you know, he didn't return. After he suffered his untimely End, the mark of the Magrafe was passed directly onto his natural descendant along with his abilities. By the way, congratulations on catching his murderer, Excariot." Boden held his hand over his uniform. To her surprise the patch he touched became transparent and Val could see on his arm, a tattoo matching hers.

"I have one of those."

"All three of us do, Val." Boden smiled kindly at her.

"So, can you pass it to someone else?" She asked.

Hadwyn grumbled, "I told you this would be the end of us. She's already giving up." He turned his back on them, placed his hand on the wall and sat down on the chair that shot out at his touch.

"I'm not giving up, but I have a lot of people depending on me back on Earth," she retaliated. Hadn't she proven herself enough to these people?

"I'm sorry. Please expect Hadwyn to be grumpy and rude most of the time, but trust me, Val, he's one of the best fighters I've ever met."

"Sam told me you've been trained since you were children. I haven't had any training so what makes you think I'm not going to put you in danger?"

"Now she's making sense," Hadwyn muttered.

Boden frowned at him. "Val, if you weren't ready for this, your mark wouldn't have activated. So even though you may not believe it, something in your DNA knows you're ready."

She instantly liked Boden; she wasn't sure about Hadwyn, but she could see why he would be annoyed by this strange little girl who had turned up to take the place of a lifelong friend and strapping Guard. She would be worried too. "Ignoring Grumpy's opinion of me," she gave him a smirk, "what can I do to help? And how long will it take? I really do have to get back to Earth. My family are in danger."

"Here's some information that should help." Boden reached his hand out and a screen appeared floating in mid-air. "The Warden was taken from a carrier ship close to the border with Necrat." He pointed to a little blue planet. "As yet, we have had no demands or even any contact with the people who took him. We have our suspicions; a group of Nyterians were spotted in the area. A traveller recognised them. Necrat is a neutral zone that's sometimes used as a meeting place for leaders, so we had no reason to give heightened protection on what was supposed to be a peaceful visit. This attack is a complete violation of their laws of conduct. We're now waiting to receive instructions."

Hadwyn was spinning what resembled a gun in his hand, "Seems like the new leader of the Nyterians doesn't have a rule book," he grumbled, "so let's leave ours at home! Wouldn't you agree Earth girl?" He pointed the gun's barrel at Val.

She held her breath. "I'm not shooting anyone." She turned to Boden. "I've never been this close to a lethal weapon in my life. I won't kill people." She was panicked at the thought.

"Val, calm down. Our job isn't to kill anyone, we stun. As a Guard you will know that the aim isn't to take life, but to possibly transform it under the right circumstance. Hadwyn, put it away."

Hadwyn shoved the weapon back onto his trouser leg where it seemed to mould itself to his shape.

"Magrafe are all unique and we all have a different weapon." Boden put his arm over his head, reached behind his back and revealed what she could only describe as something that resembled a very advanced crossbow. It glowed as Boden aimed it at Hadwyn. "They feed off our energy and take forms that suit our own personal style."

"I have a sword." Val smiled, reaching instinctively for a back pocket that no longer existed. "It's back at my room, sorry."

"You don't need it. Does this sword work well for you?" Boden asked.

"Yes, it's been great and since I got my bracelet it's seemed to have improved in power."

"That's a good start, Val. We don't have much time before we need to leave, so what we can show you will be limited, but you must learn that you are your weapon. Your uniform is made of something called Polidion. It's a material that was found in small amounts on the planet Tolak before the Great War of the Tolks,"

Hadwyn interrupted, "Those were good days." He looked at Val with a sparkle in his eye.

"Ignore him. Seriously, it was used solely to create the Magrafe's suits. It allows the wearer to pull their weapon from it. Each Magrafe is different as I said, so you need to find your inner weapon."

Val started to poke and prod the soft patches looking for a pocket. "Sorry I don't seem to have one." She could sense this was going to be complicated.

Hadwyn got to his feet, walked impatiently over to Val and grabbed her by the shoulders. "Find your weapon or I will stun you." He stepped back placing his hand on his leg. It moulded a gun to his hand, seeming to just extend from the material.

"I can't do that." She rubbed her leg nervously. "You need to give me more time please."

"Five, four, three...," he said calmly.

"Stop it!" she yelled turning to Boden for support, but he didn't move.

"Two..."

Val felt that gut feeling, the one she had when her powers were just about to take over. Suddenly and to her sheer joy, Hadwyn's gun hand dropped and he stepped back looking extremely pleased with his creation. Val looked down her arm and, on the end of her hand, was a sword pointing directly at Hadwyn's throat. It resembled the one Sam had given her, but it was coming from her suit. It had extended from a plate on her arm and engulfed her hand. It felt lighter than her normal sword. "Look, I have my sword!" she gave a sigh of relief then glared at Hadwyn. "Now you can't shoot me."

"I'm more impressed with the flames." He actually sounded impressed as well.

Val looked down and it was true, she was aflame, but not like on Earth or earlier that day. Now the suit seemed to make her flames blue, like the gas flame on a cooker. It made her feel stronger, different. "This is something I do, I'm half-witch," she said proudly.

"Can you turn it off? It's getting a little warm in here." Boden asked.

"Yes, sorry." Val took a breath to calm down. Now she had her special weapon and a little respect from Hadwyn, she could let her flames go out.

"Next, no one should see you when you're working." Boden pointed to his face and in a split second, a black helmet extended from his uniform, and enveloped his head.

"Amazing!" Val reached out to touch it. "Do I have one?" The helmet retracted and Boden nodded.

Hadwyn chipped in enthusiastically, "Just see yourself wearing your helmet." He seemed to be getting excited at the possibility of having a human flame thrower to play with.

Val closed her eyes and imagined she was wearing a helmet. After a moment she opened them again tentatively and was amazed to find something like a computer screen surrounding her head. It was like she had shoved her head into a darkened fishbowl, she could see at all angles quite clearly. She wished Jason was there.

"Hello." A voice said into her ear. She looked around turning and twisting. "Val it's me, Boden. We will all be able to communicate through our helmets without being heard or detected. We can also monitor your vital signs through your suit and keep you cool in hot places and vise-versa."

"Right," Val nodded. "How do I get it off?" Even as she asked the question, the helmet shot back.

"Just like that," he replied. He looked down at his watch and then up at Val. "I don't want you to panic, but we need to leave. We will have some time after the journey to talk, but the clock is ticking and two other groups have already left."

This was much faster than she had expected. Sam had made it sound like they were just going to hang out on the Prison for a few days. "I'm supposed to be meeting Wendy for dinner and Sam for pudding..." she was never going to get that pudding, "...but hey, now I have a sword and him," she pointed at Hadwyn. "What could go wrong?"

"They'll be informed of the basics, don't worry." Boden opened a new exit to her left. "Val, helmet on." She followed orders as Hadwyn tapped her helmet with his gun, making it quite clear he was prepared to stun her if necessary to get the desired effect.

"Get off." She pushed his hand away. Her helmet in place, she made her way out, unsure of what would be waiting for her behind the door.

CHAPTER 4

Primary Portal

Boden led the way, Hadwyn behind and Val tucked in neatly at the back. She was tense, on edge, but at the same time strangely relieved to have them with her. They walked a short distance and then came to a halt in front of a glass door. Val could see three more figures inside, dressed like her. "Are they Magrafe?" she asked.

"Yes, we must wait here until it's our turn. The High Collector will be instructing them on their mission and will send them on."

Hadwyn stood waiting on one side, Boden on the other. She felt a little like Madonna going for a jog. Suddenly the glass door went misty and when it cleared the three figures had gone. Boden stepped forward, the woman looked towards them and the door whooshed open.

"Welcome to the primary portal. It's so nice to meet you at last, Val. Your Collector speaks highly of your bravery."

Val nodded blushing inside her helmet. "Is she ok? I haven't seen her."

"She's well." The woman smiled warmly at her, making her feel a little more relaxed. "Now we must get on with your instructions. Boden, as always you will lead your group. Hadwyn, you are being warned to conduct yourself in an appropriate manner. I don't want to have to deal with the paper work you left me with last time."

"In my defence, she was crazy and wouldn't shut up before I stunned her," he shrugged his shoulders.

"You always have an answer and after two hundred years, they are wearing thin young man." She looked sternly at him as if at the end of her tether. Yet Val sensed she wasn't as angry as she sounded. "As you know, the Warden has been taken and I can now confirm our suspicions were correct, it was the new leader of Nyteria, Nathan Akar, who took him. Let me make this very clear, Nathan Akar is ruthless. He takes no prisoners and stands for no questions over his actions or authority. He has informed us he wants the power from the Prison and there is no other option. At this moment your job is simply to retrieve the Warden."

She lifted a tiny hand and a transparent screen appeared between them. She pointed to a flashing red spot. "We have been informed that the Warden is being held here, in sector thirty-four, under heavy guard. This map has been programmed into your suits. The atmosphere on Nyteria matches that on the Prison, so if you do have to remove your helmet there's no need to concern yourselves. You will now be teleported to sector thirty-two where you will be met by one of our guides. They will give you coordinates for your departure point. Do not return without the Warden." Her expression now was as serious as Val imagined it could be. "Boden, Hadwyn, you have with you the girl from the vision. She is the one who is prophesised to free the Warden. You are to protect her with your lives, do you understand?"

They nodded and Val felt relieved that they would look after her, but concerned that one of them might get hurt because of her. "Can you please do something for me before I leave?" Val asked politely.

"What?"

"Can you please tell my Collector that if anything happens to me, could she please send a message to Zac, my Hunter." Val could feel a lump in her throat as she spoke, "Could you tell him to tell my Mum and Dad that I love them." Her voice broke and she was silent.

"I will do that for you, Val. We know you are just a child in comparison to these Guards and we thank you for taking such risks to help protect us when, as a collective we may not have been so kind in return. Now go and do what your friend saw in her vision and I will be here to greet you on your return."

The Collector moved to one side to reveal the shimmering portal. Val was sure it hadn't been there a few seconds ago. Boden stepped into it and Hadwyn followed. Then it was her turn. She stood for a second, looking at her reflection in the shimmer. She looked like a wobbly version of the bikers outside Shane's tattoo parlour. 'Note to self – make sure no one sees me like this at home.' She stepped into the portal and was off.

*

Her landing was surprisingly good. She didn't hit any walls or land on top of the others which made her feel a whole lot better. They would respect her more for being in control and she was sure Zac would have been proud. She took in her surroundings through the visor of her helmet. Although she could just see the dimly lit room, it still felt odd and it was hard to focus with all the flashing lights and signals. Although she genuinely had no idea what they meant, she surmised that the red dot in the distance was the Warden. She jumped as Hadwyn walked in front of her.

"Calm down," he protested.

"Sorry." He was right - she did need to calm down. Looking around she could see they had arrived in a room that resembled a wartime bunker, concrete on all sides. Her dad had shown her one at some military museum once and told her how, when he was little, they had had one in the garden.

"Val, are you ok?" Boden asked.

"Yes. Where are we?"

Hadwyn groaned. "Were you not listening to the High Collector? Sector thirty-two." He shook his head dismissively. "I hope you listen more now we're here." He raised his hand and a beam of light radiated from his wrist, illuminating the area. "I knew the number," she grunted annoyed that he thought she meant that.

"We're on Nyteria, Val, and are now in an amber zone. That means we're in danger, but not in the main sector yet." Boden switched on his light, shining it around the closed area.

"Thank you." She was grateful someone was going to answer her questions properly.

He took her hand and lifted her wrist. She felt it click and her light appeared. "We must move quickly, the agent meeting us will be above ground waiting."

Hadwyn had reached a doorway; he placed his hand on the electronic pad.

Val watched as it started to frazzle under his palm and the door popped open. "How did he do that?"

"Explanations when we are safe back on the Prison," Boden responded as they moved out. They started to jog up what Val saw was a narrow concrete corridor leading to a staircase. She hoped they weren't going to jog up the stairs. She was wrong and by the time they reached the exit she was struggling to breathe.

"Are you ok? Your vitals aren't looking so good." There was concern in Boden's question.

"Fine – just – need – to – recover," she gasped.

Hadwyn laughed as he disintegrated another keypad on the door, followed by more smoke. She could hear the bolts unlocking and a gush of air escaping as it opened. What would be waiting for them? This was her first mission on an alien planet. Nothing Mrs Sawyer had taught her in geography could have prepared her for this. The men moved out without hesitation and she followed. Would there be trees, birds? Questions seemed to be rushing full speed through her mind. What if there were dinosaurs? As they made it clear of the exit she could now see that it was simply night time. The stars above looked similar to the ones she had seen from Earth, yet there was an odd stillness. She sensed something was missing, but couldn't put her finger on it. They moved quickly onto a large sandy area. There was nothing to see, no trees, no green and no visible life. She felt almost disappointed at the lack of view.

"Where's our contact?" Hadwyn moaned clearly frustrated, marching backwards and forwards.

"Be patient, Hadwyn." Boden was confident. She could see why he was in charge.

Suddenly there was a rustling on the ground and as Val glanced down she saw something moving through the sand. "Floor... snake!" She spluttered at the men. Holding her breath in fear she might scream and it would hear her. The rustling collected together and started to form a silhouette. She watched as it rose higher and higher. It was a good seven feet tall as the last grains gathered and came to a halt. To her surprise and relief, Val could make out the form of a man. His skin was a strange mottled shade of brown with flecks and his eyes were yellow and glowing.

"Welcome to Nyteria. How was your journey? I hear…," he hissed.

Boden interrupted. "Less of the formalities, let's get to sector thirty-four."

The creature nodded respectfully and they started to move again. Val noticed quickly that although the man looked like he was walking, his feet never actually left the sand. It was as if they were one and the same, he creeped her out.

*

Their guide informed them that they were entering sector thirty-three. Boden warned them that they had now entered a red zone and that they all needed to be alert. Val stayed as close as she could to Hadwyn; he seemed crazy enough to save her. Plus, she wasn't prepared to get lost on some random planet where the population came out of the ground you walked on. She was just about to ask how far the next sector was when Boden raised his hand. She knew it was the sign she had been waiting for. No one spoke and as her eyes scanned what had been a dark path, she realised that there was now a glow on the horizon. They moved lower to the ground. The man who had been guiding them sunk naturally up to his waist. Val felt disturbed lying on what he was made of. What if someone grabbed them from underneath? She raised herself up a little.

"This is sector thirty-four. Upload this information." He handed Boden a card. "Your maps and directions for collection are all here. We will meet in the designated teleporting bay in one hour. It will be your only chance to leave. As soon as you have your package they will close all exits. We will only be able to sustain the power for that time. Do you understand?"

"Completely," said Boden placing the card onto his suit. Val's screen lit up again, numbers and images whizzing past her eyes.

"Safe passage." The creature sunk into the ground.

"Ready?" Boden asked her. She nodded and they all started to crawl towards the top of the mound. He signalled for them to stop just short of the crest.

"Val, you need to stay really close to me. You're going to see things that aren't normal to your human eyes. Just tell one of us if you are concerned." She nodded. "Hadwyn, we need to get rid of the soldiers nearest the green sector." As he said green sector, that was what popped onto her screen. She could see several entrances and two marked clearly in green. "Do a perimeter check. Find which one will be easiest to access." Boden ordered. Val lay still next to him as Hadwyn shimmered out of view.

"How does he, and you for that matter, do the disappearing act?" she whispered.

"It's a little bit like teleporting I guess, but you don't go anywhere." Boden was clearly half listening and half waiting to hear back from his partner.

"So could I do it?" she asked tentatively, not sure if she wanted to disappear from view, but on the other hand it might come in handy.

Boden's helmet turned towards her. "You can, there is so much we can teach you and you will learn it all in time. For now, let's just finish our task. You can learn new tricks when we get back to the Prison."

She nodded. "Ok."

Hadwyn's voice filled her helmet. "Five soldiers here, another five on each intersection. They aren't taking any risks. Second option is a go for green." Val's visor automatically zoomed in on the far green entrance. "They seem to have some sort of aerial surveillance as well. I'm going to check it out."

"Will you be able to clear sector two on your own?"

"With pleasure," he laughed.

"Go for it. See you inside." This was it, they were going in. She mustn't let nerves get the better of her. She had been through worse. She had stood on a plane with a bomb, fought Excariot... "Move," Boden instructed, interrupting her pep-talk. Boden reached back for his bow and nodded at Val as he rose slightly to come over the rise of the mound they had been hiding behind. She followed without extending her sword, not sure she could even do it again without Hadwyn pointing a stun gun at her head. She wouldn't miss him when she got back to Earth – IF she got back to Earth.

"Stay close," he ordered.

She caught her breath as she saw the true landscape of this alien planet. It wasn't what she had expected. Having arrived in darkness and moved through what had resembled an Earth desert, she had expected more sand and the odd palm tree. The glow of light she had seen on the horizon was coming from humming generator-style lights on the ground. Not just in front of them, but continuing for what looked like miles, dotted intermittently into the distance. But the thing that blew her away even more was the towers. They rose out of the ground to what looked like fifty or a hundred stories high. She felt enclosed by the sheer volume of dead empty metal and concrete. What felt wrong was the fact the buildings were in darkness, completely blacked out. "What is this place?"

"Nyteria's capital, a place no one wants to live in." Boden was now speeding up and guiding Val as they moved in the shadows towards the glowing lower levels.

"Why is it like this?" she quizzed him.

"Because they ran out of power. Now please stop asking questions and just move." He pulled her along the wall. The sky scrapers towered over them like dead beasts waiting to be given the kiss of life. Val spotted a few of the sand men standing by the corner of a building. Her heart was starting to show erratic traces on her screen. She had managed to work out her vital organs whilst they were running in the bunker. "Are you scared?" asked Boden.

"Yes." Val felt no reason to lie at this point.

"Good, it will keep you alert. We're going to enter that building." He pointed towards a doorway. She could see it was Green Two. Several unconscious bodies were lying on the ground close to the door. Hadwyn had been here. "I'm going to activate a tracking device on your screen now, so you can see only the Wardens location. All you have to do is get to him Val. Don't worry about anything else."

A strong red dot appeared on her screen. Everything else disappeared; she could only see the layout of the building. For a second, she wished Jason was there to talk to. He would have said something stupid and inappropriate now to make her feel more in control. But she was here and her family and friends weren't. They were at home waiting for her to come back, so she'd better not disappoint them.

They moved swiftly towards the door. Boden spotted a soldier up ahead who clearly saw them in the same moment. He aimed his bow and a single bolt of electricity flew out and struck the soldier down. His body dropped instantly; there was no jolting and shuddering here. As they ran past him, Val turned for a moment, wondering if he really was stunned, as he lay so still. There was still a nervous pain in her stomach as they reached the door. Fear filled her body sending adrenaline coursing through her veins. She leaned against the wall while Boden examined the lock for a second, then placed his bow against the console and blew it off. He pointed up at a flashing light on the wall, "They know we're here. I'm going to leave you. Follow the red spot."

"No! You can't leave me. Why would you do that?" Panic overwhelmed her.

Boden turned to see the arrival of three more soldiers. "Val, run. Get the Warden. I promise I'll find you." He shot several times knocking the men to the ground, but not before one had taken a shot at them. Val screamed. "Go!" he yelled.

She had never experienced anything like this. Being in a shoot-out was totally petrifying. She sucked in air, looked at the red spot on her screen and turned left, running down the corridor as she had been instructed. What other options were there? She could hear shots being fired behind her and fear kept her legs moving. She took a right and could see she was close. The firing was moving away and she slowed down, knowing that the Warden was only a few corridors away. Placing her hand on the wall to steady her shaking legs she whispered, "Wendy, you're in so much trouble." She moved on, slower now, but aware of everything. One more corridor and she would be there.

"Halt." A voice from outside her helmet called. Val's heart signal went through the roof as she turned to see a soldier pointing a weapon at her. He started to walk towards her. She raised her hands in the air. Surely that was the 'done' thing on any planet if you were going to surrender. "Number?"

"Twenty-three thirteen," she said automatically.

"Throw your weapons on the ground!" he barked at her.

"Well you see that's a little difficult as I don't really have one." Damn stupid uniform was going to get her killed.

He moved closer. "You expect me to believe you have come here and you have no weapon?" He waved his gun at her. "Get your weapon out now!"

She had failed already. No one had ever been this close to killing her. She couldn't do anything. "Look, I have no weapons." She lowered her arms towards the soldier who moved forward to restrain her. To their mutual surprise her sword shot out. The soldier grabbed at it in self-defence, which was a huge mistake, and was on the ground in the blink of an eye. Val stood motionless over his body for a moment, making small murmurs of thanks for being alive, as her sword retracted. She reached down and felt his pulse; he was definitely still alive. She felt better. "Red dot." She reminded herself why she was there. Just one more corridor and she would arrive. She picked up her speed, time had been lost.

Turning the corner she saw the doorway leading to the Warden. It seemed like just another doorway, nothing special, not somewhere you would hide the most precious bargaining chip in the galaxy. Val looked at the outside it was security locked. How was she supposed to get in? "Boden, I'm here but I can't get in," she said.

"Hadwyn cleared the corridor for you. I'll send you the access code now." She could hear shots in the background as he spoke. She was tempted to tell him that he had missed one, but it didn't matter now. Her screen started to bleep and a six digit number flashed up on the left hand side. "Thanks." Quickly she punched in the numbers. To her utter relief there was a clicking sound and no alarms. She reached out and touched the handle tentatively, pulling her fingers back sharply just in case this thing electrocuted her. Nothing happened. She touched again repeatedly until she could bring herself to stop tapping and grab hold. Pushing the metal down she held her breath, waiting for the worst, but it simply lowered and the door started to open. 'Now would be a good time to get your sword out,' she thought to herself, but fear had a hold and she just pushed the door as she made her way in.

In the centre of the room, in what looked like a glass box, sat the Warden. Badly bruised, his forehead had clearly been bleeding and was now dry and crusty. Val's heart rate was showing a warning signal. She wasn't surprised. She could feel it jumping around in her skin-tight suit. She cautiously made her way over to stand in front of the Warden. Placing her hands on the glass she tapped gently.

Slowly he looked up and she saw that his snowy white beard was matted with blood. Gradually, his eyes focussed on her, but he seemed unsure how to react.

"Helmet off," Val said and the helmet retracted, allowing the Warden to see who was before him. "Hello I'm here to save you," she said hoping he could hear her through the glass.

He whispered an almost inaudible response, "Run."

Chapter 5

Trapped

Val didn't get time to run as the Warden had instructed. She didn't get time to do anything. A blinding light flashed in her eyes. It was so strong it made her stumble back from the Warden's cell. She staggered for several paces before she hit something solid. Her hand reached down to get her balance as she tried to cover her eyes with her other arm. Then the light dimmed, but she was still blind. She turned and held onto the solid object, it was that or fall down. "If you stand still it's easier," a male voice spoke into her ear.

She tried to move away, but she was now being held by two strong hands. "Who are you, what do you want?" she said, still unable to open her eyes.

"I want you to stand still like I ordered."

Val knew she had no choice; she was in no position to argue. "Fine." She held out her hands touching what must be the stranger's chest. She felt plaiting, possibly a uniform. "Now what?"

"Sit down on the floor." He pushed her to the ground. "Someone will be here soon to find out who you are and how you got in here." The figure moved away and Val sensed a barrier coming between them. Her bet was she had been left in a glass box the same as the Warden's. She reached out her hand and felt the solid sheer cold. Great!

Now Boden was going to be disappointed and Hadwyn would laugh his face off, if they were still alive.

"Val." She heard a familiar voice.

"Sorry about this," she turned her head towards the direction the voice was coming from.

"Why are you here?" the Warden asked.

Val blinked a few more times and rubbed her eyes. She was starting to get her vision back. The Warden was now a silhouette. "Well, it turns out I'm a Magrafe, and Wendy had a vision that I would save you. Which, at the moment looks a little incorrect." She shrugged her shoulders.

"You're a Magrafe?" There was a pause for thought. "Well, I'm proud to say they made an excellent choice." She could hear it in his voice; he was just trying to make her feel better. "What was this vision?"

"Funny really, I never bothered to ask. I thought I was going to have dinner tonight with Wendy and she would tell all, but as it goes, it looks like it'll be just me and you." She could now see the lines of his face, his mouth, nose and beard. Then, from the other side of the room, she heard a door opening and footsteps coming across the darkness towards her. She turned to try and focus on the silhouette, then froze with fear.

As the figure came into the light, she instinctively knew he was the leader. His presence filled the room. He walked towards her confidently and placed his hand on the glass. Val wondered if he was going to break it, but to her shock and horror he walked straight through it into her cell. She scrambled backwards into the corner. As he got closer she got a better look at him. He wasn't like the sand men. He was blue.

"Mark my words if you hurt her!" the Warden bellowed from his cell.

The man ignored him. "Welcome to Nyteria. I see the Prison has sent a little girl to free their most precious possession. Seems a little strange don't you think, girl?" He was now kneeling next to her.

"No, I'm as good as any of their Guards," she replied.

"Are you now?" he sniggered. "Are you here alone?" he asked staring into her eyes.

"Yes." She tried not to blink or look left or right, she wasn't sure which one gave away the fact you were lying.

He was now inches from her face, he smelt her cheek. Val pulled away, but she was stuck between her cell and the blue man. "You smell of fear. Why would the Prison send only you?"

She replied, her voice trembling, but what had she got to lose? "Because I'm special. I caught one of the most dangerous prisoners in the galaxy and I'm going to free the Warden."

The man let out a hearty laugh, and in front of her eyes his vibrant blue started to fade. In seconds he was the same colour as her. "You are stupid and brave, but I need information. I want to know how many people are here. Now, I will ask you one more time. How many of you are there?"

"Just me," she said again. In a single swift movement, he pinned her arm against the wall. She could feel the pain, but the suit she was wearing seemed to be protecting her from some of the force.

"You have five minutes to think about what you are going to tell me when my soldiers come for you, because what we are going to do then will hurt." He stood up and started to walk away from her.

"Are you Nathan?" she asked, her voice a timid whisper.

"Yes, I am."

"Why are you doing this? Is there no other way?"

He stopped. "I'm surprised you ask that. You have come all this way, you're going to be tortured and you don't know why?" He frowned. "My people are dying. We have no power to run our cities, we are at the end of our time, our planet will cease to exist and the Prison has the means to save us. We just want what is rightfully ours. We gave them the technology and they have repaid us with nothing."

"That's not true, Nathan and you know it!" The Warden's voice shook with anger.

"Then why are we about to destroy you?" Nathan changed his direction, marching over to the Warden's cell, changing from flesh coloured to a deep red in three strides. "You," he pointed at the Warden, "came here and took what you wanted. You left us to slowly die. You knew we would run out of energy and yet you were happy to let it happen."

"We borrowed your technology. That doesn't mean we have to sustain your planet." Nathan and the Warden were now face to face through glass. "Step into my cell." The Warden provoked him. Val could see that even though he was the worse for wear the Warden had power, and enough to keep Nathan on the other side.

"The ships are ready. They are positioned on Alchany's borders and we will attack and take back what is rightfully ours. No one can stop this."

"Nathan," a soldier entered, "we have another one trapped."

"Good. Seems our little friend was lying after all and we have more intruders. Deal with them. I must prepare to join my ship." He left them.

Val sat in the corner of her glass box trembling inside her suit. How had she managed to get into this mess? This wasn't like home where she had her friends to help her. She was alone on an alien planet, stuck in a cell next to one of the most powerful men in the galaxy and he couldn't get out. What had she been thinking? Nothing sane, clearly. To be following the vision of a Witch who had had two decent visions in her career was not a clever move.

The door opened and two large soldiers entered, carrying between them the body of a Magrafe. The helmet was still in place so Val couldn't see who it was. They threw the body to the ground and a glass cell shot up around it. She wondered if he was dead. He hadn't moved. She looked more closely. He wasn't one of her group; he wasn't tall enough to be Boden or Hadwyn. That was if it was a he? She just stared at its chest, trying to make out the rise and fall of breathing. Then it dawned on her! It still had its helmet on. She concentrated and in a flash her head was covered by her own helmet. Lights flashing, she could see her heart rate was down.

"Hello, can you hear me?" she waited a few seconds. "Hadwyn, Boden can you hear me?" still no answer. They must be out of range. She looked across the screen and saw the time. The hour for their escape was almost up. She knew there was no way out now. "Helmet off." It followed orders and sprang back. "We're running out of time," she called over to the Warden.

"You were very brave back then, Val. I and Nathan both knew you were not alone." The Warden acknowledged her act.

"Well, it's what they do in the films on Earth," she smiled. Then the figure on the ground started to stir. She knew they had sent in more Magrafe, but she didn't know them. "Hello." She moved over closer to the new cell. "Wake up," she called again. The body was moving now and pushing with its arms, trying to lift itself up.

It fell back and settled into a kneeling position. She waved a little. "Are you ok?" What a stupid question she thought, as it escaped her lips.

The helmet shot back and to Val's shock there sat Sam. He took several deep breaths.

She was now grasping at the glass. "Sam! Oh my God, it's you. Why are you here? You're a Judge. I'm so pleased to see you. I got caught, obvious really. Are you hurt? When did you arrive?" Then she stopped, realising how much she was jabbering at him.

He opened his eyes and looked around. "Hello Val." A smile crossed his lips. He turned to the Warden and bowed his head. The Warden returned the gesture. "Hadwyn, are you here?" he looked around him.

"He's not here. Are you delusional? Maybe you banged your head?" Val was worried. Then, in the corner of the room she saw movement: a shimmer that formed a body, a helmet was opened and Hadwyn appeared. He walked over to Sam. Using his watch he started to scan the cell.

"Hadwyn!" Val was so pleased to see him.

"Seems to be a continuous stream cell. It will take me a few minutes to unlock you." He headed off towards the wall, and then stopped and came to face Val. "You were fearless. I won't forget that." He tapped her glass with his gun.

She knew it meant something and he walked away shimmering once again out of sight. Sam was pulling something out from his suit. She saw it was a small electronic map. "What's the plan?" Val asked.

"We've missed our rendezvous time and so have you, so both groups are stuck here. We need to find a safe exit to a portal bay. Everything will have been closed down, so we need to make sure it's near a source of energy and the closest one to us is here." He pointed to a small room on the map.

"Can you walk?" he asked the Warden who was already standing, although shakily.

"Probably," he replied.

"Are you ready?" Sam glanced at Val who was also on her feet. "Now," he called out into the dark and the cells shut down. Sam ran to grab the Warden as he stumbled slightly. Throwing his arm around his waist to support him as the alarms started to sound. Val was running once again, but for her life. She saw the Warden getting invisible support from the other side. Hadwyn was also there. The door opened and in rushed five soldiers. Val had no choice at this point and her sword extended from her suit reaching out in front of her. She stood ready to fight. Two men moved forward, she struck the first and he dropped, just like the one she had tazered by mistake, unmoving on the ground, stunned insensible. The second one fell as swiftly, but she could see that there were too many for them to deal with.

Still she surged forward, and then they seemed to stop, before turning in retreat. She heard a noise coming from behind her and then saw flashes of energy from Boden's Bow. She struck another soldier from behind as they climbed indiscriminately over the bodies of unconscious soldiers. She followed the Warden, Sam and Hadwyn towards their only chance to escape.

"We're going this way," Sam called, leading the group with Val and Boden as their backup.

"I'm pleased you could make it," she said to Boden.

"Did you think I wouldn't?"

"Well, you never know."

They saw another two figures ahead, both standing very still. They slowed and Val and Boden moved forward. One figure waved, and as they approached they saw their uniforms. These were Sam's Magrafe. That made six of them. They must be able to get away now Val prayed. They grouped together and followed Sam's directions. Sirens had started ringing out now and Val thought her ears would explode if this carried on. He pointed to a final doorway. "It's in here!" They pulled the Warden to one side as Boden fired at the key pad. The door flew open and they all barged in. Brave as they were, the reality was that they were heavily outnumbered.

Val looked around. There was a massive computer table, but it had no lights, no power. They were in a lifeless room. "Sam, how do we get out of this?" She looked around but found no windows, no other exit. This was a dead end.

"Drake, look for the energy sources in the area." A young man's helmet shot back revealing bright red hair and a rather rosy complexion. He started to scan the area.

They lowered the weakened Warden onto what looked like the top of an electric cooker.

"Sam what should I do?" she asked feeling a little useless considering she was the one who was supposed to save them.

"Just stay with the Warden for now," he dismissed her. "Boden, how long will the door hold?"

"Four, five minutes, if that."

Val sat down next to the Warden. He was very warm and she could see how unwell he was. "Why doesn't Sam teleport us out?" she asked him.

"If there is no connection to the Prison, then no one can teleport in or out. I think on Earth you take control of the skies. Well here it's planets. So we can't teleport without permission or a portal." He tapped the ground under him.

There was a large bang on the door. Boden turned and seemed to talk to himself. "We need to block this with something Hadwyn." Val wondered how he knew where Hadwyn was when he was invisible. Then another huge bang rocked the door.

"We're running out of time - come on, Drake." Sam urged.

"I can't find anything. There's no energy line in here anywhere."

"But on the map it showed one here." Sam placed the map down on the ground.

Drake shook his head. "Well it's not here now."

Val could feel a knot building in her stomach. "The only energy here is coming from her." He pointed at Val with his watch. "Why does she have all that energy?"

Sam looked thoughtful. "Because she's special. Val, listen to me, I need you to help us."

"Firstly I have no idea what you're talking about. Energy? What energy?" Her eyes were filling up, flitting from one Magrafe to another.

Sam held her hand as another strike bent in the centre of the door. "One more blow and we're finished," Boden called.

"Val, if they get in here do you know what they'll do to us?" Sam moved kneeling down by her feet. "They will kill us all. Not only that, they will torture us. Then they will take the Prison over and your family will be left exposed to Lailah, and they will all die." He placed his hand on the side of her head. "I'm going to show you what I need you to see and I'm sorry."

To Val it felt like a bolt shooting through her head. She felt the pain of torture, the anguish of losing the Prison, of losing Sam and Wendy. Then the terror her family and friends would suffer if she failed.

"Please Val." Sam knew if he could cause her enough pain she would have the power to get them out. He had been witness to what triggered her power. "She's done things like this before," he said to the others, removing his hands. He put one hand out to the Warden. "Give me your bracelet." The Warden did as Sam asked and he put it gently onto her wrist where it automatically resized next to her own. She was blank for a moment. No expression, just tears falling down her cheeks, dripping onto her uniform and rolling onto the concrete floor. She stood up and Sam could feel the friction as the air around her bounced off her body. He knew that this was it. He called to the others to join them. They all pulled in close encircling her.

A large smash broke the door and soldiers flooded into the room. But Val's energy flashed into life, forcing them to shield their eyes with their hands. Sam and the others had their helmets on and Val just stood in the middle glowing like a sun. "Take us home Val," Sam said into her ear and they were gone.

Nathan stormed into the room moving his men out of his way with blows of anger. "What happened?" he yelled at a soldier cowering on the ground. "We gave them a false map. They should never have escaped! They should have been stuck here, but the girl... she was glowing like nothing I have ever seen, like she was pure energy. She took them out."

"Then get me that girl, NOW!"

*

Her eyes felt as if they were burning. It felt like sand grating against her lids. If what she thought had happened really had happened, then she had teleported seven people, including the Warden, from a distant planet to... where?

"Val." Sam's voice was gentle. "Can you hear me?"

She forced her voice into a response though her throat was sandpaper dry "Yes, but my eyes are killing me." He pulled her into a sitting position as she attempted to open them. The light hurt, but it was bearable. "Hello," she greeted his smiling face. "Where are we?"

"Here." He sat back allowing her to see that she had managed to bring them back into the main portal room at the Prison. They were surrounded by Guards, Collectors and a vast array of aliens. "You did a great job." He helped her to her feet. The Warden was being cared for by two Mechanics and the other Magrafe, who had their helmets on. All seemed well.

None of the bystanders said anything, but just watched as the seven collected themselves and moved out into the main Prison. They made their way into the corridor which was still seething with Guards. Gradually, the realisation that the Warden was back spread and the mass movement, driven by quiet panic, gradually came to a standstill. Then the sirens stopped. As realisation started to dawn on the Guards, a cheer went up, one Guard after another started to call out and applaud. Val was shocked at their reaction and tried to hurry on, but Sam and the others lifted her off the ground and onto their shoulders. The cheering reached a joyous crescendo. Val smiled. She had done it! The vision had come true and the Warden was free.

The Warden, who was being supported by the Mechanics, grabbed her hand. "You have taken the first step in saving this Prison. Now let's finish this battle." Turning to the Mechanics he ordered, "Take me to my office."

"Warden, you need more time to rest," one said nervously.

"TAKE ME TO MY OFFICE!" he bellowed. Val knew he was going to be ok.

Wendy was the next person Val saw running through the sea of Guards towards them. "I knew you would do it," she called up to Val over the heads of a group of Collectors.

"Did you know about Sam?" she called. Wendy nodded. "Thanks for telling me!" she smiled.

In the distance she could see a very familiar face – her Collector. But there was no smile, no cheers for the Magrafe and their success from her. "Sam, let me down," Val called. As soon as the band of Guards had lowered her to the ground, she ran towards the Collector. Guards who had previously mocked her were now patting her on the back as she passed.

"Hello, Val," the Collector greeted her.

She knew something was wrong. "What's up?"

"We must move away from where we can be seen." She walked quickly and Val followed, slipping through a doorway as the rejoicing continued behind them. The Collector, clearly on edge, made her way down another corridor and Val followed until they arrived at the glass door that led to the High Collector. Val was confused. Surely they weren't going to send her on another mission this soon? They waited as before and the door whooshed open. Val's Collector greeted her superior respectfully and moved Val into position.

"I'm sorry to see you again so soon, but you have a problem." She opened up a screen in mid-air in front of Val.

There were lines, dots and blurry images, but nothing she recognised. "I don't understand. It makes no sense."

"Look harder."

Val looked again, and then she spotted it. It was Zac. He was in a wooded area and clearly in trouble. "You will have to break the law again. I'm so sorry. Your Collector brought this to my attention, knowing you would want to help, but there is a lock down and you can't leave through the normal route. She asked me as a personal favour to help you and, considering what you have just achieved, I feel we owe you this. However Val, we will deny any knowledge if asked."

"I understand."

"To get home you must do what you did on Nyteria." The High Collector took Val's hand then touched her bracelets. "You still have the power."

She looked at her wrist and realised she was wearing a second bracelet. "What's this?"

"It's the Warden's. Seems you had a little power boost back on Nyteria. It could take you home, Val, but I must warn you, if you do, the punishment on your return will be severe."

"I don't care. I'm going home."

"If you're sure."

"I'm sure. What now?" She looked to her Collector for advice.

"Focus Val, you need to go as fast as you can. The messages I have been receiving have all been bad. It seems that as soon as the new Guard arrived and used his Dellatrax, Lailah had something to lock onto and attacked. Zac explained the situation to me only minutes ago and you need to get home now or you will have nothing to go back to."

"Thanks."

"Just try and focus on getting home."

Val pulled her bracelet out and made sure it was as close as possible to the Warden's. "Here we go." She closed her eyes and her helmet covered her face. She was going home and no one was going to stand in her way. If she could escape Nathan Akar, then Lailah was in for a surprise.

CHAPTER 6

Home Again

Val's landing sent tremors running through her legs. Her body lurched uncontrollably to one side and she opened her eyes to find herself confronted by a petite, dark haired teenage girl. Why couldn't she control her legs? And why hadn't she landed at Sam's house? Someone grabbed her from behind. She spun to find her new Hunter from Alchany holding onto her.

"Why am I here?" he shook his head, waving his watch about.

"Seems like you finally have something to do. Wherever a Guard goes, her Hunter must follow." She removed his hands from her waist. At a glance she could see that they were on a moving vehicle; the top floor of a double-decker bus to be exact. And then the reality that two people had just appeared out of thin air started to dawn on their fellow passengers.

"OMG, it's a ghost!" a young girl screamed.

Val managed to grab her mouth.

"Let her go!" another girl struck at Val.

Chaos rapidly spread as more and more kids realised that something very strange had just happened. Kids shrieked and screamed and clambered over each other in their efforts to get a better view.

"This is not going very well," her new companion pointed out.

"Helmet off."

The helmet retracted, causing even more excitement in the watching crowd.

"Everyone listen!" Val shouted above the clamour, lifting her free hand into the air. "We don't want to hurt you. We're here by mistake." She looked down at the girl who now had tears welling in her nervous eyes. "I'm going to let you go and it isn't ok to scream, alright?"

The girl nodded, her eyes wide, and Val removed her hand from the girl's lips. There was an exaggerated gasp for air, as the girl looked up at Val. "I know you," she whispered.

Val's Hunter was tapping urgently on her shoulder. "I'm sorry, but we seem to have a problem. Prisoner 248185 is here."

"Then that's probably why we're here." She turned back to the girl. "Ok, I need to know what your name is, and how do you know me?" Val didn't remember the girl's face.

"I'm Sam Brutton and I saw you fall off a roller coaster on Youtube. Do you remember, Ellie?" she turned to the girl that had tried to clobber Val, who was now once again seated. As she slowly calmed down, Val could tell by the expression on her face that she was starting to recognise her as well.

"Yeah, I remember you now. What're you doing here?"

Val couldn't believe what she was hearing. These girls recognised her from the internet, it didn't make sense. They had protected her from this back in 1645; Wyetta had made sure that no-one would remember her. Had the spell been broken when the bookshop had burnt down? That would explain her parent's miraculous memory restoral. She would need to tread carefully.

"Look guys, it seems we have a situation. Me and my friend here are military projects. We're here because there is an escaped robot on your bus. It's like a simulation that's gone a little wrong. So, I don't want you to panic. I need to know if anything odd has happened?"

"You mean like the driver?" A girl wearing neon blue sunglasses popped her head over the top of the seat directly in front of her.

"Could be. Who are you?" Val asked kindly. She needed everyone to stay calm.

"I'm Amber spelt with two r's and an h. What's your name?" She seemed overly confident for someone so young, but Val was just glad that she wasn't screaming.

Gradually everyone returned to their seats, though all eyes were still firmly on her and the Hunter. "I'm Val. Now tell me more about the driver."

"Well, me and Astacia were going to sit on the bottom floor, but he was staring at everyone. He freaked me out with his sweating, and he stank. Gross." She pulled a face of physical disgust whilst forcing her fingers down her throat as her friend nodded in agreement.

"Does smelly and sweaty help?" Val turned to look at the Hunter who was standing in the middle of the aisle frozen to the spot looking around at the kids. "Hello, they won't bite you."

"Sorry, I haven't seen so many fledglings together before. What did you say?"

"Sweating and smelly - ring any bells?" Val couldn't believe she was asking this question about a bus driver, it sounded almost normal to her.

"No, why don't you look on your Dellatrax?"

"Long story, short version: I don't have one." It was becoming very apparent to Val that they were now being streamed live, possibly onto the internet by about ten kids holding their shaking phones up in their direction. "Who's down there with the driver? Teachers? Assistants?"

"Miss Thompson and four random lost souls that haven't been on holiday for forever." The girl with the glasses answered and sat back down.

"Ok guys, listen to me. Whatever happens now, keep your belts on ok? And anyone who puts my picture on Facebook, Twitter or any other social network will be hunted down by MI5, and imprisoned on an island for life, and you," Val pointed at the girl with the glasses, "are extremely random, but thanks for the help."

Val headed for the stairs, turning to place her finger against her lips and pointing at the kids. They followed instructions. She was grateful it wasn't a bus full of pensioners; they would have been a lot less controllable.

"What's your plan?"

"I'm going to stun the driver,"

"What? Then who will drive the vehicle?" The Hunter stared at her.

"Alright. I'll stop the bus first."

"How?"

Val surveyed her surroundings. "Hey, you." She beckoned to a boy who had been watching her with astonishment. "Come here." He looked away, then back at her. "Yes, you." Val smiled at him. He undid his belt and moved over to the stairs where the Hunter and Val were crouched.

"Who are you? What do you want?" He looked suspiciously at them.

"We're SAS soldiers." Val pointed at her uniform, at last it was coming in handy. "We've just been dropped onto the top of the bus by helicopter and we need your help. What's your name?"

"Elliot, and I'm not stupid. We're a bunch of kids travelling to an adventure holiday! Why would the SAS be interested in us?" he looked at Val with disbelief.

"Ok Elliot. Truth is, the bus driver is not a good person. He's what you call a little dodgy, and we need to get him off the bus to keep you guys safe. But to do that, we need to stop the bus. How do you feel about helping us?" Val batted her eye lashes, trying to look at least a little like Delta.

"Why should I?" He now looked even less worried and more like he was going to bargain for more pocket money.

"Because if you don't, I will get him," she pointed at the Hunter, "to suck your brains out through your ear. Now go and pretend you're going to be sick, Elliot." Val pushed him forward.

The Hunter looked confused. "This does not seem a feasible act. I have never removed anyone's brains and who are the SAS?"

"Don't worry," Val replied.

Elliot hesitated in the walkway and looked back at them. Val made pulling signals at her ear. It was enough to get him moving again. They watched as a couple of adults at the front of the bus turned to look up at him. As agreed, he signalled that he was going to be ill. A short-haired woman sprang into action, obviously a veteran of schoolchild travel sickness. She moved towards the driver, shouting at him to stop and, as he turned towards the woman, Val got her first view of him.

He nodded in agreement and started to pull the bus over to the side of the road. "No one move. I'll be back in a second," the teacher called over the heads of the children on the ground floor of the bus. The door swung open and, pushing the boy in front of her, they got off.

Val waited for a few seconds for the kids to completely ignore the teacher and start standing up. She knew this might be their only opportunity, so they had to get it right. "Time to go!" She jumped to her feet, her new sword extending out in front of her, and ran to the front of the bus, accompanied by the screams of the over-excited kids who were not prepared for a young woman running around wielding a weapon. As she reached the front, it became very apparent that the bus driver was sweating profusely. The smell was almost over-powering and Val had to catch her breath to stop herself from gagging on the stench.

He looked round, "Oh, it's you," he spat.

She wasn't even sure how to respond. "Yes, it's me."

"Then let's fight." He looked her up and down and started to rise out of his seat.

"Are you serious?" Val looked back; the Hunter was still making his way down the aisle, clearly trying to avoid physical contact with the kids, who were recording Val with their phones whilst screaming. "You know what, I don't have time. I need to save my real Hunter." She touched him with the tip of her sword, stunning him. He dropped instantly, slumping onto the steering wheel.

The Hunter arrived. "Prisoner 248185, you are hereby returned to the hands of the Prison. You will come with us into holding until such time as we can return you to Alchany. Do you understand?"

"Are you mad? He's out cold." Val felt bemused.

"Protocol." He defended his actions.

"Crazy." She shrugged. Now she needed to work out the best way to end this situation quickly and without too much damage. "You," she pointed at one of the adults. "Do you have a rope or something?"

"I have a bungee." The man nodded, reaching up nervously to his bag and pulling down a thick, elasticated rope.

"We need to get out of here. These kids are having a field day and we will be all over the news by tomorrow morning." Val turned around holding both hands high in the air. "Listen to me. I must inform you all that this is a military exercise and we have all your addresses, so think seriously about the consequences if you use those pictures." She tried to look as stern as possible, not sure it was working.

Val spoke to two women sitting in the second row who looked more petrified than the kids. "Take all of their phones and delete those images, or it will be on your heads." The adults nodded nervously.

Val wrapped the bungee around the unconscious driver's hands. Then she and the Hunter hauled him off the bus. They got out into the fresh night air. A genuine reprieve from the stench the driver had been letting off in such a confined space. She spotted the teacher over in the lay-by trying to help their new friend Elliot, who was still pretending to be ill. "Elliot it's ok, were finished." She called, retracted her sword as they moved the body into the bushes. "Now let's go get Zac."

CHAPTER 7

The Novelia

Val knew that after their little meeting with the bus driver, the aliens were going to be a problem. There was no portal to take them back to the Prison, and now that Lailah was actively looking for her, she would have to move quickly. She held her wrist and prayed that she would get to her friend in time.

The landing was rougher than she expected. Being squashed against a rubbish bin by the body of the still unconscious bus driver was rather uncomfortable. Kicking him off her, she allowed him to drop to the ground as she surveyed her surroundings. It was a wooded area, trees high on each side of a simple mud and pebble track. It smelt clean and fresh after the Prison's closed environment.

The Hunter landed perfectly. If the Judges from Strictly Come Dancing had been there, he would have received four straight tens. He pointed at his watch, frowning. "Your Hunter and my Guard have a serious problem."

"What?"

"This code is for the Novelia." He was rapidly losing the little colour he had in his face. "There are three of them here."

"I've heard of them, but I thought they were in the Interspace. How can they be here?" This was bad, very bad.

The Hunter shook his head. "I don't know."

"Can you pick up Zac's signal?"

"No."

"Ok, so we need to find them fast and we don't know how big an area this is." Val and the Hunter dragged the bus driver behind a bush. "We can come back for him later."

Everything looked the same, trees, trees and more trees. Her instinct told her she should call out Zac's name, but after the grim description of the Novelia that Sam had given her, she was frightened that they would hear her first. She came to an opening in the bushes, and unexpectedly, a car park. It was empty, but this was clearly somewhere people visited, which raised another problem - random tourists. Luckily, to one side of the car park was something she knew could help, a phone box. She ran into it, pulling up the receiver and praying it wasn't just there for decoration. There was a dial-tone! She thought hard. Her parents wouldn't be home, so she needed to contact someone else who would help her: Shane. "Come on," She tapped her fingers on her head, concentrating hard. "The code is 01675 then his number was something to do with the devil... Yes 666! But what came first? Come on Val." She banged the phone with her hand. Remember the card... 849666! That was it 'The House of Art'. Val dialled the numbers, then realised she had no money. The phone took cards, but she had no pockets in her stupid special suit. If she'd had her jeans on this wouldn't have been a problem.

She searched the box for an answer to her dilemma, and found what she needed right in front of her eyes. Reverse charges call. She dialled the number given on the sign. "Please enter the number you wish to contact." She tapped away. "Say your name after the tone." The machine droned "Val Saunders." The Hunter looked at her with a quizzical expression. She pointed at the phone and smiled. "Please wait while we try to connect you." Val could feel her chest constricting with the stress of waiting. "The person you are calling will now be connected, thank you for using 0800 Reverse."

There was a silence. "Shane?" Val wanted nothing more than to hear his voice.

"Is that you mate?" It was Jason. Tears welled in her eyes. "Val, are you there?"

"Thank God. Where is everyone? Are my parents ok? How can I get to Zac? I'm in some woods and I can't find him. Please tell me what to do."

"Ok you just popped up on my screen, and in the same place as Zac. You're in Willingham Woods in Lincolnshire. Can't tell you how great it is to see you flashing at me again," he responded brightly. "Everyone's ok. We're all at Sam's. Never knew call divert would come in this handy."

She rested her head on the glass. These people were her family and she was home. "Fine, so now we both officially love BT. Tell me where he is?"

"Looks like he's about four hundred metres away. Can you see an opening and a small bridge?"

She rubbed one of the grubby panes. "Yes, I can."

"Ok, if you follow that path you'll find him on the left. Val, things haven't gone to plan. I'm so glad you've come home, the other Guard is just weird."

"Well, maybe you'll treat me a little better now then, like less training. Bye for now, see you soon." She hung up. "Come on Hunter, we have a job to do."

She started to run in Zac's direction. If nothing else, she was getting fitter. Luckily for her, the ground was soft and her approach was practically silent. She focused and her helmet came up over her head. She surveyed the area, looking for any signs of life. Over by a tree she spotted three heat sources. They looked very much like the outlines of dogs. She slowed down, holding her hand up for the Hunter to follow suit. Glancing over in the other direction she saw there were bushes, trees and two bodies, one flat on the floor the other one leaning over it. Someone was down. She raced towards them, bursting through the ferns. To her guilty relief she found that it was Zac leaning over the Guard.

His eye's lifted, distress and relief showing on his face at the same time. "Welcome. Please be careful, there are three Novelia here. I can't help you as I have to stay with my Guard, but your arrival is excellent timing."

Val realised he hadn't recognised her. "Helmet off." It shot back. "So you've got a new Guard. Let's see if we can keep him alive."

Zac looked genuinely shocked to see her. He stood up, looking her uniform up and down. "You're a Magrafe! Of all the people in the galaxy!"

Ignoring his words, Val grabbed him and held him close. She didn't care if he liked it or not. She had missed him so much. His hands patted her back, and she let him go. "Thanks for the vote of confidence, now let's sort out our friend here and yes, I missed you too." She couldn't believe how good it felt to see him again. "Don't worry, you're not going to lose another Guard. What's been happening?" They both knelt down by the Guard's body.

"We detected the Novelia taking form and came to investigate. Jason was helping us while Shane, Belinda and your father were trying to make Sam's house safe. When we arrived, they were here waiting. One bit Fourteen and I managed to drive the others away, but he's gone." Zac's voice was full of guilt. Val looked up to see the Hunter, who had allowed his Guard to leave him and come to Earth getting closer.

"Have they taken him?" he asked.

"Yes, but he fought bravely." Zac moved to one side to allow him some room to get close.

Val felt his pulse. "He's alive, Zac. He has a pulse, so why can't we save him?" she asked.

"Because no one can escape from the Interspace, they keep you…"

"…I know, suspended in eternal pain, but if he's suspended then surely he's still alive. He has a pulse!" she repeated, feeling annoyed with this Interspace.

"Say you could save him, and that's not the issue, the problem is I don't believe you can get his body back to the Prison. You can't teleport him there as he will show up as dead. Remember when we tried to get Flo back?" Zac reminded her.

"Have you ever heard of someone getting attacked by a Novelia outside the Prison?"

"Well no. It's rare to find them anywhere else."

"Then let's stay optimistic. We need to get him somewhere safe for now and work out how to reunite him with himself."

Val suddenly felt a presence. She turned to see three dogs creeping forward. She had seen their silhouettes before through her helmet, but now they were only a few feet away. "Labradoodles!" she exclaimed. "For heaven's sake, they're like the cutest things ever." She retreated into nervous silence when one snarled. Its saliva dripped onto the ground and she was horrified when it sizzled the grass into ash. "Labradoodles with acid dribble. Nasty! Are you ready to teleport?" Zac nodded and she grabbed hold of the Guard on the ground. "I'll take him, don't worry." They were all extremely still; no one else was going to the wretched Interspace today. "Now." she said quietly and they teleported out.

*

Val was relieved to see that at last they had arrived in Sam's office. She had hoped this would be the case. They had all come to this house seeking refuge after Lailah had destroyed the bookshop and challenged her at her parents' house. On arrival, she had found a letter that Sam had left for her, explaining how he had tricked her into programming her fingerprint into the door of this special weapons room. To her delight, she and Jason had managed to replace all their equipment that had been destroyed in the bookshop fire, from her sword that Daniel - Delta's little lackey had destroyed, to several new laptops, some slim-line phones and a new necklace.

It was a sleek looking room, everything in chrome; clean and precise. Sitting at the desk looking extremely pleased to see her, was Jason.

"Mate," he jumped up, rushing over to grab her in a bear-like hug, lifting her off the floor and planting a kiss on her cheek. "Where were you? And what are you wearing?" He released her, lowering her to the ground, and only then spotted the body next to her. "What's wrong with David?" He knelt next to the Guard.

"He was attacked by the Novelia," Zac answered.

"Looks bad and who's this guy?" Jason smiled at the Hunter.

"He's David's Hunter. This is Jason, he's like our Mechanic on Earth," the Hunter returned the smile, "We need to get David's body somewhere more comfortable," Val instructed. "Jason, where are my Mum and Dad?"

"Are you seriously asking me where your Mum is? She's in the kitchen, of course. Does that woman do anything but cook? I swear my jeans aren't going to fit if she keeps trying to feed me, and your Dad's in the garage. Heads up. I didn't tell them you were back; just in case your Mum got all stressed out and you didn't survive."

"Thanks for that, Mr Positive."

"Shall I come with you?" Zac asked

"That would be nice. Jason, can you guys move the Guard on your own?"

"Sure, see you in a few minutes."

Val walked down the landing with Zac at her side, she wanted to see everyone, but she needed some honest information before her emotions got the better of her. "Ok, tell me what's been going on?"

"Well, after you left, I was the first person your parents informed. I tried to explain to Susan that we had no way of communicating with the Prison. May I add at this point, that she has a very loud voice, for someone so small. Luckily for me, it was literally minutes before David arrived to replace you. He told us about the lock-down on the Prison and that was all he was prepared to say, which is normal procedure. However, it didn't go down well with your mother. She also has quite a temper."

Val smiled. "She doesn't mean it; it's the mother lion thing she's got going on."

"I see. Then we sat down with the others to work out how best to carry on and I was just so pleased David had a Dellatrax." His shoulders dropped. "Val, I picked up a signal within an hour of you leaving and didn't think about the consequences. We went flying off after a Prisoner and when we arrived, there was nothing. David was as confused as I was. That happened three times, but now I see it was a trap. Lailah must have been testing us. She knows we have a Dellatrax and I can only guess she thinks it's you that's been teleporting with me. It's my fault that David's now in the Interspace."

"How were you supposed to know what she was doing? Don't forget she has Eva -a witch- and a powerful one at that. Then let's not go there with my nemesis, Daniel, son of Excariot. Mix that with Delta's natural evil streak and a very dead Flo and, I'm sorry, but you pretty much have an army."

"It was my job! David knew little of the happenings at the bookshop or of Lailah and her threats. I should have informed him that things had gone wrong, that the Dellatrax was lost, and that we were hiding in the house of a Judge. It just seemed easier to tell him less, rather than more. I didn't want him to know we had failed. Then when he was bitten, I had no other option than to use his Dellatrax to send a message to the Collector to tell you what was happening. I was blinded by the fact that he was so professional and he knew the rules."

"Thanks for the indirect insults." She nudged him. "And I'm glad you did send that message. You did what you thought was best and, let's be honest, when have you come across the Novelia on your travels? I'm sorry about David, but we have to focus on the future and stopping

Lailah. If she thinks I have our Dellatrax that may work in our favour. We'll deal with the Interspace later."

"Well, I know your friends will be very pleased you have returned safely, and look at you, a Magrafe." Val noticed how he seemed sad.

"So, do you have a problem with me in this delicious suit?" she asked.

He avoided eye contact. "Magrafe don't need Hunters."

Now she understood. "You listen to me Zac Efron, I need you more than you will ever know. There's a good chance I'll get extracted in the next few days just for coming here, so let's do what a new friend of mine suggested and leave the rule book on the shelf for now."

"What...?"

"No questions, ok. Let's just get this situation under control." He nodded in agreement as they reached the bottom of the stairs.

"I will leave Shane to tell you about the maps," he said.

"What maps?" She asked as they went into the kitchen.

"Val!" Susan spotted her first. She ran round the marble topped central island, apron covered in flour, which was also sprinkled liberally into her black hair, making her white streak look less alone. Val reached out her arms grabbing her just as Mike came into the kitchen from the garage door. "Dad!" Val couldn't control her emotions. Tears started to fall down her cheeks as they both pulled her in tight. Mike's moustache tickled her forehead.

"Don't you do that again!" Susan ordered through matching tears, wiping her eyes and spreading the flour.

She felt someone grab her hand and looked up to see a tearful Fran holding onto her, looking as beautiful as always with her thick auburn hair and deep green eyes. This must be so hard for her, knowing her twin sister, Yassmin, was still controlled by Lailah. Susan and Mike released her and she greeted Belinda with a very witchy welcome and then Shane with a heartfelt embrace. Shane's huge arms wrapped around her and Val just loved how massive and imposing he was. Yet she knew he was the kindest, gentlest person she had ever had the good fortune to meet. This was what she wanted. The Prison wasn't her home. These people were what counted; now she was going to keep them safe, even if the cost was her life.

"I've only been gone a day and look at us. Honestly!" she laughed.

"Take this." Her mum handed her a tissue. Val wiped the tears from her face and just stood for a second, breathing in the familiarity.

"Well, I see you've decided to dress up as cat woman now. Given up on the good guys?" Shane pointed at her uniform.

"No. Get this: I'm a Magrafe - that's like the SAS of the Prison." Val flipped her helmet to her mum's astonished gasp. "Helmet off. It's so cool."

"I'm impressed," Shane agreed.

"Are you hungry?" Susan asked.

Val hadn't even thought about food, her brain had switched off to anything normal, but as she said the words, her stomach jumped for joy, rumbling for everyone to hear. "I think starving just about covers that," she said to Susan's delight.

"Tell us what's going on Hunny?" Mike pulled out a stool for her to sit on.

As she sat, Val spotted that the kitchen table was covered in what looked like astrological charts. "Well, there's this blue guy called Nathan Akar who has just become the leader of a planet called Nyteria. He wants to take over the Prison because they have an endless supply of clean energy, which in some ways I can understand. Trouble is, he kidnapped the Warden - he's the one I told you about who looks like Father Christmas, my boss. Then Wendy had a vision."

Belinda's eyes lit up at the mention of her daughter's name.

"Don't worry, she's fine," Val reassured her. "She saw that I would save the Warden, and that's why they took me away and you got the other Guard."

"Where is David?" asked Shane.

"He's upstairs and not well. He was attacked by a very dangerous alien. Problem is, we can't fix him here. I need to get him back to the Prison. Just out of interest, why's he called David?"

"I named him after David Beckham, didn't you see the resemblance?" Jason answered as he walked in wrapping his arm around Fran's neck.

"Not really." Val frowned.

"Same resemblance as our friend here to his namesake?" He patted Zac on the shoulder. "Anyway he liked it." He grabbed a sandwich from the side and winked at Susan.

"Point taken. Now back to my story. In the beginning I didn't want to help the Prison and was on my way home when Sam took me to a place called the Space." Val shot Shane a glance.

"You've been to the Space?" Shane perked up, eager for news.

"Yes and Taran is fine. Why didn't you tell us about them?"

"It was safer not to, Val. Sometimes you have to keep these things to yourself; that's what the army taught me. If what you have to say isn't relevant or necessary to keep you alive, then don't say it. Anyway, it reminded me of Beth too much."

"Mum?" Jason interrupted.

"You know my history with Sam spans a very long time son, and talking about your mum always hurts. It wasn't safe to tell you about our work when you were little, children tend to repeat everything they hear. When Beth died I bought the tattoo parlour here to be closer to Val. I told Sam I would help this girl he said was so important, but no more moving as I had you to bring up alone. Yes, I have visited the Space with Sam and taken gifts for the children. Son, you'd love it there. They're a unique bunch of people who have so much to offer, yet they're prisoners in their own planet. I promise, now you're old enough, I'll tell you all about my past, but right now we've more urgent matters to deal with."

"Anything you can tell us that you think could help would be good Shane, because they're in trouble and far from being out of the woods – no-one is. Even though we managed to save the Warden, Nathan is still planning an assault. So really I should be there now, but my Collector told me you guys were in trouble. So, does someone want to tell me about the maps?" she pointed at the table.

Mike moved over and turned one of the star charts towards Val. "Shane, you're the man with the knowledge."

Susan landed a sandwich in front of her with fresh bread that made the word 'doorstop' sound like 'wafer thin'. Val grabbed it and tucked in.

Shane picked up one of the maps and placed it on the counter. "See this?"

She nodded, whilst masticating.

"My wife drew it in 1645." Val's chewing slowed. "She was there the day you were born; she travelled a lot with Sam in the beginning."

"Right. Go on."

"After Beth's death, the charts were hidden by Sam to keep them safe here on Earth. They hold information that only a few can decipher. Some of them show where energy sources are positioned on Earth; we call them ley lines. Others hold planetary alignments. After you left, I received a message from Sam to fetch them and check to see if there were any alignments due. He had a hunch."

"Uh huh."

"He was right, there's an alignment coming, and I suspect that Lailah's becoming active all of sudden has something to do with it. Our concern is that Lailah's trying to find this point here." He placed his finger on the map.

"But that's just a star, I don't understand, and how does Lailah know about this?"

Belinda explained, "Val, a planetary alignment brought me and Wendy to you eleven years ago. Eva is a very powerful and intelligent witch. I wouldn't be surprised if she hasn't been informed of this alignment. I'm sorry to say that the skies look the same for all of us and so we can't stop them finding out."

"Belinda's right," Shane said. "Val it's not a star, it's a point here on Earth. As soon as I saw where it was, I knew I had to share it with everyone. Seems we're in for a huge surge of magical power."

"So Lailah wants it to do what exactly?"

"Sam will be able to answer that, but we have more problems. Before David and Zac left they picked up a glimmer of a signature. Tell her about it."

"It was worse than that," Zac said. "It seems that Lailah has been busy while we have been waiting. Earlier today when I picked up the last signal, the one for the Novelia, I got a glimpse of her plan. It seems that she has also got more prisoners waiting." Zac tapped at his watch. "Look at this." He pointed to the screen. There was a white spike from the top to the bottom. "That's when the Novelia appeared. Lailah clearly wanted us to go and get them; she knows just how deadly they are and knows you wouldn't let them go." He pressed more buttons. "More worryingly, this appeared a second after. It seems that Eva's been cloaking her activity." He held out his watch once more for Val to see as the screen went solid white.

"Just explain that one more time to me," Val asked, frowning. "One line on your screen was three of the most dangerous aliens in your galaxy and a full page of white is what?" Her gut was already telling her, but she needed to hear it from Zac.

"It's *full aliens*, and a lot of them all together."

"When you say *full aliens*, are we talking prisoners like the bus driver I just left in the woods with the Novelia, or something else?"

"Something much worse. Our friends have found a way to allow the prisoners to use humans to revert to their natural forms. That's probably why they have been so quiet, it would take a few days for them to transform."

"Are you sure?"

"The Novelia can't take on human form, they can't tolerate large amounts of human DNA. So to get them into another vessel, you must cross them back to their closest alien form, and your dog seems to be the next best thing. So yes, I'm almost positive."

"So, let me get this straight. We have a magical alignment predicted in 1645 coming, mixed with a mass of full aliens, and three dogs that could kill us with their spit? But why?" She placed the sandwich back on her plate, her appetite gone.

"Portals - ways to other planets or times," suggested Shane. "I'm not a hundred percent sure yet. I was hoping to speak to Sam, but it seems he's a little occupied at the minute."

"I agree with Shane," said Zac. "Plus when David got the first signal as we teleported home, they would have been able to track us down, which means they are probably on their way here now. They will also think that the Novelia have killed you, not knowing it was David." Zac informed her. Susan gasped in the background.

"Too many facts Zac," Val told him. He would never get subtle. "But let's get ready for the fight."

CHAPTER 8

Unwanted Guests

She hoped Zac was wrong, that Lailah had no idea where they were, but she knew better. She also knew that they would be coming for the Dellatrax thinking she was dead, and that some magical alignment that Lailah and Elizabeth had known about was happening and soon. The only problem was, she didn't have the Dellatrax, and they still had no idea who did.

Belinda's voice broke the uncomfortable silence in the kitchen, "Is that who I think it is?"

Val walked over to the window. "Well, unless you mistook Delta for the bin-man, I think it is. Belinda, now would be a good time to get a protection spell up and running." Val's helmet closed over her face and she dashed for the front door. They weren't going to get in that easily. She was closely followed by Zac, Jason, Mike and Shane.

"Don't forget it's Yassmin!" Fran called as Val pulled the front door open to find herself in a western style standoff with her adversaries.

"Give us the Dellatrax and we will let you live. We know you have it," Delta announced.

"Delta, leave now while you still have a chance." Val's sword slowly extended.

"Who are you and how do you know my name?" she demanded.

Val's helmet sprung open. "Surprised to see me?"

"More disappointed you're not dead, but look who went to town on her uniform. Get it from Pri-marni?" Delta faked nonchalance, but Val could tell they had genuinely expected to waltz in and get the books. Meanwhile, Daniel moved closer to Delta while on her other side, Lailah and Flo looked even more menacing - if that was possible.

Lailah's expression was one of anger and hatred, even in Yassmin's body with the long blond hair and blue eyes, she looked like a villain. "Magrafe... interesting. Kill her," she ordered.

Val heard a noise in the distance like feet, mixed with hooves and howling. Quickly she stepped out in front of the others and, raising her hand, she created an impressive blue ball of fire. "If you want to try?"

Daniel raised a ball of energy but held it, as if unsure of what to do next.

"Do it! What are you waiting for?" Lailah yelled at him.

"Daniel wait, we don't have our Dellatrax. You're not going to win, and you need to know I've just comeback from spending time with Wendy." His eyes twitched, like he had been knocked off track. "Yes, Wendy. She's alive and living at the Prison. You could go and see her. I could take you there if you would just stop this madness." The approaching noise was getting louder and Val could see that this was going nowhere.

Delta touched his arm in an attempt to refocus him. "Daniel, she's lying. Eva told you Wendy's dead. She's the one you should trust, and you saw the signals from the Dellatrax. Now kill her."

So they had been tracking them as Zac thought. Val, watching him closely, saw that Delta's words had had the desired effect on Daniel, who went from questioning the truth, back to being her potential killer. He lifted his hand and threw the ball of energy at her. But she had been prepared for it and was already running at him. His ball of energy missed her head by inches as she grabbed him and teleported them out.

She gave no thought to where they might end up, but just acted to protect her family. Their landing was hard, but she was lucky as her uniform protected her as they fell. She felt hard walls knocking her from left to right, then steps, down which she tumbled, unable to stop her jarring descent. Through the gloom she could just make out Daniel suffering the same fate a few yards ahead of her. Desperately she turned, dug her sword into the ground and gripped the edge of the next step with her fingers. Finally she managed to come to a halt. Jumping to her feet she saw Daniel was still rolling into the darkness. She ran after him, lifting her wrist to light the area.

It was clear that they were underground, and this place looked oddly familiar. Then it came to her. Of course! It was the cave passage in Devon from the landslide. Daniel's body had finally come to a stop at the bottom of the steps. There was no movement. Val approached him cautiously, keeping her distance. It could be a trap; he could be tricking her into thinking he was out cold. She nudged him with the edge of her boot, her sword pointing at his neck. Nothing. She crouched, shining her light in his face and spotted the blood. It was seeping from his head, covering the ground, mixing with the mud. She felt for a pulse, it was slow, but at least he was still alive. She decided that she had to leave Daniel here. She knew that Lailah and the others didn't have powers like Daniel, but they were still dangerous and her first responsibility was to her family and friends.

She teleported out and arrived outside Sam's house to find that Lailah and her followers had gone.

"VAL!" The urgent shout came from behind her. She spun to see Jason and Fran leaning over Shane's still body. She started to run and had almost reached them when she was suddenly struck from the side by a massive blow; it was how she imagined it must feel to be hit by a car. Her head shook. Her helmet covering her like a safety airbag going off as she hit the ground, skidding three or four feet on the concrete. The pain was intense and the thing that had hit her was now coving her whole body, panting on her, steaming her visor. Her sword retracted as she used both hands desperately to fight it off. Scrambling backward, she attempted to get up, but the alien beast wasn't going to let her go that easily. It grabbed her with its huge gaping mouth and started to shake her like a rag doll. Her uniform hardened in an attempt to protect her. She could only see blurry images of the others as she put her hand out to grab what she could just make out as an ear. She ripped at it aggressively and the creature cried out in pain and shrank back long enough for her to get to her feet again. What was it? And were there more? She didn't have to wait for answers: a group of alien beasts leaped down the drive towards Sam's house, bouncing off the parked cars and jumping hedge rows as they came.

She ran back towards the door. "Get back inside!" she called to the others. Zac already had the door open as something resembling a lizard threw itself onto Jason's back. Mike beat at it with his fists until it released him, scrambling away over the hedge. Val grabbed

Shane's arm; he was still unconscious on the ground. With Zac dragging him by his jacket, they hauled him towards the house. They still had a couple of metres to go when a smaller figure grabbed at his leg. Fran ran to help, and they managed to pull Shane through the door. Val turned swiftly, her sword extending at lightning speed, she stunned the stumpy, elf-like creature and kicked it away from the entrance.

How could this be happening? She heard a large bang as another alien with huge hooves charged the doorway. She crouched over Shane's body, hoping her suit would also protect him. The creature raised its front legs and came down with tremendous force. Its hooves made contact, but not with Val; instead it appeared to hit a barrier of bright red light. It recoiled in pain.

Another one attempted the same and received the same jolt, howling in anger. They couldn't get in. Val looked around to see what had created the barrier and saw Belinda standing by the door, chanting, her lips were moving in a stream of words that Val couldn't comprehend. As they pulled Shane fully inside, Belinda, poised in the doorway, raised her right arm and cried, "So mote it be!" The door slammed shut in the aliens' faces.

Val glanced down at her uniform and knew that the stuff all over her was Shane's blood. "MUM!" she called out. Susan was already there, knelt down at Shane's side. She started to carefully pull at his top.

Jason, still half-stunned by the attack, stood by the wall, covered in his dad's blood, his face ashen.

Pumped up with the adrenaline flowing through her veins, and full of fear for Shane, Val headed towards the door once more. Zac followed her. "Where are you going?" he asked her.

"I don't know. Where did they all go? Look what they've done to Shane! They'll pay for that!" She moved backwards and forwards like a caged lion as three more aliens attempted, but failed, to get in at the hall window.

"They didn't; it was Daniel. When he missed you the energy ball hit Shane." he grabbed her arm making her stand still. "Where's Daniel?"

"I left him in Devon. He's injured, out cold, he won't be going anywhere."

"Go and get him," Zac ordered.

"No, look what he did to Shane."

"Val, go and get him. You have no choice; it's your duty."

She stood her ground as her dad came over. "Where's the boy?" Mike asked.

"Mike, Daniel is wounded and your daughter is refusing to fetch him."

"But Dad, he hurt Shane. Shouldn't we be concentrating on him?" Her voice trembled with anger.

"That boy is just a child and we need to help him as well. Valerie, please go and get him, quickly." Mike's tone was firm.

Val couldn't fight with her dad, not when he spoke to her like that. "Fine."

*

When Val returned with Daniel, Belinda and Fran were still in the hallway, helping Susan tend to Shane amid a litter of first aid packs and bloodied dressings. Val struggled to support the unconscious Daniel and Zac and Mike hurried to take him off her, laying him on the floor. Shane now lay next to the boy who had wounded him so badly.

"Val, it's not good, we need help. Go and get your uncle Julian."

"Are you serious, Mum? Why not get them to a hospital?"

"And tell them what? Here are two alien attack victims. One of those attackers was my daughter, please arrest her now! And dissect her while you're at it!"

"Ok, I'm going."

*

She had been to her uncle's surgery several times over the years for one thing or another, but this was going to be interesting. She teleported into the toilet opposite his office, praying no one was in there. She was lucky. She pulled the door ajar. The surgery was shut and there was an elderly lady vacuuming the waiting room, but that was it. At that moment her uncle came out of his consulting room. Val did her best to look as if she really had been using the facilities and plastered a smile on her face. "Val, what are you doing here? I had a really odd call from your mother the other day... what are you wearing?" His normally jovial expression was quickly replaced by a look of confusion.

"I need your help. This'll make no sense, just hold on." She grabbed his arm and they were a blue spark.

Her uncle staggered several times and was deftly caught by Mike, who smiled and patted him on the shoulder. "Hello, Julian. We've got a bit of a problem here and we need your help."

Her uncle surveyed his surroundings, clearly unsure whether to run or just faint. Val was most impressed that he hadn't been sick after his first teleport.

"Julian, please help me." Susan looked up, her hands covered in blood, sweat running down her face.

"I...just...Star Trek..."

"Honestly! Star Trek? Is that the best you can do? Now get down here and help me."

Seeing the wounded on the floor his medical training took over and he knelt at Shane's side. Completely focused on his patient, he inspected Shane's wound and took his pulse. "We need to get him somewhere more comfortable. What about the boy?" He crossed over to Daniel. "He has a nasty trauma to the head. Both of them need to be off the floor. Do you have any beds?"

Mike nodded. "Upstairs. Jason, help me."

Jason still hadn't moved.

"Jason we need you," Mike insisted.

He shook his head.

"Listen son, I know you're scared, but we still have a chance. Don't give up."

Zac moved to help Mike and Jason slowly shuffled forwards. He touched his dad's arm and tears filled his eyes as they lifted his limp body. Val thought her heart couldn't hurt anymore and, yet watching her friend's pain made it break into a million painful pieces.

"Val," Fran spoke, "I know we don't have the Dellatrax, but what about Sam? He saved you before. Can't you get him now? Maybe he could help Shane."

She was right, Sam had healed her. She needed to get him without being spotted, but that would be almost impossible and she couldn't risk losing the Warden's bracelet. She needed Wendy and Sam here right now to help her. "Do you know how Shane contacts him?" Fran shook her head. Then the only way to get close to them was through the Space. She needed to get back to Enoch.

"I'm going to go get him." She gave Fran a hug and made her way up the stairs two at a time. She felt that there was still hope. She made it to Sam's weapons room. She would stand a better chance of focusing here; teleporting so far away from home wasn't easy. All she could do now was pray that she would arrive in the Space. She closed her eyes, holding her bracelets. "God, if you really like my Mum as much as she thinks you do, then I'm calling in a favour. Get me to the Space."

CHAPTER 9

Shane Walker

Val was relieved to find herself standing on the rocks of the Space. Glancing up she made a little thank you gesture to the unseen sky. "Think - was it left at the grey rock or right?" she quizzed herself as she turned around. This wasn't exactly what she had wanted. She had expected to arrive at the big metal door, but now she was totally disoriented. Looking from one cave wall to the other she suddenly remembered that they had cameras. Sam had shown her one, but how many did they have? And where? Were they working? If she could get spotted by Enoch and his friends, hopefully they would come and find her.

She searched for signs of technology, but everything was still, grey rock. There was no point in moving if she was heading in the wrong direction; that's what her dad always said. So she stood and waved, turning in slow circles. Ashamedly, this was the best idea she had.

She had been waving for three or four minutes when she heard a whizzing noise, like sparks flying off a knife sharpener. Then she spotted a figure getting closer. Wheels spinning full speed, she recognised Alsom's blond hair floating in the air behind him as he glided up and down the rock walls.

"Hey Val," he called "good to see you." The boy spun in mid-air clearly showing her what he was capable of and came to standstill a few inches away. Val smiled, relieved. "So what brings you here?" he asked.

"Big problems and time is running out. Could you please take me to Enoch? By the way, where's the camera?"

"There." Alsom pointed to the floor under Val. She had been standing over it all the time. She would have been embarrassed if her life wasn't falling apart.

Alsom moved with ease over the surface, Val not so gracefully. Taran was waiting by the door to greet her, his arms wrapping around her waist. She returned the embrace. "I need to go, but I promise when I can, I will come back and see you, ok." Taran nodded, releasing her. She ran up the grey hill towards Enoch's. "Alsom, tell him I'm coming," she called out as the boy spun away from her.

By the time she had reached the top, Enoch was heading towards her. "Val, what's wrong? Why are you here?"

"Shane's - dying." The words came out between gasps for breath.

Enoch grabbed her arm, helping her to stand on his level. "How can we help you?"

"I need Sam and Wendy. They are on the Prison and I can't go back there at the minute. Sam can cure him; he did it for me before."

"Val, the only way I can get Sam is if I go onto the surface, and they are under attack."

"I know I'm asking you to take a huge risk, but I really need them," Val pleaded.

Enoch nodded. "Of course I will. Shane and Elizabeth have given us so much in the past. I can't tell you how long it will take, I can only hope for success. Go and be with your friend, I will do my best." They said their goodbyes and Val followed Alsom back to the door.

"Good to see you again," he said and was about to close the door when Taran appeared. There was something about this boy that Val couldn't resist. He was so innocent.

"Please give a message to Shane for me," he called. "I need new crayons, my red has all gone." He waved as the door slowly shut and Val crumbled inside. She grabbed her bracelet ready to return to the others and to wait for Sam and Wendy.

*

The landing was too quiet for her liking. There was no noise. If people were screaming or talking it meant they were still alive. She walked towards one of the bedrooms not knowing exactly where Shane was. Opening the door she found Daniel lying on the bed. There was no one in the room with him, but a bowl with steaming water and a towel showed someone had been there recently. He lay motionless, his head in a bandage, yet she could just make out his chest rising and falling. She made her way over to the side of the bed. "I hate you," she whispered fighting back the tears of loathing she felt for him. "Why did you come here? Why couldn't you just stay in the past?" She knelt down at the side of his bed, "I didn't lie to you. Wendy IS alive and she's coming here to help Shane."

"Val," Daniel rasped.

She stumbled backwards.

"Val," he spoke again.

She had no choice but to respond. "What?"

"Wendy," he coughed.

"Yes, she's coming here, to help Shane." She needed him to know that.

He laboured to open his eyes; the sheer effort was clearly draining. "Can the Dellatrax heal Shane?"

"Yes, but we don't have it."

"I do." His voice was getting weaker.

Val just looked at him. Was he seriously going to do this to her? "What's wrong with you? Aren't you happy enough with almost killing my friend that you now want to taunt me with something that could cure him?" She stood up.

"It's at your parent's house…" His eyes shut, scrunching with the pain he was suffering.

"Nice try, along with an ambush."

Daniel took a huge breath as if it was possibly the last he was going to take. "Look in your room. It's with the gold shoes. I just wanted to see Wendy…" The words faded and his body seemed to slump deeper into the bed.

Val knew exactly what he was talking about. She had a hideous pair of gold shoes her Mum had brought her. They were in her 'don't go there' box. Surely he wasn't telling the truth. But could she take the risk? She had made that mistake before when Wendy had told her she was her guardian. She quickly left him, making her way down the landing pushing each door open until she found them all. Jason was sitting on the floor as close to the bed as possible, without actually being on it, holding Shane's hand. Fran was grasping onto his arm and her uncle Julian was monitoring his patient. Zac was standing with Mike in the corner. It was as if they were frozen in time, like a painting.

Fran spoke breaking the grave picture. "Any news?"

"I'm working on it; just keep him alive." She signalled to Zac to follow her.

"Yes?" he asked, joining her on the landing and closing the door behind him.

"We need to go somewhere." This time she took his arm and they left.

*

Trouble seemed like a bland word compared to what she would be in when she went back to the Prison; with all this teleporting and rule breaking she knew she was going to be extracted, but she was past caring. They arrived in her hallway. She saw her jacket hanging on its usual peg. It was like stepping into a bubble, everything was familiar, but she felt like a stranger in her own home. Sadly it no longer felt like the place she had grown up in.

"Why are we here?" Zac asked.

"Daniel said he left the Dellatrax in my room."

Zac sucked in air. "Clever move."

She shrugged her shoulders. They moved quickly, but cautiously. The front door was closed, but still had marks where Lailah and the others had attacked. A pile of post lay on the floor, unopened. It didn't seem important right now. She made her way up the stairs towards her room, pausing to extend her sword outside the door. If this was a trap, whoever was waiting for them would come off worst.

Zac grabbed her by the arm. "Do you trust him?"

Pushing the door gently she looked through the crack. "Bit late for that question." Unless there were invisible aliens in her room they were clear to go. They move in to the room, and she switched on the light. Her bed was still made, everything how she had left it. Her poor mum and dad must have wondered why they had a teenage girl's bedroom, but no teenager. Edging towards the wardrobe she saw her reflection for the first time in her new gear. "Heck! I do look like cat-woman," she exclaimed. Opening the wardrobe door she knelt down next to the box her dad had made her. This was it. If this was a trap they would soon find out. She placed her fingers around the lip of the lid. Lifting it gently, she peeked inside. To her shock, filling the box were her Dellatrax, all of them. She sat back. Daniel had been telling the truth, but why? Why in her room?

Zac began pulling the volumes out. "You need the healing book, the one Wendy used on you. We can come back for the others later."

"But they all look the same."

"But they don't feel the same." He handed her one of the volumes.

Val placed her hand on the top. She wasn't the best at this, and the person who was, wasn't with them. However, it was only a few moments before she felt the book, like a tingling sensation under her fingers. Like it was talking to her in waves of energy. "This isn't it. Hand me another." Zac pulled out another one. "No, another." She had sensed at least five when she hit on the right one. She knew it was the book. A feeling of wellbeing washed over her. "This is it, now what?" But she wasn't going to have to wait. A noise from outside the door told her that someone was about to join them.

"They must have cast some spell on the house. They know we're here," Zac said, grabbing at the books. Val followed suit.

An explosion rocked the bedroom, the door disintegrated, sending shards and splinters all over her bed. In the still smoking doorway stood Lailah, her hands glowing a deep purple, which spread half way up her arms. She looked crazy with anger. "How long did you think you could hide them from me!" she yelled at Val.

"Odd that. I didn't. It was Daniel." Val clutched her books, knowing Lailah was getting her power back. She had to get the Dellatrax back to Shane. Now was the wrong time to fight, but Delta entered behind Lailah and Val needed to make her feelings known. "By the way, Delta, the whereabouts of the Dellatrax were Daniels dying words...," she added and was about to embellish his painful passing, when Zac, who was holding as many copies as he physically could, took her arm and they were gone.

*

Val landed clumsily, dropping the books along the landing as she ran. She didn't care; she had the one she needed held tight to her chest.

Zac was following with more style. "Why did you feel the need to tell them Daniel was dead?" he asked her as they arrived at Shane's door.

"I wanted them to hurt like we are." She barged in. Sam and Wendy weren't there, but she had the next best thing. "Belinda I need you to do something."

"What's that?" she asked as Val shoved a book at her.

"Zac, tell her how to make it work. Uncle Julian, step aside."

"Belinda these books are a life force, very much like your trees." Zac took Belinda and guided her towards Shane. "They can sometimes heal people if the connection is strong enough."

"But Zac, I don't have a clue what to do."

"Belinda, I will guide you don't worry. You are the only person here with the right intuitive skills." Zac knelt down at Shane's side. "Hold the book out and place it on his chest."

"Won't that hurt him?" Fran asked.

"Nothing could hurt him more than he's suffering right now," Zac reassured her thoughtlessly.

Belinda held the book above his body.

"I need you to search for your healing powers. Like Wendy, you have been focused students for many years, you more so, as you are clearly old. All I want you to do is tap into that river of power."

She looked at the book, and across the bed at Jason whose eyes pleaded for something – anything to help his dad. She laid it to rest as gently as she could on Shane's body. He coughed, a gurgling sound in his chest, making them all hold their breath.

"Place your hands on the book, Belinda." She followed Zac's instructions. "Now focus. The book will tell you what to do. You must listen with your magical senses not your human ones. As you are the mother of Wendy, then this will be strong." Belinda closed her eyes and, as Val had predicted, the book knew what she was and started to create its holograms. Lightning blue images rose up from the cover. They wove up her hands and circled her arms. It was such a mesmerising image, beautiful yet painful at the same time. The air in the room was still and they could have heard a pin drop. They climbed and climbed and then, to everyone's horror they stopped. Like someone had switched out a light.

"What's wrong?" Val asked.

"It's not enough," Zac replied. "She's not had enough practice we need…"

"Me. You need me." The door was open and in the entrance stood Wendy.

"Wendy," Val hugged her. "Is Sam with you?"

"He's coming," she reassured her.

"Please help us. You know what to do," Fran pleaded. Belinda moved aside to give room to her daughter. They smiled briefly at each other; there would be time for reunions later. Wendy knelt down placing her hands on the book. It only took a few seconds for the holograms to start lifting into the air once more. They were vibrant blue floating out into the room. Wendy was obviously doing the best she could, but nothing was changing.

"Wendy come on," Val urged.

"Please Wendy, save my Dad," Jason pleaded.

A familiar voice broke the air of desperation. "Let me through."

Val twisted. "Sam, where've you been?" She wanted to hug him out of relief, but knew it wasn't the right moment.

Sam looked at the holograms. Then, to Val's surprise, he reached out, catching one in his hand. It floated in his palm for a moment as he observed it, then faded away. "Wendy, you need to stop. It's too late."

"What exactly do you mean it's too late? You can save him. Use whatever you used to save me," Val insisted.

"His injuries are too severe." Sam moved past her, and her body went from hopeful to defeated in a second. "Jason, look at me?" Sam knelt next to him at the bedside.

"No, save my Dad. I don't know what you two have done in your time, but you owe him this. Please save him," Jason said, still refusing to take his eyes from his dad.

"If I could, I would have already done it. I do owe him my life, many times over. I won't take this time you have left. Don't waste another breath on me." Sam kissed Jason's head and stood back.

"You're lying," Jason sobbed.

Wendy stopped, the holograms faded away and she lifted the book gently from Shane's body.

Shane's eyes opened. "Son." Wendy had done enough to allow him to return to consciousness.

"Dad, hang on, I can get you to a hospital. Let's get him in a car." Jason's voice was hoarse his throat closing with the pain as he attempted to stand.

"Stop, listen to me." Shane's voice was faint. "This is out of your control son. Sam's right, he can't heal me." He took a laboured breath. "Before I go, you need to know the facts. I don't have much time, so just listen." He coughed, blood coming from his wound. Val was now crying openly and Susan pulled her in close.

"I'm a soldier son, I'm a fighter and so are you. I've lived a life beyond imagination." He reached for another deep rasping breath and Val could see how much pain he was in just trying to hang on. "I have fought with Sam to keep this planet safe for you, son. I've faced Death and he's missed me far too many times. Sam will look after you now." Jason's head rested on his dad's chin as he cried uncontrollably. "Val, come here."

She moved over, almost scared to reach out for him. "Yes?" the words seeped from her lips almost as quietly as Shane's voice.

"It's been an honour. Keep fighting, Val. A soldier never asks why, they know in their heart that they were

meant to protect those who can't do it for themselves."
He reached out for her as she knelt next to Jason. "I'll see
your Mum soon son. I bet she's just as beautiful as the
last time I was with her. No more paintings. I love you
boy." Shane closed his eyes as Jason cried out in pain.

"Stay with me, Dad, I don't want to be here alone."
Jason hugged Shane, blood soaking into his shirt.

Val stood, her world smashed to pieces, her heart
broken and unable to deal with what she was watching.
Her dad walked up to her, but she couldn't cope with
this. She walked out past them all. Why Shane? He'd
never hurt anyone. It was her fault, but blame wasn't
what she needed right now. Now she wanted revenge.
She would capture Lailah and anyone else who stood in
her way in the process. She walked downstairs towards
the front door. Pulling it open, she stepped out into the
dark.

Her pain filled body burst into flames, lighting the
garden as she bellowed, "COME FOR ME COWARDS!!"
Her heat burned her tears into vapour before they fell. She
closed her eyes and there was darkness.

CHAPTER 10

Coffee Then Revenge

The tattoo parlour was lit only by the street light outside its large front window. Val's flames reflected off the barber shop floor as she walked over to Shane's work chair. In her mind's eye she could see him tattooing the beautiful girl with the Rock'n'Roll red hair Zac had been so taken by. Kneeling down next to his chair, she allowed her flames to die out, sobbing uncontrollably until it felt like she would drown. She felt so full of pain and confusion. No one could tell her this was ok, that taking Shane was something that was just one of those things, that she didn't have the right fight to back. They were going to taste their own medicine.

Pulling herself up she headed towards the swing doors. As the air rushed through, she could smell his aftershave. She remembered the first time she and Delta had been here and Shane had joked about Bruce Wayne. She had known him for such a short time. How could he be gone? Would he still be alive if she had never come here? As she walked into their space, the stunning pictures of Elizabeth filled her with sadness. 'No more paintings' he'd said. She wandered over to the coffee maker. It was filled and ready. She pushed the button and sat down at the glass table, passing her hand over its soft cold top. One more word, that's all she wanted, one more chance to say she was sorry. But death was so final.

The coffee whooshed and glugged. Val went to get a drink. It seemed like a good plan: coffee first, then she would hunt them down and imprison them all. Yes, she would have a drink then go and deal with Delta.

The hinges of the swing doors gave her the heads up that someone was coming, but she had no fear. No one else would take anything from her today.

"Hi." Sam greeted her. Walking over to the percolator he poured himself a drink and sat down. "Just taken your uncle home and thought I'd find out what you were up to."

She glanced at him. "You won't stop me." She took a sip.

"Doing what?"

"You know what. They can't get away with killing Shane."

"I agree."

"I know you're going to tell me it's not right to want revenge, and that I'll be just as bad as them if I do something stupid. But I'm not going to stop until I capture them because they didn't think about Shane when they took him."

"Yup you're right. Jason wants revenge as well. He's going to hunt them all down, and he has no powers, so 'best of luck' I said to him." Sam took another sip glancing at Val from the corner of his eye.

She sat up straight. "Are you crazy? He'll be killed, stupid idiot. Where's he gone? We need to get him."

"Why? Everyone wants justice here. What makes you think you're hurting more than Shane's son? Let him get on with it. You seem to be doing ok on your own."

"Are you mad? They'll shred him. At least I have powers."

"You don't get to choose who takes revenge, Val. Let's all take it, then we'll all feel better. Lucky for Jason that Shane didn't take revenge on the people who took Elizabeth, because if he had, Jason would have had even less time with his dad, and you wouldn't be here, and the journey you're on to save so many lives would never have happened." Sam looked at Val for a response.

"I don't understand."

"Shane has been in endless situations that put his life in danger before you knew him, and he lost loved ones, but he never lost sight of the final outcome: your arrival."

"So you're saying it's my fault?"

"No! I'm saying that if Shane never took direct revenge on the people who took what he most loved, but strove to bring the one thing that could release us all to the light, then I know he wouldn't want you or anyone else to avenge his death by dishing out the same rough justice. He would want you to honour your power and position. He would want you to be there for Jason, to protect him through everything, and respect who he was. To look to a brighter future and not be stuck in the bitterness of the past."

"But it hurts so much. I don't know how to deal with this pain. I can't breathe." Her eyes overflowed.

"Use the pain to bring us all together, and let's get this situation under control. I have some explaining to do and I need you and Jason to listen to everything I'm going to tell you. Are you ready to go back?"

"Not yet."

"Ok," he nodded.

Val sat for a moment in contemplation. Sipped the last of her drink quietly and then wiped away her tears. "Sam?" She put her coffee cup on the table.

"Yes."

"Do you think he's really with Elizabeth?"

"Definitely."

"I need to tell you something."

"What?"

"Daniel's lying all alone, dying, back at your house." Val knew now that whatever had happened she didn't want his death on her hands.

"Then we'd better leave." He took her hand. "Let's go and do the right thing."

*

"Where is he?" Sam asked pulling the office door open.

"Just there," she pointed to the door.

"I'm going to get Wendy. You go and talk to him. Remember what it feels like to be away from your home and different without wanting to be." Sam headed down the corridor leaving her to go in.

She pushed the door open hoping someone would be there, but they were obviously all still looking after Jason, although now there was a fresh glass of water next to the bed. Daniel was still alive, just, and he clearly wasn't going anywhere. "Hello," she mumbled awkwardly as she moved a chair from the corner over to the bed. "So, you're out cold still? Then this would be a really good time for me to say maybe I was a little harsh earlier when I said I hated you. I really don't know you at all. I was stressed and, well, stuff comes out. We got the Dellatrax, thanks."

The door opened and Wendy came in. She looked like her eyes might fall out of her head from crying. Gripping the healing book, she rushed to Daniel's bedside. She needed no instructions and quickly placed the Dellatrax on his chest. Val watched as the holograms skipped up and around. In her heart she knew he wasn't as badly injured as Shane, and that he would survive.

Sam came to watch over them. "Wendy, just be careful. We don't know what Daniel will do when he wakes up."

She nodded and sat back as the holograms faded. "I know it'll be ok."

Daniel's body began to shake violently. He took a huge gasp of breath, his chest lifted and his back arched from the bed. Val was scared. Was he dying or living? He fell limp onto the sheets and, for a moment there was no sign of movement. Then slowly he opened his eyes and looked straight at Wendy. "I'm so sorry I left you," he whispered.

Val found it hard to watch as Wendy kissed his cheek. "I know; I saw you in a vision. It's time to do the right thing," she said to him.

"Yes it is." His eyes closed again and he just lay there passively: no movement, no aggression and no teleporting.

Sam signalled to Val to follow him out of the room. "You need to see Jason," he said as they joined Zac, Mike, Susan and Belinda on the landing.

"Mum, I'm sorry I bailed on you all." She looked at the floor not sure if she could make eye contact without crying her heart out again.

Susan's voice was shaky, "Go and see him, Val."

"Ok Mum." With Zac following her like a lost dog that had been left home alone, she entered the room to find Jason still holding onto his dad's hand.

"Hey, you're back," he greeted her softly.

"Yeah. Sam came to give me the talk on revenge not being an option, and I'm here to pass it on." Fran released Jason and stood to hug Val.

"I'm going to get Jason a cup of tea, do you want one?"

"Yes that would be good." Val made her way to Jason's side. "I'm so sorry." She laid her head on his shoulder and just breathed in and out.

"You did the best you could and he knew that."

*

Fran returned with hot cups of tea and they just sat in silence together. They were joined a little later by Sam, holding what looked like a glass sphere. He stood very still and she could see it was slowly growing in size.

"Are you ready?" he asked.

Jason nodded. "Yes, are you coming Val?" he asked as if she knew what was happening.

"I'll do whatever you want me to, but what is it we're doing?"

"We're burying Dad." The glass ball was growing faster now.

"What?" Val was shocked. It seemed so sudden. Didn't they have to fill in forms and stuff? The glass ball began to cover Shane, then it engulfed Zac, Sam, Jason, Fran and finally Val. It didn't hurt, just gave her a feeling of oneness with the others inside. The bubble grew and the world outside seemed to darken. She stood and Jason stood with her. Then their cocoon of protection began to disappear and Val caught a breath of what smelt like the sweetest scent she had ever inhaled.

"Where are we?" She looked around.

"We're inside the Space Val," Sam replied.

"But it's so green."

"Yes, we're in an area made of something very similar to your volcanic soil. To respect our lost friends we have created this place for fallen soldiers."

Val looked around, but there were no gravestones, no memorials, and nothing to indicate the purpose of this place.

Sam made his way over to Shane's body. "I will miss you old friend. You were a truly inspirational warrior. I swear to protect your son and Val with my last breath." He touched Shane's face with affection. "Zac, come with me, I have something to show you." He left Val, Fran and Jason alone.

As they stood by Shane's body, Val began to wonder what was going to happen. Then she saw a glimpse of a leaf weaving up towards Shane's ankle. "Jason look!" she whispered.

He moved towards his dad, kneeling by his head. "Dad, if you can hear me, I love you. I didn't say it earlier, I'm sorry." Jason was choking on his words. Fran sat next to him, placing her hand on his. "I want to make you proud. Please help me do that. Watch over me, Dad." He placed a kiss on Shane's cheek. Vines now covered almost all of his body. Jason looked at Val. "He loved you, Val. He said that to me once when I asked him why he was taking so many risks to keep you safe. He said you would make the world a better place to be in. Will you?"

Val placed her hand on the vines that were now taking Shane completely away from them. "I swear I will."

Jason's tears fell as they watched the land take Shane back. Then, out of the mass of green, there appeared one white flower. It was a lily. The lily opened and the sweet smell engulfed them as a breeze, that hadn't been there before, washed over the three of them.

"He's gone." Jason stood up, pulling Fran to her feet. "I want to go home now." She nodded.

Wanting to give Jason and Fran some privacy, Val went to join Sam and Zac who were standing to one side.

"How's it going?" Sam turned to them.

"Painful. How's it going here?" Val responded. She could see that Zac's face was full of emotion. "Are you ok?" she asked him.

He pointed to a mound. "They found my Guard and brought him here, an honourable resting place."

"Oh Zac." She moved over, putting her hand through his arm and pulled him closer. She knew that this would mean so much to him. He had been prepared to be extracted for his Guard and she knew how much it had hurt him leaving his body on an alien planet. They all stood together for a moment's silence and then, without need for words, Sam created another bubble and they were all returned to his house.

Susan walked in with a new tray of drinks and, seeing that Shane had gone, she placed the cups down and held Jason as he sobbed into her neck.

Sam waited respectfully for Jason to compose himself, and then they drank. "Ok, are you ready to make plans?" Val and the others nodded.

"Can I be in on this?" Wendy asked from the doorway.

"Of course. How's Daniel?" Sam asked graciously.

"Asleep." She came in and sat down.

"Good." Val hugged her and they all sat together on the bed.

Sam summoned the others and, for the first time, Belinda was able to welcome her daughter, greeting her with a kiss on each cheek.

"Where's Fourteen?" Sam asked.

"You mean David Beckham?" Val raised her eyebrows at Jason who mustered a sad grin. "He's in one of the bedrooms with his Hunter. Had a run in with a Novelia and the rest is history. But like I said to Zac, if he's still alive in the Interspace, we may be able to save him."

"Well it's never been done, but most of the things you do have never been done."

"Yup that's me – professional galactic rule breaker."

"So where do we go from here?" Mike asked.

"We go to Mistley Heath," Sam replied.

Chapter 11

Manningtree

"Where?" Val asked.

"Mistley Heath is the place of the coming alignment. Its location is a place called Manningtree - one of the most powerful energy points on your planet. Do you recognise the name?" Sam asked.

"Should I?" Val shrugged her shoulders.

"I do," Belinda said with sadness in her voice. "It's not a place for witches, Val. It's a place full of painful memories. It was where more than eighty-five of our sister and brother witches were killed: healers and simple folk hunted down by a man called Matthew Hopkins who ran amock. He was known as the Witchfinder General."

"Sounds bad, but what has that got to do with us?"

"The events that Belinda, so correctly talks about, happened between 1645 and 1647," Sam told her.

Val had definitely heard those dates before. "I was initiated in 1645. That's when Wyetta said that witches were being killed by Excariot."

"Yes, you were born at Manningtree, but the story starts after your father arrested Excariot, and Lailah. Excariot managed to escape to Earth, knowing his chances of survival here where much higher. When your father came after Excariot, he met Wyetta and they fell in love. Shortly after that, you were born and news travelled of the birth of a star child. As a consequence, Excariot was one of the main instigators of the witch-hunt devastation. He wanted to find you and destroy you before you became too powerful. He knew even then that a witch mixed with a Guard would create something special. But he also had other motives."

"Are we talking about Lailah?" Val asked.

"Yes, he wanted to free Lailah, but to begin with had no way of achieving his goal. Do you remember I was there?" She nodded. How could she forget? "Elizabeth was with me at the time. We were also sent to Manningtree. The Prison had seen a great deal of energy emanating from there and wanted to see if it was possible to use Earth as an extension to the Prison. They had proof that a human could be possessed, with Flo making it look easy. We both knew that this would be the end of the Earth if they also knew about the alignments Elizabeth had mapped out, and so we hatched a plan to keep her maps safe."

"How did Excariot know about the alignments?" Val asked.

"Excariot knew the power that Mistley Heath held for the witches, and was brutal enough to interrogate sufficient witches to find out that your initiation would be held on a special date. That's why I got involved. It wasn't my job, but I got emotionally attached to the situation." His eyes met Val's for one second and she blushed. "When he failed to open a portal the first time, and we sent you to the future to Susan and Mike, he was determined to take you back in time. Luckily for us, he didn't know the maps existed, or he would have known not to bother with all that hard work of taking you back to your initiation in 1645. He would have had other opportunities, like the one Lailah is about to use. As soon as you told me Lailah was here, I contacted Shane and told him to get the maps. I knew she was crazy enough to do something like this."

"Crazy is an understatement," Susan said.

"When the Prison saw what Excariot had achieved second time around by teleporting a couple of hundred prisoners, they were so excited, I had to convince them that this half-hearted attempt was the only chance they would have to transport prisoners in bulk to Earth, that they should look elsewhere for a holding planet. Elizabeth and I had never told them about any of the other alignments, but some of the information Excariot had at the time, he passed to his followers - one in particular."

"Who?"

"Flo. She was with him, willingly or not, and remained with him until the arrival of Delta and Lailah. Flo knows everything about Manningtree and the power of the Heath and, from what I can see, she has - with the help of Eva - worked out the next date powerful enough to open a portal and passed it onto the others who will be heading there tomorrow night. Without the Dellatrax, this could be Lailah's only chance at opening a full portal, so she will be there, no question."

"How do you know that?" Fran asked.

"Elizabeth's astrology charts told us that tomorrow will be one of the major dates for the crossing of energy paths."

"So Shane was right?" Val said.

"Yes. You see there are more than one or two alignments. They happen on a regular basis, but some are special. This time Earth is the planet coming into alignment with the Prison. Which means Lailah can open a large portal to Alchany."

"Will their attack be the same as Excariot's?"

"Much worse I'm afraid. If the Prison didn't have enough problems with the Nyterians attacking, they would still struggle to fight this one. It could mean devastation for everyone. I don't even think Lailah knows what she's doing. She's looking for a way to release her subjects, a group of powerful sister Ranswars who were imprisoned hundreds of years ago, but with this sort of power they won't be able to pick and choose what they get, or how many."

"Great, we met some of the wonderful creatures she's created already today. So, how do we stop her?" Val asked.

"We need to block her, which means we can't step in until she opens a portal. It's vital that we halt her and anyone who's with her. She must not succeed."

Val looked at the others. They had been through so much and yet they all listened attentively ready to make the next move. "Tell us what you want."

"Everything you can bring to the table at this point. We'll need to leave in the morning."

"Are you sure about all this?" Mike's voice had a faint shadow of fatherly concern.

"Dad, Shane's gone and I'm not going to lose you or anyone else on this planet to some messed up alien invasion, so let's get a plan before they get to us, because it's going to happen."

"No disrespect, Mike, but I actually don't need you or Susan to come with us. I only need Val, Wendy, Belinda and Zac," Sam apologised.

"What about me?" Jason asked.

Sam patted his arm affectionately. "We need you here. Your eyes will be the only way we'll know they're coming."

"Ok."

"But tonight we need to rest. Tomorrow we will make our way to Manningtree. We'll travel by car, we don't want Lailah to know myself and Wendy are here. It will give us the upper hand."

"How long will it take?"

"It's quite a journey, several hours by car."

Mike piped up, "Then you're going to need me to drive. Val hasn't quite mastered the art yet." Val rolled her eyes.

Sam nodded. "You're right Mike, I do need you. Susan, if you and Fran could look after Fourteen and his Hunter."

"And Daniel?" Wendy whispered.

"Don't worry, we'll look after them all," Susan replied.

Belinda stood up. "Although the house has a protection spell over it, I think we should all stay close tonight, maybe take it in turns to watch. I can take first watch with Wendy."

"I agree." Sam stood. "Mike, we need to get the car ready for the morning. Everyone else, rest." Mike and Sam left the room.

"I can't sleep here." Jason looked at the bed.

Val could understand how he felt, the room felt so empty and cold now Shane was gone. "Let's take some mattresses downstairs."

*

They all worked at making the living room look like a fortress of springs and duvets. Mattresses from wall to wall, they all sat together, Fran curled up in Jason's arms. They looked drained, but incredibly close. Susan had made a space for her and Mike, who had just returned from sorting out Bessie, the big yellow Dodge Nitro. Val sat alone, watching her family and friends. Zac went to check on David and his Hunter. "Are you ok?" Sam asked Val when he returned from checking Bessie.

"I'm worried, Sam. There's so much going wrong. The Prison is under attack, we're going to battle with a planetary alignment and a crazy bunch of aliens, and we still haven't had time to grieve Shane."

Sam sat close to Val on her mattress, and although she felt confused about the universe, she knew exactly how she felt about him. "Sometimes we can't see which way to turn. Life is confusing and it throws us in a million directions, but these people, your family, will always anchor you to who you are. We can do this together."

"Do you have any family?" she asked.

"I did, but they were all lost a long time ago. I was found by the Judges. They took me back to the Prison and I was brought up as a Guard, until they noticed I had gifts that made me different to the others."

"Gifts?" Val was intrigued.

Sam smiled. "Yes gifts, just like Wendy. I had abilities that allowed me to become a Judge."

Val tried to coax Sam into revealing more by raising her eyebrows, but he clearly wasn't reading her womanly expression to tell all. "Look, I don't want to spend all night pussy- footing around, what can you do?"

"I love your directness. I have the ability to affect people's minds." He looked uncomfortable telling her.

Val instantly had images of hypnotists, and Delta strutting around like a chicken. "How?"

"I can take away memories, or give them back. Sometimes I even have to change them."

Val frowned, "Have you done that to me?"

"See, ask too many questions and you may not like the answer," he replied, concern in his voice.

"Well?"

Sam fidgeted. "I have, yes. There have been times when I have found it necessary to remove memories to keep you safe."

"Can you give them back?" She felt odd, knowing he knew things about her that she didn't.

"Some had to be removed completely so that no-one can ever access them."

"Tell me one?"

"Now?"

"Yes." Val wasn't going to let this go. He had taken her memories. She didn't know whether to be angry with him or not.

"It's just a memory." He placed his hand on her eyes, she felt a tingling buzzing sensation and was about to ask what he was playing at when everything went dark. As her eyes got accustomed to the new light she could make out trees. It smelt familiar, fresh air, cool breezes rushing in between leaves. "Hey," a voice made her jump, releasing a small and embarrassing squeal, she swung around. It was Sam, thank goodness.

"What memory is this?" she asked.

"Sorry?" he looked confused.

"Nothing." She smiled. Clearly she was acting something out that was in her past and this Sam wasn't aware of what she was doing.

A woman approached her, wearing a familiar floor length sackcloth cloak, Val held her breath. Was this her mother? She would love to see her, even if just in a memory. As the hood came down, Val was even more surprised.

"Hello V," the woman with the blackest hair and deepest green eyes greeted her.

"Elizabeth." Val knew who she was from Shane's paintings. It was amazing; here she was with Jason's mum.

"How are we doing?" she asked Sam.

"Gabriel has just left to find Excariot, we can now move into position."

"Oh no, that's not good. Excariot's going to kill him."

"V, your father is one of the greatest Guards, don't worry." Sam patted her arm like she was mad. God, he was annoying sometimes.

"Listen to me, my father is going to be killed, *right now*, by Excariot, and then you too Elizabeth. Sorry to drop that one on you. Your son is one of my best friends and..." Val blinked and was once again sitting in the room with her family.

"Val, you can't change the past." Sam removed his hand.

"Why not? They were real, I saw..." she lowered her voice another notch, "Elizabeth."

"Yes, you did and you knew her, but you didn't need to remember her. The memories I give you are like watching a re-run of a film. It doesn't matter what you say, they will still turn out the same way."

"Why did you take that memory? It didn't seem all that important to steal it from me."

"Wyetta and I decided to take them all before we sent you to the future, in the hope you would be safe forever. There is nothing of relevance in your early life memories."

"So, taking away memories of my birth parents, Elizabeth and you, seems ok?"

"No, it's never ok, but sometimes it's for the best. If you had known what you were capable of, you would've been in danger from day one. Your Mum and Dad would also have been at risk. Wyetta chose your parents because she knew that they were the right ones to take care of someone as special as you. Excariot would have found you much faster and you wouldn't have been ready to protect yourself. Wendy wouldn't have been ready for her visions and Shane and Jason wouldn't have been in place to help train you. We planned for the worst possible outcome, every person and place you have come into contact with was considered before we took your memories, and you consented to it Val."

"So why were you there?"

"I was there…because of the maps." Sam stopped and Val could almost see his brain ticking, working out how to explain why. "And also to see if Elizabeth's predictions were correct."

"Did she see me in her predictions?"

"No. Before we left Alchany she saw the Prison taking over Earth, through one of these alignments. She changed the future at the cost of her life." He stopped, taking a breath. The memories of Elizabeth clearly caused him pain. "The Warden still needs more space now and is under pressure again to find a place for our overflow of essences. Using a weak planet outside our galaxy means that the Prison will no longer need to put criminals back out into our own planets – they could just release them. But my biggest concern now is that I still don't think Flo or Lailah know what they're doing. All Lailah wants is to free her sisters. This could be the end of Earth as we know it. If she opens the portal completely there would be a plague of prisoners large enough to fill Earth twice over."

"As much as I love the end of the world stuff, explain something. If the world is full of prisoners and some are left over what will happen?"

"Look at Flo."

"Dead people?" Val felt a shiver run down her spine.

"Exactly, but it gets even more complicated. The Prison was suffering the first wave of an attack from Nyteria when Enoch came for me and Wendy, and I fear the worst. If they have already failed then it will make it even easier for Lailah."

"What about Hadwyn and Boden?"

"They'll be fine Val, you really couldn't have been chosen for a better team. They're the real soldiers."

"Good. Then we'd better get this sorted tomorrow because I don't fancy living on a planet full of dead and living criminals. But before I face the end of the world, and I don't need you to go telling my family that one, I have another question."

"More questions."

"Delta? How come I met her when I was so young and she turned on me?" This was a question that had bothered her a lot. After everything she had done, somewhere Val still felt an attachment to this girl who had once been her best friend.

"Excariot knew who you were from early on, but he needed you to reach your full potential and powers by your eighteenth birthday, so that you matched your original age of initiation, on the alignment date back in

1645. Imagine how twisted and tormented he was after over four hundred years of waiting for you to come of age, never knowing just when you would be re-born. Delta would have been easy prey for him. To convince her to turn on you was simple. Excariot had the ability to charm anyone and Delta clearly craved the one thing you had that she didn't."

Val let out a laugh, grabbing the attention of the others who were settled. "Sorry." She lowered her head. "Are you serious? What did I have that Delta didn't? Her parents are millionaires, she's travelled the world several times over, she has dress sense to die for and a mane of hair that makes most grown models cry."

"You had love. From the moment you arrived here your family loved you. She never had that. Excariot knew that if he gave her the right attention, that would be enough for her to follow his orders. Plus, I hear he promised her your powers. Delta regretted following Excariot, but she never felt remorse for what she did to you."

"How do you know?"

"Because I saw Delta in your mother's village when you left her, she was looking for shelter with Excariot's baby."

Val felt guilt for what she had done, but at the time she'd been so angry. "Surely she has the ability to be good again?"

"No, Val. You need to understand that Delta has never been good."

"So why did you let her come back to the future?" Val was confused. They could have avoided so many problems.

"If I had thought for one minute she could make it back here, I would never have left her, but she wasn't my mission. Judges don't get to choose, they just follow orders and mine was to simply find out if Earth was the next Prison overflow."

"So, we still don't know how Delta got back to the future?"

"No, but she did. And now I think we both need a little rest before the morning."

Val agreed. After rescuing the Warden and losing Shane, she felt completely drained and numb. Jason and Fran had fallen asleep already. Her dad was snoring quietly in the corner, wrapped up with her mum in a sleeping bag, making them look like a giant caterpillar. Val lay down on her mattress. Pulling the duvet up around her, silent tears rose in her eyes for her lost friend. As she drifted off, she thought that if this was to be her last night's sleep on a free planet, she had better make it a good one.

CHAPTER 12

The Gathering Crowd

Val woke to a torchlight's beam piercing her eye lids. She winced, raising her hand to protect herself from the glare. She had been woken by her faithful Hunter to take her shift guarding the house. Zac reached out a hand, pulling her up to a wobbly standing position on the mattress.

"We're on duty," he stated the obvious.

"Ok buddy, what's going on?" she whispered her response as they made their way towards the kitchen.

"We seem to be gathering a crowd." Zac pulled opened the blind to reveal a dark street.

Val peered out. "Where?"

"Look at this." He pointed to his watch and Val could see the lines, that she guessed indicated aliens. "They're out there." He pointed. "Look harder."

She placed her nose on the glass, staring into the nothing, then she saw a glimpse of an eye. Like the cat's eyes in the road, then two more flickering between bushes. "I see them. What are they?"

"356725, 4009876, 3267453. Would you like me to go on?"

"No, you're ok, but now we have the Dellatrax, can't we look for their weaknesses? And why haven't the people living on the street called the police or something? It's like it's not happening."

"They can't see them. Look at how well Eva concealed Excariot's hideout, that witch could hide anything from plain view. Belinda could break this spell, but my advice would be to leave it the way it is."

"So why can we see them?"

"Because she wants us to see them. It's a good tactic, meant to cause fear in the opposition. Are you scared? Do you think your family and friends fear for their lives?"

"Well, yes."

"Then it has worked." He looked out again. "Look at them all, waiting. In a few hours, Val, you will have to make your way through them. It will come down to the strongest surviving."

To her amazement his expression stayed completely emotionless. "Thanks. You know Zac, sometimes here on Earth we like to do something called sugar coating. Do you know what that means?"

"No, is it important that I do?"

She took a moment to think about her answer. "Not really. It would take far too long to explain and you'd just ask too many questions." Val released the blind as Zac pulled them up some stools.

"Then, as we may have only a little time left together, I would like to learn more about you. Before you, I knew every detail about my Guard. We arrested, drank and teleported together from an early age. I felt pain at losing him and then yesterday, I felt pain again at losing Shane. Going to this place they call the Space, something in me hurt when Sam showed me his place of rest, like being struck in the chest." Zac placed his hand over his heart. "Yet I had feelings of relief after I knew my punishment on Alchany wasn't wasted. Now I want to spend the time we have left learning about who you are. Not just the reject I studied in the memory banks on Alchany, but you."

"Really? Well, if you promise to never call me reject again I will, although I'm almost starting to like the title. Where shall we begin?"

"From the beginning, if it holds interest."

Val walked over to the kettle, made herself a coffee then sat by the window spinning the tale of her very simple life up until her birthday, of funny childhood antics and lazy summer holidays with the girl who had been her best friend. Of relatives past and present and how she had been so lucky to have such great parents. Of her pet goldfish, Frank, and the hamster that had never arrived, along with the cat and dog she had waited for all her childhood. As she talked, every so often she would see the glimmer of a set of eyes or the reflection of light off slithery skin. It was scary, but not as scary as telling an almost emotionless Hunter about the time in her school play when she was supposed to be a motionless star, yet she had managed to organise all the wise men and shepherds, and had then taken the baby from the manger and dropped it off the stage.

She told him the little she remembered of going back in time and meeting her real mother, of how the world was in the past, her sackcloth dress and the fact that she had no shoes. About all of the people she had saved and how difficult it had been, knowing her parents had forgotten her, but that she had learnt that sometimes you have to sacrifice the things you love to keep them safe. She talked about meeting Shane, his kindness, and that somehow she had known he was always on her side. Her eyes filled up and the words caught in her throat. "I will make him proud."

"He was a very special person and I feel honoured to have known him." Val looked at Zac's face. He was looking out of the window, attempting to hide the fact he was as sad about Shane as she was. It must be so hard to have emotions without knowing what they meant. He really did have a heart.

The story came to an end as her mum entered the kitchen. Susan's voice was a welcome break from her own. "Morning." She placed a kiss on Val's head and patted Zac's arm. To Val's unease the sun was rising. They had made it through the night without any incidents, but what would follow?

Slowly the others surfaced, but it was a subdued group who gradually assembled in the kitchen.

"So is anyone hungry?" Val's mum asked, pulling out some frying pans.

Fran held her belly. "I'm not sure. I'm feeling a little bit queasy."

"I think we should all have something," Mike said. "You'll be fine after some of Susan's pancakes and bacon, Fran, it's her speciality. Never go to war on an empty stomach." He knew Susan found cooking calming and also knew she needed to feel like she was making sure everyone was ok.

"Then breakfast it is." She flicked on the hob's rings and went to the fridge.

Val turned away from the window and did a double take at what Sam was wearing. "So is this your uniform for the day?" Today he wasn't wearing the Magrafe uniform. He was all in green, the same as Wendy. He looked smart and she had to admit she wished she could get out of her cat suit for a breather, as it made going for a wee virtually impossible.

"Says the woman in Lycra, I thought you loved Spiderman, not his clothes." He pulled at her uniform which was stuck to her skin.

"Harsh. If this suit wasn't my only weapon I'd be in my jeans right now." She pushed him playfully. Was this real? Were they all really standing around the kitchen as her mum cooked pancakes waiting for the end to come?

"Zac," Susan called holding out a glass of his vitamin gunk.

"Thank you, Susan."

"Now you can't say I don't feed you." She gave him a warm smile.

Wendy was last to arrive in her green Judge's ensemble; it was all starting to look very official. "Morning hunny. How's Daniel?" Susan enquired.

"Still sleeping." She looked ashamedly at the floor.

Jason walked over to her. Gently he placed his hand on hers and the other under her chin to lift her face. "Wendy, we can't take back what happened yesterday, and today's not the day to talk about it, but if he's joining us because he loves you, then I'll accept that. One thing my Dad taught me was to give everyone an equal chance. Let's see how he uses it."

Her eyes welled up. "Thank you, Jason. I promise you he won't fail us."

"Ok. Who's first?" Susan flipped the pancake as in walked David's Hunter.

"Hey, come on in but don't eat or drink anything," Val greeted him. "How's David?"

"He can have this." Susan passed him a glass of Zac's gunk.

"Thank you for your kindness." He took it, drinking it straight down. "Fourteen is stable; he doesn't seem to have changed. It's as if he's frozen. I just wanted to offer you my services for today." He turned and bowed his head in respect to Sam and Wendy.

Sam responded, "You'll stay here and help protect the house with Susan and Fran. Jason may need you. He'll come and collect you as soon as we leave." The Hunter nodded and left them to make their plans.

✳

After they had eaten and the sun was up, the true extent of the crowd gathering outside the house became clearer.

"Your neighbours must be used to some weird goings on, Sam! If I saw something that looked that much like a Minotaur in my garden, I would be running for help or calling the police. Why does no one seem to be reacting?" Fran asked.

"Zac says there's a good chance that Eva has them cloaked to the humans."

"So why let us see them?" Jason asked.

"Intimidation, they want us to be aware of their power."

"Interesting," he nodded shoving a piece of bacon into his mouth.

They all stood around eating pancakes in an oddly upbeat frame of mind. Val was wondering if this would be her last meal when Sam tapped on his watch. "Right, it's time. We have quite a drive in front of us."

"That's if we get out of the garage alive…" Zac stated.

"Zac, sugar coating!" Val glared at him.

Mike jangled his keys and they started to make their way out towards Bessie. Wendy and Sam jumped in the back, crouching down out of sight. Belinda joined them. Mike embraced Susan and kissed her. "See you later." He smiled as tears started to fill her eyes.

"Don't be late for dinner." She forced a smile for him. He released her and walked quickly away, aware that they had little time. He and Zac got into the front of the truck.

Val was next in line to hug her mum. "Valerie Sheridan Saunders, you come home tonight, or else." Susan's voice trembled.

"Ok, if you promise to make me my favourite dinner."

"Hawaiian burgers it is." She hugged Val and then it was time for them to leave.

Val closed the connecting door on her mum as Zac impatiently beckoned her into the vehicle. "No, I need to deal with the crowd first." She pressed the button to open the garage doors. Mike started the engine. The truck door swung open as Zac leapt out. "Stay there, I'll be fine. Anyway, Hunters don't fight." She shoved him back to the car. The last thing she needed was him getting her knocked about. He did as ordered. With the door fully open she could see the crowd of creatures gathering. Her stomach tightened as her helmet sprung over her face. Her sword extended as she readied herself for the fight of her life. "Please let me get through this battle alive," she murmured to herself.

Her screen showed her vitals were strong, apart from the fact that her heart was dancing a Samba. She was about to the leave the garage when a huge blue flash of light knocked her off her feet, throwing her forcefully onto the bonnet of the car. Val shook her head, trying to clear it then looked up and saw the shadows of two large figures in the open garage door. She had to get up and take care of them before they harmed her friends in the truck. Then Mike was grabbing at her arm, pulling her to her feet.

A large, dark figure strode towards her, made difficult to see by the bright light spilling through the garage door. Mike dragged her backwards, but she shrugged him off, trying to summon her sword again. "Did you call?" A familiar voice asked.

She gasped and her helmet sprung back. The figure's helmets followed and to her utter joy there stood Boden, with Hadwyn close behind him. "Oh my God, it's you! How did you get here? You're alive! I'm so pleased to see you." She embraced Boden and turned to greet Hadwyn. "I won't hug you, don't worry."

"Good," he replied turning his nose up at the open displays of affection.

"We didn't get here, you brought us here." Boden returned the embrace.

Val called to the truck and its occupants. "Hey, this is my team, well I'm sort of their follower!" she said loudly so Sam and Wendy could hear her.

"Pleased to meet you," Mike said as he shook their hands. "I'm Val's Dad from the future."

"What's the problem? We got a distress call from you and then we were teleported out." Boden asked.

Val nodded to the scene behind him.

He turned around to face the gathering crowd of full aliens. "Ah! Right, I see. So what's your plan?"

"Looks like she was planning on getting killed," Hadwyn butted in.

Val ignored him. "We have to get to a place called Mistley Heath where Lailah and her followers are gathering to open a portal to the Prison, big enough to teleport all the prisoners to Earth at once."

"Are we talking about Princess Lailah?"

"You can call her Queen Lailah for all I care, although I prefer psycho. We need to stop her."

Hadwyn looked concerned. "She's been in Prison for a long time, Val, and she's one of a group who attempted to free the Ranswars before. This isn't going to be easy."

"Nothing is in my life," she responded. Zac tapped on the windscreen, making pointing signals to the back of the car and another to the outside. "I'm pleased you're here guys, but I think it's time to make a move."

CHAPTER 13

On the Move

"Val can you hear me?" Jason's voice was clear in her ear.

"Yes I can. Tell me what you can see," she asked as they stood on the garage's threshold.

"Whose voice is this we can hear?" Hadwyn asked, twitching his head.

"It's Jason. He has equipment to help us see how many aliens and where they are."

"Why do we not teleport?" Boden enquired.

Val glanced back at the truck. "Because our secret weapon's in the truck and we must protect it with our lives."

"Good enough for me." Hadwyn drew his gun, Boden released his crossbow and Val's suit flared blue flames. "I do love it when you do that," he laughed.

"Let's get going." Val stepped out, and something fell from the garage roof onto her back, only to scream in pain as it came in contact with the heat of the flames radiating from her body.

"Looks like there are at least fifty surrounding the house, more moving in," Jason relayed. "Hadwyn, six to your left."

But Hadwyn was already taking care of them. Flashes shot from his gun, leaving the creatures stunned and motionless on the ground.

Val could feel the adrenaline rushing though her. The aliens charged at them in an uncoordinated rush, from all directions. If Hadwyn didn't get them first, then Boden was close behind. Val struck some creature covered in fur with a fire ball. It lit up like a twig, the smell of burning hair filling her nostrils. Then she knocked down two more with a blast of air. More surged forward, as the truck started to leave the garage, Mike steering cautiously behind the fighters, clearly aware of the danger. Inside the truck they heard a thunderous noise as a four-armed alien landed on the truck roof, denting it with its weight. Its skin glowed aggressive red with lumps that looked like boils.

"Belinda, can you protect the car?" Mike called back to her.

"I'm trying." She began weaving a small blue ribbon between her fingers as the beast struck again at the roof. "As I wind this string I bind, the alien from another time. Take his power, give it to me, and keep us safe, so mote it be." Then Wendy started to chant from the floor of the car with her mother. "As you wind this string you bind, the alien from another time. Take his power, give it to thee, and keep us safe, so mote it be." They got louder and faster as another blow struck the roof and Zac's side of the truck was so dented he was almost sitting on Mike's lap.

Boden was dispatching an alien when he spotted the truck's plight. He headed back towards them, ready to fire at the creature on the roof. He was too late. Belinda and Wendy's spell caught the creature, sending it flying into the air. Yelping in confusion, it floated spinning above the roof, not able to get away. Boden leapt onto the truck's bonnet and took aim. The stunned creature dropped to the ground. Boden jumped back down, moving to one side allowing the truck to slowly edge past him. He nodded respectfully at Belinda who acknowledged him in between chants.

Val was knocking the beasts down one by one. Boden had now positioned himself behind the truck and Hadwyn was on the far side. They seemed to have been fighting forever, and she was starting to tire. The aliens were relentless and extremely strong. Jason kept them informed of what was coming, and so they kept fighting until the mass slowly became a rabble and the rabble became a few desperate fools.

"They're finished," Hadwyn called over to the others as he fired at yet another crazed alien. "I'm sure I've met him before. Got him that time as well," he guffawed.

"Is it normal that he enjoys this so much?" Val asked Boden.

"Would you prefer it if he cried?" Boden punched a six foot dog-like thing, then fired on it at close quarters.

She had to agree, he was right, and the aliens were only being stunned. Suddenly something grabbed her from behind. It was immensely strong and knocked her off her feet, but she didn't fall. Instead she found herself being lifted up by her shoulders into the air. She hadn't seen the flying creature coming, and it was evidently untouched by her flames. She screamed in pain as it clamped its talons onto her shoulders. Boden and Hadwyn watched in horror as she rose into the air. Both started firing over her head, but whatever had hold of her simply deflected the shots. Val looked up, readying her sword, but to her amazement all she could see was clouds. Whatever had her was invisible and as hard as she tried, her arms just couldn't reach high enough to strike anything, and now she was rising far too high to even contemplate making it drop her. The top of the truck and the men disappeared as it flapped, carrying her away into the distance.

"Val, can you still hear me? Are you ok? I can't see what's got you." Jason said urgently into her ear.

She was breathless and the pain in her arms was intense. There was the most stomach wrenching stench coming from whatever was holding her. She struggled to speak. "Yes, I'm ok, but I don't know where it's taking me." She took a painful breath, "We're far too high up to do anything now, just track me and tell the others to head for Manningtree. Tell Hadwyn and Boden to protect the packages."

"Will do. I'm here with you Val," Jason responded.

"I know," she said.

*

As the alien soared into the sky, the top of the canary yellow dodge became a spot in the distance. With the wind rushing past her body, she wanted to be sick; her lack of stomach for heights was only beaten by her fear of flight. This was as close to truly flying as she could imagine and it felt bizarre.

The buffeting the wind was giving her was exhausting; they seemed to have been flying for ages. There was a sudden change in the creature's direction. It was coming down, circling over a wooded area, gliding in ever-decreasing circles. Val could make out a clearing in the trees. Then a pond. She could recognise it even though she was hanging under an invisible flying alien. She was home. This was Mistley Heath. As she got closer to the ground she saw Lailah with her mass of blond locks and Eva with her Brazilian bronzed face waiting for her arrival. Eva raised her hands towards Val. The creature that had been holding her immediately became visible. Val looked up. It had metal-like claws attached to legs that looked armour plated. It wasn't a bird as she had imagined; it was more like a flying cockroach. It seemed to be secreting some sort of mucus from its mouth area, which Val was pleased she hadn't seen before. She struggled to escape its grip, but she didn't have to try for long as it dropped her right in front of her enemies.

Lailah approached, eyes blazing with pure hatred. "You are a problem to me."

Val stayed silent, rubbing her sore arms and taking a moment to survey her surroundings. There were hundreds of creatures making camp. She glanced over at the pond, remembering the dreams, or memories, she had lived. She knew that through the trees, behind Lailah, was the place of her initiation. They would take her there again tonight for sure. "So is this your big plan, a picnic?"

"Shut up Guard!" Lailah tossed her hair over her shoulder then closed in on Val until she was standing up close to her. Viciously, she grabbed her by the arm, lifting her up. "Do you know how powerful I will be very soon?"

"Excariot said that too." She shrugged.

Lailah started to glow. Her nostrils flared. "I'm far superior to that idiot." She banged her delicate fist on Val's helmet. "It's bad manners to wear those things in the presence of a Princess."

Val's helmet shot back. "You know kidnapping is bad manners and you alien types don't seem to get that."

Lailah took a deep breath, refocusing herself. "I don't like being called alien, don't do it again. Anyway, you're one. Now let's get down to business. Do you know why I have brought you here?"

"I have an idea," Val replied.

"Tonight, I will free my sisters, and then I will allow them to destroy your weak pathetic planet before we go home. I could have done this with your Dellatrax, but you wouldn't hand it over, so now I have to use some ancient mystic alignment."

"Yes, and when you do, you're going to create hell on Earth. Do you really understand what you're doing?" Val quizzed Lailah.

"Of course I know what I'm doing!" she roared into her face. "I've had four hundred years imprisoned in a box to plan it!" She took a deep breath. "Deal with it." She threw Val towards Eva.

She knew better than to try and get away from Eva. They had come face to face before and Eva had helped Val and the others to escape. But that had clearly been part of the bigger plan. "So how are you going to deal with me then?" She asked the Brazilian witch.

Eva touched Val's cheek. "I hear you killed my son."

Val had forgotten about Daniel, She couldn't let them know he was alive or that would put her mum in even more danger. "So what if I did? It was a fair fight. He killed Shane."

Eva's next move was unexpected. Val didn't have time to step away or try to dodge the swipe. A claw like nail struck Val across the face. She felt it digging deep into her skin from just above her left eye down to the top of her cheek. She wanted to cry out, but knew weakness would be fed upon. She kept her mouth tightly shut. "When you see that scar, if you live long enough, remember why I put it there."

"What is it you want Eva? Always the puppet? Never pulling the strings?" Val deliberately needled her. Even through her pain she knew angry people talked too much.

"Puppet, hah! You have no idea of the power I have. Each and every one of these aliens does as I order. And soon you will be joining them. So sit tight and be patient." Her finger directed Val to the ground and she found herself unable to resist her power. Her knees buckled and she fell to the grass. Eva walked away, unconcerned with Val.

Val tried to stand, but whatever power Eva had over her was strong enough to keep her down. She had to escape. There was no way she was letting one of those prisoners into her body. The reality was that the future wasn't bright. It was her, here, captive and dripping blood from her forehead. The situation was grave and yet she found herself wondering where Delta and Flo were hiding. Surely Delta should have been here, taking great pleasure in her suffering.

*

Val had been sitting for hours, worrying about how and when the alien prisoner was going to take her over and whether she would even be aware of it happening. Did they go up your nose or in your ear? No one had come near her. She wasn't sure if it was fear of her or of what Eva might do to them. She might have been physically alone, but in the back of her mind she kept believing that the others were coming - if they had managed to get out of Arksdale alive. The aliens seemed to be readying for the evening's events. Fires were now being built and groups were gathering together to eat the things they had caught in the woods. Their unusual forms were starting to look familiar. Val had seen a snake-like woman come past at least five times and had named her Bertha. Her back was aching from being crouched on the floor and, although her uniform was keeping her warm, she had lost contact with Jason. Her ear piece was blocked, either by magic or loss of signal.

A small pebble hit her head, bringing her out of her self-pity and back to reality. She looked around to see who was going to be sorry. "So, you got captured." A voice whispered in her ear. It was Hadwyn. He was down next to her - invisible.

"You know, I'm sure if you'd been picked up and carried away by an invisible flying roach you'd have been captured as well. Why did you throw a stone if you're next to me?" she whispered between pursed lips.

"I would never have been captured, and the stone entertained me," he replied.

"Whatever. Just get me out of here." She wriggled her bottom, trying to get some sensation back into her legs.

"No. We've been here for a while and are all in position. We know what we're doing and we will step in if we think you're in danger. The packages have arrived and we have cut communications with you for our safety. You are to stay here until the time of the alignment."

Val couldn't believe what she was hearing. "They're going to shove an alien in me!" she growled at him. "Like snake girl." She flicked her head in the direction of her newly named pet, Bertha.

"They won't; you're too valuable. Stop making a fool of yourself. I like your scar; it makes you look more aggressive. I'm going - be ready."

"How the hell do I do that when I'm magically strapped to the ground?" She was so mad. "When I get out of this, Hadwyn, I'm going to burn your hair off," she mumbled, knowing he had already left. Tears of joy started rising in her eyes. They were safe. Her dad was safe. One of the aliens walked over to her. Getting brave, it prodded her with a stick. "Yes, you prod away. I'll be sending your sorry alien backside back to jail very soon." She grinned at it, not caring if it understood her or not. All she knew was it would soon be time to end this relationship she had with people wanting to use humans as sock puppets once and for all, and she was ready for it.

CHAPTER 14

The Battle

As mist started to roll onto the Heath, Val sensed the time had come. The aliens that had taken form were howling and cheering at the rising of the moon, prancing around their fires. One of the uglier ones came over and pulled Val to her feet, then started to drag her towards the woods.

"You know you could let me go?" He sneered at her showing his doglike teeth and black gums. "I'll take that as a no then." She attempted to pull free, falling onto her knees next to the pond. Her reflection clearly showed the scar forming over her eye and the dried blood on her cheek and neck. It made her think of Daniel. It seemed Eva was right: it would always remind her of him, laying asleep back at Sam's house, while they all went to their deaths at the hands of his crazy mother and Princess Lailah.

The alien pulled her up, forcing her past the bushes and into the woods. Val looked around for signs of the others, but no one was there, or they were extremely well hidden. She really didn't want to be here again, once in sixteen forty-five and again just the other week felt like quite enough for one lifetime. The dark green scaled thing who was pushing her was getting impatient with her slow movement and shoved her, causing her to stumble. His dry skin brushed against her hand, making her shudder in revulsion.

"Don't you like the way I look?" He pushed his face next to hers.

"So, you can speak." Val squirmed at the end of his fist. She wanted to flare up, but nothing was happening. She was seriously going to take some magic lessons after this. He pushed her on, and she didn't trip again; one sniff of his fishy breath was enough to keep anyone on their feet.

The clearing was full of life, alien life, or more accurately, possessed Earth life. Val had to stop herself from feeling completely repulsed and remember that each one was a human being or an animal possessed by a prisoner, just like she would be if her friends didn't step in soon. The man who had guided her threw her to the ground. She was getting sick of this 'let's throw the Guard into the dirt' entertainment. Then, from her lowered view point, she spotted a pair of red soled stilettos - Christian Louboutin if her memory served her right. Her eyes rose up a slender pair of legs to a torso wrapped in what she saw was a Burberry Jacket. "Delta." She uttered the name.

"Hello Alien, nice to see you home again," she taunted. "Remember this place? Remember that tree?" She pointed to a majestic oak.

"Not particularly," Val replied, lifting herself onto her knees.

Delta let out a slightly crazy laugh. She touched its trunk. "This was the tree I hid in with Daniel, until your people came for me. They didn't know who I was, and were kind enough to take me and Daniel in. They were even accepting of the fact that he grew at a ridiculous rate. You know it took him thirty days to reach the age of eighteen. They told me how you had been the same.

That he was special, a star child, and he was." Her words came out with venom and hatred.

"Then surely they told you about being a good person, and not killing the people who protect you, like Shane."

"What?" Delta flinched.

"Yes, Shane's dead."

Delta paused for a moment in thought. "I'm sorry for Jason, but not for you. You deserve everything you get." She didn't wait for a response, she simply walked away.

That was it: no explanation; no options. For Delta this must have been sweet revenge, and now Val understood how wrong she had been to leave her behind. Bad person or not, she had made a critical mistake. But, now wasn't the time for trying to make things right. She couldn't begin to imagine what it must have been like for her with Daniel. She had evidently had Val's mum and coven trying to help her, and yet she had still turned against her. Sam was right, there was no give or take with Delta, she had always been bad.

Val watched Delta nodding as Lailah spoke to her, and then they embraced. Lailah placed a parting kiss on her cheek. Then Delta walked towards a clearing where Val spotted the red tail-lights of a vehicle. She thought this was odd. Why would they be letting Delta go at such an important time? The door opened, Delta climbed in and the vehicle set off, its lights bobbing and weaving over the rough terrain and off into the night.

Eva was the next to approach her. "The portal will be opening in exactly five minutes, so I was wondering if you wanted to say anything before you lose your body and soul." She grabbed Val by the hair and pulled her aggressively to her feet.

Val squirmed with pain. "You're not the first to try. Taking over Earth has a very low success rate to my knowledge."

"We will see about that." Eva laughed out loud, ignoring Val's warnings as a chorus of aggressive howls rang out in the darkness. There was frantic movement in the distance. Val couldn't see anything and Eva was far too focused on removing half her scalp.

"Eva!" Lailah demanded her presence and, to Val's relief, she let her go.

Val was starting to feel the energy rising in the air. Her fear was now mixed with a sense of something huge coming. She looked around once more now she was on her feet, but there was still no sign of any movement.

They stood talking and then Eva started to gather a group of aliens, making them form an orderly queue. Then to Val's amazement and terror Eva grabbed the first one in the line by the face, her eyes turning black she seemed to suck out its life force. The creature never had a chance. It was as if Eva was rooted to the ground, pure energy. She dropped the creature's body, lifeless, and it was quickly dragged away by other aliens who were surely thanking their lucky stars they weren't in the queue. The others, who were now trying to bolt, were being held in a pen by Lailah and her purple light. They yelped and screamed to escape, but there was no way out. Val had no idea what the purple glow was, but they clearly weren't going anywhere until Eva sucked their lives out. This went on until she had consumed twelve of them. Val was petrified. She had witnessed some crazy stuff, but this was major magic.

Eva was now sparking, full of energy. Then she jerked her arms above her head, palms facing the night sky, her hands letting off sharp sparks into the atmosphere. Val could feel the hairs on the back of her neck standing on end. Why weren't the others doing anything yet?

"Can you feel it?" Lailah caught Val's arm and started to drag her towards Eva, "Soon, very soon, you will have the privilege of housing one of my sisters and we will be the most powerful people on this planet. Does that not fill you with excitement?"

"I can think of better things." She tried to resist Lailah's pull, but she was seriously powerful. She needed to prevent herself from being possessed for a few more minutes. She glanced quickly over her shoulder.

"What are you looking for?" Lailah asked her.

"It's just such a nice view." Did that sound as stupid as she thought it did?

"Or are you looking for these people?" She pointed and a mass of creatures dispersed to reveal a group huddled on the ground. Val's worst nightmares had just come true. There they were: Hadwyn, Boden, Sam, Belinda, Zac and her dad. "Because they will all be joining us as well, in a roundabout way, as you say on Earth."

"Dad!" Val called. "Are you ok?" Mike nodded. She could now see they were all bound together in a tight circle.

"These are my offerings; some ritual Eva says will please the gods. I don't care much for gods but it makes her happy. Quite a catch if you ask me." Val was trying to force her way over to them when Lailah tightened her grip on her arm. "No, you're not to be with them, they're not like us. We are to rule the Ranswars. Come, take your place here in the centre."

"I'd rather die with my friends." Val dug in her heels.

"That is not the answer I wanted to hear, you ungrateful useless Guard!" Lailah's response was filled with agitation. Her hands glowed a deeper purple. Val could feel the magical energy coming through her suit.

"Well guess what Princess? Sometimes you just have to take no as an answer. I'm not going to go down without a fight." She slammed Lailah with her shoulder, knocking her off balance and ran towards the group, throwing herself onto her dad. "I'm going to get you out of here Dad, don't worry. Sam, teleport out," she pleaded. Why were they just sitting there?

Mike looked into Val's eyes. "Don't worry about us. Just remember Spain." That was all she got before two creatures dragged her off him, pulling her back towards Eva.

Eva lowered her hands and spoke, but her voice was not human anymore. It sent shivers up Val's spine. "I told you she would be a problem; no one will be teleporting in my presence." Eva spat at Val, calling to Lailah who was being helped up, "She won't submit. I will not give her one of your sisters."

"Fine. Stick the ugliest beast you have in her after we have used her." Lailah brushed herself down, aggressively pushing the aliens away from her.

'Spain? What was her dad talking about? Spain had been one of those 'surprise' holidays that hadn't happened because her mum had found the tickets two days before they flew. Val looked back at her friends probably for the last time. Spain, why had he said that? Think Val, come on.

"Hold her down here," Eva instructed, pointing at the ground.

'Spain.'

"Now I get to avenge my son." Eva reached her hand up and light shot into the night, then her other hand followed. Two solid beams shot out. Who knew where they would strike, but Val had a bad feeling it would be the Prison.

Then the light bulb went off in her head. "I get it!" she shouted. It wasn't the holiday; the surprise had been Susan's Auntie Bianca from South Africa, who had turned up out of the blue. That was the big surprise. Wendy! She wasn't with the others. Why hadn't she realised that sooner?

Eva was glowing like a light bulb; Val was still held down at her feet, but she could see enough to witness the arrival of what Sam had feared: essences from the Prison, and many more than in Excariot's attempt. Above them was a huge swirl of energy in a sparking, buzzing cloud. Whatever her witchy friend's plan was, it had better kick in soon. Val was suddenly aware that her feet were very warm. She looked down, to see small blue flames skipping off the toes of her very unattractive boots. Was this part of the spell? Eva was too busy weaving her magic to notice Val light a tiny flame in her hand. 'Thanks Wendy,' she thought. Somewhere nearby Wendy was opening things up for her. Val concentrated on willing her sword to extend just the smallest amount. It complied.

Eva looked down at Val. "It's time," she said in her creepy voice.

"Yes it is." Val allowed the helpers to lift her to her feet. She was now face to face with the enemy. Eva was totally possessed and Val had to believe that this would work. Reaching up, Eva summoned one of the essences. "Tome este corpo agora," she called to it. Val could only guess this meant it was time to get a body. As Eva slowly lowered it down towards her, it whipped back and forth, eager to find a new home. Val's vision rose up momentarily to witness the main circle growing in circumference, filling the sky above them, increasing in size with every second. This was Sam's worst fear spilling into reality.

Eva allowed the essence to rest on her hand, her black eyes inspecting its form. The two creatures held Val firmly in front of her. Eva stepped closer. Val knew this was going to be her only opportunity. Eva pushed the light out towards her, and in that instant, Val flamed blue flames, It was like being a foot away from a bonfire in all its November 5th glory. Val wasn't sure whether fear or magic had caused the exploding flames, but they threw, not only the creatures holding her, but also Eva three feet away from her.

The essence evaporated and Val aimed a flame-ball directly up towards the larger collection. Although her plan was good, she hadn't factored in Lailah hitting her from behind. The surge of purple energy knocked her forward. Lailah was extremely strong, but Val's uniform saved her from the worst of the blast. As her armoured patches became rigid; she felt the tension in her arms, chest and legs.

"Four hundred years. I won't wait another day." Lailah grabbed Eva, pulling her back up onto her feet. "Do it now. I will deal with her!" She shouted her orders seemingly unconcerned that half of Eva's hair had been burnt away. Her attack was remorseless. She struck Val three, four, five times. Each time, Val found herself being knocked a few feet further away from her friends. This was bad, she needed to get to her friends and release them so they could support her. Then she heard a blood curdling scream. She managed to dodge the next purple assault and spotted Wendy coming out from the bushes with something she recognised. It was Sam's wand. He had used it to stop Excariot in 1645, saying he could only attack when the dome Excariot had created was down. Well right now there was no dome.

Lailah was now aiming in both directions, but Wendy was ready for her. "Subsisto," she said sharply as each shockwave bounced off an invisible shield protecting her. Pulling herself to her feet, Val ran towards the others. Throwing herself into their midst and grabbing Sam's hands she burnt through his rope first, then the others. Hadwyn was first on his feet, his gun extended and he reached over Val, using her as a firing platform as he disabled four aliens. They were all now on the move.

"Protect Eva!" Lailah fired again at Wendy. Val could see that she needed to distract her long enough for Wendy to stop Eva.

"Val, cover Sam," Boden called as he drew back his crossbow. She extended her sword catching an alien as he attacked. Stunned, the creature fell at her feet, but more were flooding through the bushes and what had felt like a feasible plan was now falling apart because of the sheer number of attackers. Belinda and Mike were already being restrained. Val tried desperately to get to her dad, but her sword and powers just couldn't cope with the volume of enemies.

She watched as Sam and Boden were smothered by the crush of unnatural beings, some now the size of horses. Eva's circle of light had reached proportions far greater than before. Suddenly Val realised that Wendy was being dragged to the ground. Wendy called out to her friend, but she was knocked unconscious. Val raised her hands into the air – retracting her sword. "STOP!"

she shouted. Her companions came to an immediate standstill.

"STOP!" Lailah echoed the message to her own followers. The aliens came to an instant halt. Lailah was left standing in the middle of the fight, proud of her achievement, floods of alien creatures still pouring into the opening. Lailah had won. "Did you seriously think I would show you how many followers I had! Always save the best to last!"

In moments they were all once again tied down and Val lay at Eva's feet, her destiny face down in the grass. She would become a vessel for a prisoner and her friends and family would have to watch.

CHAPTER 15

What Happened Next

The group stood huddled together under the street lamp.

"Are you sure this will work?"

"Well, based on the information I have, you are the only ones who can do it."

"How do we get there?"

"I will take you."

"Doesn't that put you two at risk?"

"Nothing matters more now; we have to rescue them."

*

It seemed to be taking Eva a while to recover her powers fully after Val's group's failed assault. Val knew this was the end of the road. She had no other great plans. She was overwhelmed by a sense of responsibility; of the realisation that she had brought her dad into all this trouble. He would die because of her, and her mum would end up alone, taken over by a hairy alien.

Lailah was now in possession of Sam's silver wand, which she had placed in her pocket. She walked around, looking up towards the energy cloud floating above their heads and then back down at Eva with a satisfied expression. Everything was going according to her plan.

They pulled Val to her feet again. Understanding that her life was about to end, she allowed her body to go limp, she wouldn't give them the satisfaction of her helping them to drive her from her own body.

She could see Sam in the distance; their eyes met. What would life have been like for them? She suppressed the thought. This wasn't the right time to be thinking about wedding bells and little Sams running around.

Meanwhile, Eva pulled another prisoner from the glowing mass. The aliens who were supporting Val forced her to lift her head and she was compelled to look Eva directly in the eyes. She stared back boldly, refusing to cower before her nemesis. She had the random, comforting thought that it would take Eva years to grow her hair back.

As the essence got closer she closed her eyes, waiting for the inevitable, wondering if it would hurt; what it would feel like. She almost wished Eva would hurry up, that it could be over with so she didn't have to think about what her friends were going through. A sudden commotion in the background caught her attention, but she kept her eyes closed. They must be getting ready to celebrate her death and she had no desire to look at them.

The noise got steadily louder, punctuated by screams and yelps that, even to her despairing mind did not sound much like a celebration. Her eyes flew open and she tried to turn her head to look, but a hairy hand held her fast, forcing her to face Eva. Then the first explosion hit. Blood-curdling cries of pain filled the air.

Val started to struggle. What was going on? Eva looked past her, her face blackening with anger. "Deal with them!" she yelled at the alien spectators. "I will not stop!" she screamed at the two creatures holding Val. "Hold her still."

From behind her she heard her dad call, "Susan!" she froze. Her mum was here. How on Earth had she managed that? She still couldn't see what was happening and Eva was still far too close for her liking. In that moment another explosion threw Val sideways several feet onto the ground. Clearly the one restraining her had been struck. She was now face down in the mud.

"Daniel what do you think you're doing, you fool?" Eva released the essence.

"What's right." He gave a resounding response. Val rolled over to see him now standing over her, energy ball in each palm ready to protect her.

"You can't stop us, we're too powerful," Eva insisted.

Purple lightning struck Daniel in the back and he was thrown down next to Val. He began pulling himself up.

"Stay down if you wish to live," Lailah yelled, purple energy skipping all over her body.

"NOW!" Daniel yelled.

"Get away from my daughter!" Val heard her mum before she could see her.

Lailah's expression changed to one of fear. How could her mum be having this affect? Val managed to lift her head enough to see the answer. Susan was striding across the grass with three Labradoodles on leads. She was backed up by Fran and Jason, both holding tazer swords.

Val felt hands grabbing her under her arms. The face of David's Hunter was a very welcome surprise as he pulled her to safety. Now Eva and Lailah were alone under the glowing portal.

"You need to learn to behave on someone else's planet," Susan told them sternly. She knelt down and removed the leads. The dogs sniffed the night air and their eyes focused on the women. There was no Flo to teleport them out; they were surrounded. The dogs were on them in a few short leaps of their agile bodies.

The first leapt at Eva, its teeth sinking deep into her arm as it pulled her to the ground. In seconds the venom was coursing through her veins and she started to shake. As Eva became motionless her portal of floating prisoners began to retract. Val sensed Eva's power fading. They would all be free soon.

The other two dogs corralled Lailah, stalking her like they would a small deer. She aimed the wand she had taken from Wendy, striking one of the dogs with a fatal blow, but the other took the opportunity to attack. It sprang forward, seizing her leg. She fell onto her knees.

"Val, don't do any magic, they feed off of it," Susan warned her.

Since when had her mum become this feisty alien fighter? She let the Hunter help her to her feet. Daniel was already releasing the others. Fran and Jason were warning the aliens to stay back.

"Come. Heel," Susan called to the two dogs that were still standing. They pricked up their ears and made their way back to their new owner's side. Val was stunned by what was happening, but very proud at the same time. Susan put them back on their leads.

Fran ran towards Val throwing her arms around her neck. "I'm so glad you're ok. We really had no choice." Val reciprocated the embrace.

They headed to Lailah. Fran knelt down next to her sister's body. "We'll get Yassmin back, don't worry," Val said as she positioned herself to protect them, aware that the crowd was starting to gather and grow into a mass, something that once again looked like a force to be reckoned with, Lailah or no Lailah.

*

The group assembled, Mike hugging his wife hard. Hadwyn and Boden patted Val vigorously on the back. Relieved to be together and relatively unscathed, they formed a circle around the wounded, trying to stay out of reach of the two remaining Novelia who seemed quite happy to sit placidly by Susan's feet dribbling acid.

Sam made a direct line for Val. She watched as he moved closer and didn't stop at what would have been the appropriate distance. He just kept moving, his arms reaching out for her and then he pulled her in close to him. Val wasn't ready for this and looked up to see his deep black eyes staring down into hers. "I won't live without you, Val Saunders." His lips pressed down on hers. She wanted the moment to last forever.

It couldn't and Sam stepped back releasing her, turning to address the group. "We can't leave this situation as it stands. The humans are at great risk from these creatures and they now have no one to control them. Wendy and Belinda aren't strong enough, so, ideas please, people."

Zac made his way to Val's side. "I do not wish to join mouths with you, I hope this is acceptable, but I was concerned and I'm pleased you are ok."

"I don't wish to join mouths with you either, buddy," Val laughed, nudging him.

"Is it possible to create a reverse portal?" Boden asked. "Because there are too many of them for us to deal with even with the amazing Susan and her Novelia."

Susan blushed, "Thanks."

"The portal Eva opened was only going in one direction and that was here," Sam said.

Hadwyn stepped in. "Val got us all off Nyteria. Why can't she do the same here?"

"I wasn't conscious of doing that and I'm not sure I can do it again with hundreds of aliens," she replied shaking her head.

"What if we boosted your powers a little?" Boden looked at Daniel. "He seems powerful."

"Yes, Val, Daniel can help you; you have similar DNA," Wendy added, now conscious and being supported by Daniel. "Sam, is it possible for me and Mum to create some protection to allow them to work?" He nodded.

"Then let's do it." Belinda said as she and Wendy joined hands and Sam gave them instructions. Boden and Hadwyn began to fire warning shots at the creatures closing in.

Val watched as a veil of light surrounded them, not dissimilar to the one Excariot had created with the coven. Daniel moved closer to her. "So what should we do? I'm new to this?" he said.

Val looked at him and smiled. "Thank you, Daniel. You took a huge risk bringing the Novelia here and facing Eva."

"Val, I love Wendy and they lied to me. When they made me burn down your bookshop I knew I was doing the wrong thing."

"Guard instincts. It's in our blood."

Wendy called out. "Val, we have a problem!" She was pointing outside the protective dome.

Val could see the mass getting closer to the barrier between them. "What?"

"Oh my God!" Fran screamed and sprinted to the edge, placing her hands on the glowing wall that was keeping them safe.

Then it became horribly clear to Val: Sam was on the outside. How had that happened? "Wendy, take it down. NOW! Please, take it down," Val begged, feeling more fear now than when she had believed her own life was about to end.

"If I do we can't put another one up Val. It's not that simple."

"Boden what can we do?" Val pleaded.

He looked around him, but the shield was all encompassing. Sam looked at them through the glowing haze as the first wave of aliens got the courage up to attack him. With his sword extended in one hand and a plasma ball in the other he defended himself.

"Why isn't he teleporting out? We need to get him." Val's blue spark flashed, and as she reappeared she found herself standing in the same spot, she couldn't get out. "TAKE IT DOWN!" she screamed at Wendy.

She watched them piling on top of Sam. He pushed them back, but it was just a matter of time.

"Val, you need to teleport the aliens out of here, they're going to kill him." Zac said to her, his voice, as always in these situations, was even and persuasive. "Are you going to allow them to do that, Val? Are you just going to stand there and watch?"

She rounded on him furiously. "How could you say that to me!" she yelled.

He merely smiled and nodded.

Then she knew why. Her body was heating. She couldn't see Sam any more, through the wall of flames that surrounded her. But it wasn't enough. Desperately she turned to Daniel. "Take my hands," she ordered. He didn't question her, placing his hands onto hers.

"Stand back," Hadwyn warned the others. "It's going to get bright in here." His helmet covered his head. The others turned away.

In Val's mind at that moment there was no longer any anger, no desire for revenge, just an overpowering need to protect Sam. She gripped Daniel unaware of the pain she was causing him with her flames. Then she felt his energy surging through her. She felt like a Catherine wheel ready to spin. The others watched as her light grew. Mike grabbed Susan and turned her face into his chest as he turned his head away. Fran and Jason had crouched on the floor together. Outside the protection of the bubble, Sam was down on the ground, under a pile of aliens.

"Come on Val, come on," Boden whispered to himself wondering how Sam could possibly survive the onslaught.

Suddenly the protective barrier that had been keeping the alien creatures out was broken. Beams of light shot out from Val's body, hitting each individual alien flinging them skywards. The mass of creatures covering Sam was torn upwards, so high they disappeared. Val was now vibrating and Daniel seemed to be the only thing anchoring her to the ground. The light that had caused them all to cover their eyes was growing in ferocity, faster and faster. Aliens that tried to run were grabbed by the light and thrown into oblivion.

Zac called out to her as he edged his way cautiously in her direction. The creatures where now growing thin on the ground, the light dispersing, as one by one the creatures rose into the atmosphere and disappeared.

As he got closer, the final few shot into the air. "You can stop, now," he told her. Daniel's face was full of pain from his severely burned hands. Seeing that she hadn't heard him, Zac touched her flaming arm quickly, pulling it away sharply and, at last, her head turned towards him. "Val, Sam's safe," he reassured her. "We're all safe, stop."

She couldn't feel her body as she came down from wherever she had been in her mind. "Daniel!" She looked at their hands, hers perfect and his burned and blistered. "I'm so sorry. Wendy!" She called for help, but it was already there.

Hadwyn moved in, lifting Daniel off the ground as his weak body gave in to the shock and pain. Then Wendy was beside Daniel reassuring him it would be ok.

"Val," She heard her mother's voice. Susan was with Mike holding two empty leads. It seemed that even the Novelia had been cast out by Val's power. But to where?

Moving felt odd. Her legs seemed almost reluctant to take her. Her body ached from the sheer power that had been surging through her. She glanced from David's Hunter to Boden; they were making sure that every last alien had gone. Then she spotted Jason and Fran kneeling next to a body - Sam. She moved as fast as her legs would go, tears already streaming down her face as she reached them. She couldn't lose him, she wouldn't lose him.

Fran moved backwards to let her in, and Val threw herself onto his still body. "Sam, don't leave me. You said you wouldn't leave me ever again," she sobbed.

"Ok," he exhaled.

Val sat back. He struggled to open his eyes, a pained grin on his lips. "Then we have a deal." She pushed forward kissing him with a confidence she had shied away from before.

"Time and place people," Jason coughed.

"Honestly!" Fran grabbed Jason's arm and dragged him away.

Val stroked Sam's hair out of his bloodied face. "How?"

"What?"

"How did Wendy's force field miss you? Were you busy looking at the view? How on Earth did it happen?" She slapped his chest in annoyance.

He coughed. "I told her not to include me. Don't be angry, Val. It was the only way to get you to the maximum of your potential. I know it was a crazy trick, but it worked."

"Idiot." Val pushed at him and he winced in pain. "Don't you ever do that to me again."

"Well, after all this it won't be necessary."

"I wouldn't count on it. Two major players are missing. We have two soulless bodies over there, but Delta and Flo weren't here. And where did all the creatures go?"

"I don't know, but I'm sure Zac will know if they're on Earth. We need to get back to my house." Sam started to lift himself up. "We have a Prison to take care of."

CHAPTER 16

Breakfast TV

They had left Mistley Heath; Val hoped for the last time, taking Lailah's and Eva's bodies with them. Teleporting back to the house was their quickest option so they left the truck in a secluded area and trusted it would be safe until they had time to return.

Sam's house was eerily quiet when they got back and they all moved around in silence, exhausted by the trauma they had just lived through. There was a definite sense of relief, but also a sense of apprehension about what would be waiting for them back at the Prison. Sam instructed them that Mike, Susan, Belinda, Jason and Fran should remain at the house and wait for them to return. Wendy had taken the healing book to help Daniel with his burns.

Zac had gone to pack the rest of the Dellatrax for transport back to the Prison and the Hunter was back with his Guard David. Eva and Lailah were laid out in the lounge on mattresses and the rest of them we're gathered in the kitchen. Val looked out of the window to see the sun rising. Another day on planet Earth; how very different it could have been.

Susan fluttered around Val with a damp piece of tissue. "Look at this scar. You'll have to get Wendy to get rid of it." She rubbed off some of the dry blood.

"Stop." Val gently took Susan's hand away from her head. "Ok Mum, what were you thinking?"

"Well, looking after you of course," she said retreating to her comfort zone by putting the kettle on and pulling out cups.

"What possessed you to go and risk getting the Novelia after everything we told you about them?"

"David's Hunter came to us and told us that there were a lot of aliens massing in one place. He guessed that with the loss of communication that you were losing the fight. It was him that came up with the idea. He said that the Novelia wouldn't hurt us because we were humans, but that they could kill Lailah and Eva, but we would need to be careful as they could kill you lot as well. He told us they feed off power so if we could get to the Heath and stop you from using your magic, then we stood a good chance of sorting them out. But Daniel took the greatest risk. Teleporting us all, the Novelia could have bitten him at any time, but he didn't care. You know, Val, he's just a boy." She shoved a coffee in front of her daughter.

"Well, you were awesome and I can't tell you how cool Boden and Hadwyn think you are; I'm going to have to pull a serious stunt to impress them now."

"I think you already have. When will you leave?" Susan asked pouring milk into a jug.

"Soon; maybe an hour," Sam interrupted, piling the astrology charts together.

"When will you be back?"

"I don't know; I can only promise I will keep Val safe."

She gave him 'a look' one that warned if he didn't, he would be extremely sorry. "I'll hold you to that," she said seriously, then finished filling the mugs. "Who wants a drink?"

They chorused their orders and sat at the counter. "Put the TV on, Dad."

"Do you have the sports channels?" Mike asked as he took the remote.

Val tutted. "Seriously, we've just saved the world from an alien takeover and you want to watch golf!"

"It's therapeutic," he grumbled. "Now I'm going to make you watch the news."

"I'm not sure which is more depressing?" Val whined, sipping the drink Susan had passed her.

The widescreen TV strapped to the wall lit-up and there, in full HD with surround sound, was Delta. She was dressed to kill and talking to a presenter on Breakfast News. "Eamonn Holmes," Susan squealed. "I love him. What's going on?"

"Mum, shh," Val instructed. "Turn it up, Dad."

"So tell us, Miss Troughton, what exactly has been happening? We have been watching these videos posted yesterday on Youtube of some children being approached by an aggressive female dressed in black and a strange docile male. The most disturbing fact is that they seem to appear from thin air. Now we also have this film, taken from your house, and we can see that this is the same woman we saw in the Youtube video, shooting in the street this morning." The footage began and it was immediately apparent that Delta had been filming them as they left the garage, but because the aliens weren't visible on the footage, it made it look like they were just randomly shooting in the street.

"Well Eamonn, where do I start?" Delta flicked her long blonde hair for the cameras. "I thought this woman was a good neighbour, so you can imagine how shocked I was to see this. However, I can't lie and tell you I didn't have my suspicions. Her family, Mike and Susan Saunders," at this point she held a picture of them up to the screen, "mistreated her from a young age. She would beg me not to tell anyone. I just wish I had done something to help her back then, maybe then these things would never have happened."

A mug smashed on the kitchen floor, making them all jolt out of their silent horror, "Liar! You little…" Susan's outburst was a shock to them all. She was shaking with anger.

"So you're saying she comes from an abusive background. But how did she do this? It looks like she appears by magic." One of the children on the bus had been filming his friend doing air guitar when Val arrived. "She then goes on to kidnap the driver and threaten the teachers." They played another clip of Val running down the bus.

Val defended herself, "I had no choice."

Delta lifted a tissue to her eye wiping away a tear. "I know you'll think I'm mad, but she's been mixing with some really dangerous people, as you can see from this film, Eamonn. Those men in the video she's with are so scary. I haven't slept in weeks and this is going to sound crazy, but I think they have been mixing with…" she took a deep breath, "…witches. I think she may have been used for experimentation, or rituals I think they call them, along with some of our other friends."

"Goodness me, that does seem a very farfetched allegation, although we can see on our screen something out of the normal is happening. Now you have kindly supplied us with photos of these suspects which the police have agreed for us to show on our website. Do you have any more information for the general public?" He patted her hand over the desk.

"Yes. The last time I saw them they were doing some kind of ceremony. I think live animals were involved." She hung her head mopping her crocodile tears. "They took my puppy." She held up another picture of a tiny Chihuahua. "Just don't go near them," she sobbed.

"UNBELIEVABLE!" Sam slammed the charts down. "Get on that website now Jason," he ordered.

"On it already," he said standing in front of a silver laptop at the table. "Looks like she's got pictures of us all."

"Finally, Delta, before we speak to our military expert, Captain Smyth, are the police following this up? Do you know if anyone has been arrested or if they'll just disappear again?" Eamonn grabbed his earpiece. "I'm sorry to interrupt; we're just getting some breaking news. It seems that there is yet another video of this particular girl." Eamonn nodded. "We now have some more footage of her trying to harm some tourist on a roller coaster in Skegness and we are going live to the woman who was actually on it with her."

"I was saving them." Val looked around the room for support.

A nervous-looking brown haired woman stood next to a bright red front door, microphone held to her face. "Good morning, Michelle from Lincolnshire, can you tell us exactly what happened?" Asked a male news reporter, out of shot.

"I saved your life, that's what happened," Val pointed at the television as if the woman on the screen would respond. The worried looking woman told him all about how Val had levitated the roller coaster, trying to shake them all off. Then the cameras went back to Eamonn who was starting to talk to Delta again.

"Can't we switch this off?" Val grumbled.

"We need to get out of here," Belinda warned them. "We have visitors."

Val looked out the window and there was a group of armed police in full body armour heading towards the house. The street had been closed off. As if they didn't have enough problems, she thought angrily.

"Look here, we're all on this page." Jason swung the laptop and it was like the FBI's most wanted page. There were pictures of them all.

"Val, I think we have a problem." Zac came in waving an envelope at her.

"Zac, seriously! You think? You've just missed us being made out to be Chihuahua abducting, rollercoaster smashing, teleporting murderers and the police are here!" Val threw her arms into the air.

He handed her the envelope. She recognised the hand writing instantly. "Where was it?" she demanded.

"On David's bedside table."

"How on Earth did she get it in there?"

"What are you two talking about?" Sam interrupted.

"Seems Delta's been in the house - or had someone drop off a note."

"Open it."

The envelope was addressed to 'The Alien'. Val peeled back the flap and pulled out a card.

"What does it say?" Wendy asked.

Val turned it to them, "It says, 'Welcome to plan B'."

Everyone just stared at the card. What was plan B? Well, it clearly started with Delta making them enemy number one, which she was doing right now on national television. Val was sure that by tea time Delta would be on Blue Peter showing kids how to make traps for them with double sided sticky tape and a wire clothes hanger.

Sam broke her internal mental meltdown. "We need to get out of here and fast."

"But where can we go, they have our pictures? Everyone knows what we look like now." Susan looked to Mike.

"I don't know, but it's going to be fine." He put his arm around her.

"We need to get off this planet," Val said to Sam.

"I agree. The only place to take them is the Space. Get everyone and everything we need into the lounge. We're going on a trip." Sam directed Boden, Hadwyn and Zac. "Bring David down and put him with the others. Susan, get any supplies you need together. Fran and Jason, take anything you think will come in handy from the office. We're leaving. Hurry!"

Val glanced out of the window. The police were still there, gathering in groups, in full protective kit. It wouldn't be long before they were battering the door down.

She quickly helped Sam to roll the charts up. Each held an abundance of secrets that she would possibly never understand, but they were important and Sam needed them. "These charts, Val, are all I have left until Wendy gets her full powers. We need to keep them safe." They had five tubes. "Where would you put them if you had to hide them from the world?"

"Tough question. I've got to hide my family and you're right, the Space seems like the best choice. Why not take them there?"

"I agree, for now they aren't safe on Earth." He tied the tubes together and rested them over his shoulder as the first blow on the door echoed through the hall. "We need to go!" he shouted urgently as he made his way to the others. They had all congregated in the lounge with their piles of equipment. "Zac, Boden and Hadwyn, I need you to ask me no questions; I need you to simply forget what you see before you see it." They nodded.

"What about our families? Surely when they can't find us they will look for them?" Susan asked him.

"At this moment I can do no more than protect you. Your families may be questioned, but they will not be locked away or treated like Val will be if they get their hands on her."

Susan saw his point. "I understand. Let's go."

Sam strode over to a small oak chest of drawers; he pulled open a drawer and brought out a sphere similar to the one he had taken Shane away in. It started to expand.

Val grabbed her mum's hand. "It's going to be ok." She held it tight. The bubble engulfed them all. Everything went dark and they felt the sensation of brief motion. After a few moments the bubble slowly receded and Val saw the grey rocks and markings of the Space. "Well, that wasn't so bad," Mike said, a note of relief in his tone.

"Where is this place?" Hadwyn looked around him.

"You're in the centre of Alchany." Val patted his shoulder. "Come on, let's get everyone inside."

Sam led the group in a procession towards the door. "It's very grey," Fran commented to Val.

"I know, but wait till you see what's behind that door."

Their arrival had been observed on the cameras because Alsom had the door ajar as they approached. Val waited for the others to repeat her reaction to the boy with wheels. He wasn't alone and he came speeding out with Taran in tow. This time Enoch was with them. "Come in now!" he urged.

"Val, they have wheels," Susan said as Taran spun around her.

Val ruffled Taran's hair as he came around a second time. "I know. Awesome aren't they?"

"What's wrong?" Sam asked Enoch as he hurried them through the metal doorway.

"It's the Prison. It all happened too fast. There was nothing they could do; they didn't stand a chance." Enoch welcomed each one as they came in. "Sam, Nathan has control of the surface."

"What are you saying?" Boden became restless. "What has happened to our Prison?"

"They came in ships. We watched it from our screens. There were a lot of them, but I honestly didn't think they could win. How could they take down the whole planet? The Prison is so strong. But they did and it took only a few hours." Enoch was visibly shocked and in no way relieved to see the cavalry arrive.

"Sit down and tell me what's happening on the surface, my friend," Sam encouraged him gently. They all grouped together to listen.

"A virus. They surrounded the planet and released some kind of airborne agent. No one stood a chance. They were breathing it in before they knew how Nathan would attack. He tricked them into believing he was going to launch an assault, and offered then the chance to surrender, but that was never his plan at all."

"Do you know what sort of virus?"

"No, I don't know. We haven't dared to go onto the surface to try to get a sample. But it was like everyone gave up. They became docile with no will to fight. Then the Nyterians arrived and just rounded them up. Follow me." He stood and beckoned them up the grey hill.

"Taran, Alsom, please take our friends and find them somewhere to rest," Sam instructed. "Val, Zac, Daniel, Wendy, Boden and Hadwyn, come with us."

"Val." Susan looked to her daughter.

"Mum, it'll be fine," she reassured her.

There was an air of concern around them as they ascended and Wendy gripped Daniel's hand. They were welcomed into the main chamber where Enoch and his followers ushered them into the room of technology. "Look for yourselves." He pointed at the screens.

Oddly, everything looked normal. Nothing was destroyed or ravaged by weapons. There were no dead bodies lying around or any sign of what Val had come to expect of war from television and movies. These people had used an invisible weapon to bring the planet to its knees. Val watched as streams of Guards were led away by Nyterians. The Guards seemed powerless to resist them. "Well, he wanted the power and he clearly has it, but why aren't they fighting back? What is Nathan going to do?" Val asked.

"I don't know, but we're going to find out," Sam said.

"How?" Val asked him.

"By going to the surface."

"That's crazy. What if they capture us? What about the virus? What if they find out about this place?"

"We have no choice. Enoch, get ready for us to leave." Sam gave his orders.

"Val," a nervous voice called from the entrance.

"Hello," she greeted David's Hunter. "Is everything ok?"

He was out of breath. "Well, no," he panted. "Not really. David just stood up and teleported out."

CHAPTER 17

The Surface

Val looked at the Hunter. "Did you just say that David teleported out?"

"Yes, he just stood up and was gone." He exhaled again, shock and horror written across his face.

"What's going on?" Sam asked.

"I think we may have brought a passenger with us. Please excuse me. Take me to the others. Come on Zac." The Hunter led them briskly down towards the group who were standing in a state of confusion, now aiming weapons at Lailah and Eva's still bodies.

"He was lying here." The Hunter pointed to a now vacant spot.

"Zac, when you originally checked for Flo, did you keep her signal?" Val asked.

He began moving his watch in a circular motion. "Yes, all new signals are recorded for later analysis. Do you think she was in David?"

"Well, you said that dead people couldn't go back to the Prison, but this was the perfect opportunity to escape Earth and it explains the arrival of the envelope from Delta."

Mike moved in. "Is Flo the dead girl with the long curly hair?"

"Yes, she's also one of the oldest, but why come with us?" Val asked Zac.

"I'm not sure. Delta clearly wanted us off the planet, so was this planned. But what did they hope to achieve? They have no magic; Flo has no powers apart from teleporting - they were taken from her by Excariot." He looked puzzled.

"What about the books?" Jason said. "Would they be of any use to them?"

"Oh my God!" Val's eyes darted around looking for them. "Where's the Dellatrax!?" she cried. Everyone moved, frantically looking for the books, but Val already knew it was too late. She pushed her head into her hands and sunk to the floor. "She's won again."

"Yes, it was Flo." Zac sat next to her allowing her to see a completely non-descriptive white line on his screen.

"Why does this keep happening to us?" She stared at her stupid black boots.

"Because we are on the right track. If we weren't then no one would bother with us," Zac said.

"What's going on?" Sam, Boden and Hadwyn approached the group.

"Flo stole the Dellatrax from under our noses," Val moaned.

"Fine, we have bigger things to worry about now. We can deal with them later."

Val buried her head deeper between her knees. "Seriously, Sam, I spend my life dealing with things later."

He clearly had no time for her self-pity. "We'll break into two groups. Wendy, Daniel, Boden and Hadwyn stay here. Jason you go to Enoch's with your equipment; we'll need your ears and eyes on the surface. We really don't know what's happening up top and we need a strong force here in case we don't return. Zac, Val and I will go up. There's no time to worry about Flo or anyone left on Earth because if Nathan has his way, Earth will be one of his targets."

Val knew Sam was right, and she liked the idea of the others staying to protect her parents. She stood and searched the group for her mum, where was she? "Sam, can I say goodbye to my Mum?"

"Of course but be quick," he replied, whilst giving orders to the others. She raised her eyes to see over the crowd, but still nothing. Had Flo taken her as well? "MUM!" Val yelled as she walked away from the others.

"Val, she went with the little boy with one wheel." Mike signalled to Taran's little room in the cave side.

Peeking through the entrance Val saw her mum sitting on the stone bed as Taran proudly showed her his pictures. "So where are your Mum and Dad?" Susan asked.

Taran turned on his wheel and moved closer to Susan, "I don't have any parents, but it's ok because Shane comes to see me and I have Sam and everyone here." He leaned on Susan's leg and Val watched as her mum moved his hair behind his ear. Someone was going to have to tell him about Shane, but she knew her mum wouldn't do it now. It was still too raw for them all.

"Guess what? I'm going to be here for a while, so what about you showing me how things run here and I'll look after you in exchange? I'm a very good cook."

Taran leaned back out of her reach. "You want to stay with me?" his voice held fear and hope.

"Well, my daughter is all grown up and is busy saving the world and your Prison, and I guess I need someone who needs me right now, so how's about we make that you?" Susan's words were full of love, soft and gentle. Val loved her mum so much. She realised Sam was right. She did have something special. No wonder Delta had wanted to take it away.

Taran wheeled closer. "I would like that." He placed his head on her shoulder and they were just still. Val turned, she would go and sort the problems on the surface out now.

✳

Sam and Zac were ready to leave when she returned. "Dad, I left Mum with Taran. She was busy; tell her I'll be back later." She embraced him.

"You know, Val, this place has potential," Mike grinned. Val could see his builder cogs spinning.

"No time like the present to build the world of your dreams, Dad."

He hugged her. "Remember you're always my little girl," he whispered in her ear.

"Dad." She nudged him. "I'm ready to go. What's the plan?"

Sam interrupted, "Val, Zac we head back to the surface through the room we entered before. Zac will be able to monitor the situation from there. We find the Warden and any of the High Judges who have survived the attack. They would have been the first people Nathan went for, because they're the most powerful."

They made their way to the door; it was already open. "Seems Flo was born in a barn," Val said.

Alsom looked at the door in surprise. "I closed it!" he said in his teenage defence.

"It's ok." Sam patted him on the shoulder. "Close it after we leave."

Hadwyn made his way over to Val. "I think your weapon is weak. You should try to manifest a gun; they're faster and more precise." Val took this as an emotional goodbye. "Maybe one of your cannons or a machine gun?"

"Her weapon is fine." Boden nudged him out of the way. "Be brave, be strong and come back. We will be following your every move."

They made their way out into the greyness and stood together in a circle. "Val, are you ready?" She nodded. "Zac?" He bowed his head. "Then let's go." Sam took their hands and they were on their way to the surface.

*

Sam pushed open the door to the Prison and the atmosphere they entered was one of despair. He signalled for them to move and they joined a line of Guards who were being transported. There were several hundred all moving together along the corridor. No resistance, no fighting, just moving.

"What's going on?" Sam asked the Guard next to him, who had allowed them to enter the line. "Judge, leave now, get out." His eyes met Sam's and they were full of fear. "He has killed our souls. We can't fight, we have no power. There is nothing we can do. The only ones left with power are the High Judges and has taken them prisoner." They kept up the pace not wanting to draw attention to themselves.

"Tell me more about what's happened. Why can't you fight?"

The young man glanced down the line to make sure they weren't being observed. "They are saying it came in the air. They filled the Prison with poison. Not enough to kill us, but enough to immobilise our inner Guard."

"How's that possible?" Val asked.

"We have looked at a similar airborne technology, but we never used it for fear of the consequences. That is why we opted for extractions. We couldn't be sure of the effects on the masses," Sam explained.

"So if the Nyterians invented the extraction process this is going to be their other way of working..." Val knew she was right, "...which means if they can keep you all docile and unable to fight, they can use the physical form of extraction to increase the energy levels."

"If this is affecting all Guards, will it affect Val?" Zac asked Sam.

"I don't know, but it seems the Judges have kept their powers or he wouldn't have kept them separately from the others. Where's the Warden?" Sam asked.

The Guard's head dropped. "He's the example for us all."

Sam grabbed his arm. "What are you saying?"

The Guard pointed up. "He fought to keep control, but we couldn't help him." Sam saw him first. Then Val gasped out loud. Zac pulled her to keep moving. At the highest point of the corridor a flickering image of the Warden was projected for all to see. If Val had thought the way he looked before on Nyteria was bad, this beat it a hundredfold. He was slumped, suspended in a cage, battered, bloody and bruised.

"We need to get him out," Val demanded.

"We will, when the time is right," Sam said, grabbing her hand and pulling them through the crowd. He knew the planet better than Val and in the flick of his wrist they had moved from the line into another room.

"Did you see him?" Val's face filled with anger. "What are we going to do?"

"First check your powers are intact. I'm hoping your human witch DNA will hold you together."

Val started a flame on her hand. "Seems ok." Then she extended her sword. "Well at last being a reject has come in handy."

"Zac, the Warden. Where is he?"

He checked his watch. "He's in the teleportation room."

"Good, there are far too many people watching him. We'll need to find the High Judges and get them out first. Do you have a sample of the air?"

Zac tapped at this watch. "Yes, but how can we work with this in the place you call the Space?"

"You would be amazed at what they can do. I need you to take that information back to the others."

"You want me to leave, Val?" His voice filled with concern.

"Without that data, we don't stand a chance. Tell Boden and Hadwyn they mustn't come to the surface."

"Zac, he's right, take it. I'll be fine," she insisted.

"If you need me I will hear: we're connected." He made his feelings known.

"So, you're playing the connected card? Good move." Val hugged him, he stepped away and disappeared.

"Ok Sam, what now?" She felt on edge without Zac, but trusted Sam knew what he was doing.

"We can't teleport without them picking up our signals, and we need the element of surprise. We are going to head to where I think the High Judges are being held. I need you to be ready when we arrive for an attack. They won't play with you like they did on Nyteria. They were trying to trick us then and now they have no need to keep us alive. They want to kill you. Do you understand what I'm saying Val?" He was more serious that she had ever seen him.

"Hey, people want to kill me all the time." She grinned trying to lift the mood.

He gripped her arm. "This is no game! I can't save you again. We have to get to the High Judges at any cost."

She wasn't keen on the pain he was inflicting. "Ok! I get it. People will try to kill me and I need the High Judges."

"Good, then let's go."

They left the room once more and mingled with a passing group of Guards, who were quick to spot Sam and surround them, standing tall around Val to cover her. They marched past the Nyterian soldiers and slipped away at the next corner. Val's pulse was racing; when Sam pushed her though another doorway into what looked almost like a torture chamber.

"Where are we?" She looked around at metal beds and equipment. A noise came from behind a shiny chrome cupboard.

Sam put his finger up to his lip to deter Val from saying anything. "It's ok. We're here for Alchany's freedom. Show yourself." Reassured by Sam's voice, a tall, thin, woman edged out from behind the cupboard. She was dressed in what looked like some kind of rubber suit. It had an odd skirt at the front and covered her whole body, from her neck, to her fingertips.

"Judge." She bowed her head.

"Are you ok?" Sam moved closer.

"We have had better days." She responded.

"Do you have any information that could help us, Extractor?" Val realised now why the woman was dressed as she was, and why the room looked like a surgery.

"Only what we have seen with our own eyes." She shook her head. Val could see she was shaken by what had happened. "They came in ships, standing off in orbit from the planet. They threatened us. We were afraid, but the Guards were ready for them. The Warden rallied us and made us feel powerful again, and when they arrived we were sure victory would be ours, but in hours it was over. The Guards could not fight. It was as if they had lost their connections to their life force. Like clone bodies they were gathered by the Nyterians who marched them around for everyone to see, and now the Guards cannot help us."

"Are you saying this thing has only affected them?" Sam asked.

"They didn't want our kind; we're no threat to them. I heard the poison only affects the Guards."

"Are you sure? It's important that we understand as much as possible."

"The Collectors are still on duty and they have the Hunters and Mechanics ready in the docking bays and beyond."

"How could they have a poison that only affects the Guards? They would need to target them at DNA level."

"We heard that they are keeping the Warden under heavy guard." She looked cautiously up at Sam.

"What do you mean?"

"They have him close because he was the first, that's exactly what a Collector told us."

Sam's eyes darted to Val's. "That's why they took him, he's the first."

"I'm sorry, but you've lost me." Val shrugged.

"Nathan created something that only affects the Guards." Sam grabbed her shoulders and shook her in excitement. "That's why he took the Warden before. All Guards share a common DNA with the Warden. He needed something from the first Guard. You're all related."

"What? I'm cousins with all those people out there?"

"Sort of, but the one thing you all have in common is the Warden."

"But how can this help us?" Val asked as the door started to open. She held her breath, and felt an instant tightening in her chest. Relief flooded her as Zac appeared. "What are you doing back?" Val asked him, relieved but annoyed that he had scared her.

He seemed as excited as Sam. "I have vital information. You were right, Sam. The Space is most impressive. It seems the poison is a Nyterian-made virus which contains the Warden's DNA."

"We'd were just working that out," Val said.

"Why have you returned?" Sam asked.

"Because to create an anti-virus, Enoch needs some blood from the Warden."

"Fine, if he needs it then we will get it. Val, you go with Zac and get the Warden, or at least some of his blood. I need to get to the High Judges. Striking separately at the same time will help to cause confusion, and if we all get captured now then the battle will be lost. We are much stronger apart."

"I won't let you down," Val said. Zac coughed. "Sorry. *We* won't let you down."

He smiled. "You need to move quickly. Teleport. He's surrounded by soldiers. It will make no difference if they pick up your signal since you're heading straight into their midst. Use the element of surprise to your advantage. Once you have the Warden, get him to the Space. I'll meet you there when I have the others."

Val's helmet closed over her face and she said goodbye to the man she knew she loved, not at all sure that they would ever see each other again.

CHAPTER 18

What Alien?

Val's touchdown didn't quite work as she had expected. She thought it would be a battle from arrival, but as she landed she was struck in the helmet by the fist of a familiar figure. It was her pet, Bertha the snake woman. She landed hard on her bottom and was initially dazed, finding herself in the middle of what seemed to be a huge battle between the aliens she had expelled from Earth and the Collectors. Then a small hand reached out, but without making contact lifted her off the floor. She looked through the chaos of bodies fighting and shoving to see the tiny face of her Collector. "Hello Val." She shouted.

"Hello." She searched for Zac who was crouching two feet behind her shaking his head in amazement. "Helmet off. What's going on?" she yelled over the noise of animals and shots.

"Turns out some fool on another planet decided to send several hundred prisoners in one teleport. Something that has never been done before. Any idea who did it?" she frowned.

"In my defence..." Val shrugged. "No, I have nothing. Where are the Nyterians?"

"Over there, on the edges. Seems they have never witnessed anything like this and don't know how to control it so they had to bring us in. But Val, be warned, they know who did it. Nathan Akar has put a high price on your head."

"We can deal with him later. We've found out that the virus that has left the Guards defenceless is made with the Warden's DNA and I need to get him out of here. Where is he?"

The Collector pointed towards the ceiling; they were directly below him. "What exactly is your plan? And where are you going to take him?"

"Well, I'm going to rescue the Warden and take him back to the Space." She said as a large, hooved alien knocked her sideways. She clung to the floor, grabbing the Collector's hand.

As she pulled herself back up the Collector was just staring at her. "Did you just say the Space?"

"Yes, it's an amazing place at the centre of the Prison and they have everyone who was going to…"

"…the Interspace," the Collector finished her sentence, her expression softening as she deflected Bertha from another assault with her petite hand.

"Now's not the time to talk, but is there something I need to know?" Val enquired.

"NO!" The Collector looked up at the cage. "The time to talk will come; you must get the Warden out of here."

"Zac," Val called through the chaos to her partner who was busy dodging blows. "How am I going to get the Warden down?" she pointed up to the ceiling. "How do we get up there without them spotting us?" She didn't have to wait for his response as the Collector stood and started to raise her off the ground. Quickly she made her helmet cover her face: to prevent herself being recognised.

The Collector called to two other women dressed like her. When they saw what she was doing they started raising some of the aliens into the air alongside Val to cover her. She was near the cage now and she could see the Warden in the flesh for the first time. He looked terrible. His beard was matted with blood and one eye was shut from the bruising around it. How could someone this powerful have been beaten in this way? No one was safe.

Using his good eye, he stared at the strange performance outside his cage. Then he spotted her.

"Hi, it's me - Val." Her voice sounded muted through her helmet, but she was too scared to take it off. She could see the Nyterian soldiers watching the goings-on and starting to question some of the Collectors who were trying to distract them. "How do I get you out?" she quizzed as she bobbed up and down.

"I need my bracelet, which I believe you have?"

"Ah yes, well you see…"

"Val, you came back here when you could have stayed on Earth. I need no explanation, just give me what is mine." He raised his hand.

"I came back because you're family and….. I'm explaining myself aren't I?" She reached her hand out taking off his bracelet. "Here you go."

His eyes lit up. "Can you get it through to me?" He couldn't get his hand through the bars.

Val looked down at the Collector and signalled for her to get closer. She nodded and Val started to move nearer. Her hand was close enough to pass it now. As she reached out she heard the order to fire being yelled. The bracelet left her hand as the sound of shots rang out. She felt a blow and a sharp pain flared in her side. An energy shot had been deflected by her suit. She dropped to the ground. She could only pray the Warden had caught his bracelet. Zac was by her side instantly. The Collector grabbed her arm. "I'm sorry. Dropping you was the quickest option."

"They are coming for you. Defend yourself." Zac started to pull her up.

"Did you release the Warden?" the Collector asked.

"I hope so. Now stand back," Val ordered, allowing Zac to pull her fully to her feet. She shook herself down and lit up like an Olympic torch, ready to cross any path. Failure could no longer be in her vocabulary; too many people's lives depended on her right now. Her sword extended as the soldiers headed for them. She blew a clear path in front of her, scorched hair and scales moving out of the way of her flames. She began deflecting what looked like bullets of energy as they came towards her, "ANYTIME NOW WOULD BE GOOD!" she shouted up to the Warden.

The soldiers were getting closer and the Collectors were desperately trying to stop them, but with no weapons they were losing ground by the second. Then Val heard a thunderous bang. The floor behind her shook and she turned to find a freed Warden standing behind her. Sam had told her the plan: get the Warden and get out. But if she left the Collectors now she would be leaving them to die. She couldn't save them all. What could she do? They were trying to help her and she was going to abandon them.

Almost as if she had read Val's mind her Collector was next to her. "Leave. Take him and go."

"But..."

"Val, she's right, we must go." Zac offered her his hand.

"I promise you I will come back for you." Her voice cracked inside her helmet.

"Keep the Space safe. I believe in you." The Collector positioned herself in the line of fire, moving aliens into the mix to distract the soldiers.

Val grabbed the Warden's and Zac's hands and prayed that her Collector would survive.

*

"What are we doing here? And where is here?" The Warden asked looking around him at the grey and unfamiliar surroundings.

"Well, it seems that the Guards have been rendered useless by your DNA. So we've brought you here to get some of your blood." She heard the cries of her brother Magrafe. Boden was first to greet the Warden, with her dad following.

"Have you heard from Sam?" Val asked tentatively.

"Jason has been speaking to him. Let's get the Warden inside where he will be safe and someone can get the samples we need." They led them swiftly back into the interior of the Space where Susan and her new friend, Taran, were waiting. Val embraced her mum.

"So this is your boss?" she asked. "Big man," she observed.

"Yes, and very powerful. People are going to be very upset that I've taken him back again." Val told her.

"Val!" she heard the Warden calling her.

"Yes?"

"Where is this place?" He was now sitting while a young woman pulled at his uniform.

"You're in the Space. You're safe for now and all these people..." she moved back so he could get a good view, "...are rejects like me. They're the things you, on the Prison choose to put in your rubbish, or to be more precise, the Interspace."

Taran wheeled his way over to the Warden and handed him a glass of green liquid.

The Warden took the drink. "Thank you." Taran acknowledged him and spun back to Susan. "I knew nothing about this. I hope you can believe me. I know we have strict laws on Alchany, but this isn't my doing. Thank you for helping me. What is happening now on the Prison?"

Enoch was heading down the hill with Hadwyn when they spotted Val and her guest. They stepped up their pace. "Warden," Enoch greeted him respectfully.

Hadwyn beamed. "Val, you made it back."

"You doubted it?" she said hands on hips. "Where's Jason? I want to know what's going on with Sam."

"Sam is still on the Prison?" the Warden asked.

"Yes, we split up. Zac got the air samples, whilst Sam and I were looking for the High Judges, then Zac came back to tell us we needed your blood and the rest you know. But Sam is still on the surface looking for the others."

The Warden turned to Zac. "You have shown great bravery, more than is ever expected of a Hunter. This will be rewarded."

"Thank you," Zac replied.

Enoch pointed Val in the direction of the hilltop. "Jason's working with Fran."

"Come on Zac. See you all in a minute." She excused them and they started their ascent at speed.

She arrived in the cave to hear Jason shouting. This wasn't quite what she was hoping for. "Get me back online now!" he was raising his voice at a woman who was clearly trying her best.

"Jason." Val put her hand on his shoulder.

The relief on his face was only momentary. "Val, Sam's in trouble. I'm going to lose him."

Val understood straight away why he was in such a state, but this wasn't helping the woman. "Jason, we aren't going to do that. I have the Warden and Nathan wants me, so we have two bargaining chips. Where is he and what's he doing?"

"He was heading down an empty corridor. He said something about High Judges and then we got cut off."

"He's back!" The woman jumped out of the seat to let Jason back in. Val patted her on the shoulder and she looked relieved.

"Sam can you hear me?" Jason asked.

There was a moment of static, "Yes. Have you heard from Val?"

"Here boss," she called out. "Want some help? I can come back and meet you."

"No, give me another few minutes to find them. Well done, Val. There are sirens ringing out all over the Prison so I hoped you'd been successful."

Jason was tapping away on his laptop which had large glowing crystals all around it. "What's with the rocks?" Val asked Fran.

"They're a form of power source; it's like Duracell from another galaxy."

"Jason, tell me what's coming around the corner," Sam asked.

Jason tapped looking at his screen, "Next one's clear, mate, but there's a large area that I can't see after that."

"That could be because that's where they're holding them."

Zac was tapping on his watch. "That is one of the main containment areas outside the docking bay. It will have storage for large and powerful prisoners. It is an ideal place to hold them."

"Thanks Zac. Jason, mark the coordinates to this location."

"Ok." He made a mark on the virtual map.

"It looks..." The signal was gone.

"Sam," he called. "Sam." Jason looked up at Val.

"Give him a second. You said he was going into an area where there was no signal." They stood together. The seconds ticking so slowly it felt like time had slowed to a standstill.

Enoch's entrance made them all jump. "How's he doing?"

"We've lost his signal, but he was just going into an area that he thought was holding the High Judges."

"How long has he been offline?"

"Almost three minutes now," Jason answered.

There was static. Val felt her heart skip inside her chest. "Hello."

"Sam!" she shouted.

"Well, hello there and who are you?" A voice that wasn't Sam's enquired.

Val pushed Jason to one side. "I'm Val Saunders, prison Guard Twenty-three thirteen and who are you?"

"I am someone who would very much like your presence."

"Nathan," Val said.

He laughed. "I'm pleased I made an impression on you. You stole something that was very important to me and I want it back."

"I think the Warden is more mine than yours."

His voice became tense. "Not the Warden, although I would like him back as well. You have powers that no one here seems to be able to match and annoyingly, you have given the Guards hope, taking away their fear. I need to quash that before it goes any further. Now that I have your, Sam, I think you may be interested in co-operating. It seems we can't locate your signal, so unless you hand yourself and the Warden over to my soldiers, Sam will die along with the Collectors who were stupid enough to help you. So, bringer of hope, what do you say to that?"

Val looked at Zac. He shook his head. She signalled to Jason to turn off the mike. "He thinks we're still on the Prison. He knows nothing about this place. If we go back, it'll give you time to sort this out." Enoch was now also shaking his head. She knew as well as they did that if she went back with the Warden they would be lost. Sam would have looked at the bigger picture. He wouldn't care if he died to make sure the prisoners had hope, but she loved him and that was making her weak. She signalled to turn the mike back on.

"Well?" he sounded annoyed at having to ask twice.

"I think I..." she started to speak then pulled one of the crystals away from the computer and it instantly shut down.

"What are you doing?" Fran gasped.

"I've just given us a few minutes grace. Now get another computer up and running with a different frequency. Zac, find out how close we can teleport. I'm going back to the surface."

Chapter 19

Natural Resources

"Well, if you're going through with this, let's get our troops ready," Enoch said.

"Do we have troops?" Val felt a little more confident at hearing that.

Jason had a laptop in his hands. "I'll get another link to the planet, but you'd better have a good plan, Val."

"I will find you the best place." Zac tapped at his watch.

"Come with me, let Jason and Zac do what they need to do." Enoch led her out of the room and back towards the exit of his hilltop cave. "Don't worry, we will do everything in our power to get Sam back, he's our brother." He lifted what Val could only describe as a primitive drum stick and hit it against the rocks. The sound wave that came from the stick vibrated through the air. Val couldn't hear anything, but she felt it running through her body, like the vibrations of a speaker when you put your hand on it. He kept striking and to Val's surprise people appeared and started heading towards them. "Sometimes you only need to feel the calling," Enoch said.

"That's amazing." She saw them all lining up together.

Enoch stopped beating and raised his hands to get their full attention, "Family, as you know the surface is under attack. I know how you feel about them. I know you were rejected and sent to your endless deaths, but our brother Sam has been captured and his life will be taken." There were gasps of shock from the group. "We may not be quick enough to save him, but we have to try."

A young man with a metal arm called up, "What will happen to us? We are seen as the weaker ones and I have heard there's a virus that has taken away their power."

"I can answer that in part." A young woman Val hadn't met before joined her and Enoch. "Hello Val, I'm Hereswith, but you can call me Eswith." She smiled and her face lit up. Val was momentarily taken aback by her natural beauty. She had an athletic build complimented by her flawless skin, pale from living under ground. "We have an answer," she spoke to the crowd. "We can reverse the virus, but to free the Guards already infected will take at least half a cycle, twelve hours." She told them. "However, because we haven't been subjected to the virus here, we can protect you now, before you go to the surface."

A cheer went out amongst the gathering. Enoch brought them back to silence once more. "You need to understand that this will change everything. At this moment we're invisible, but in doing this we will become visible to the Prison. We have the advantage, but after we're done, things will never go back to the way they were." His words hung heavy in the air.

"May I speak?" Val heard a familiar voice. To her surprise she saw the Warden walking into the crowd.

"We all have an equal right to speak here," Enoch said respectfully.

The group turned towards the Warden.

"I have been overwhelmed by the information I received on arriving here. This virus comes directly from me, so I feel responsible for my men and now for you. Despite the way you have been treated by the Prison, you have welcomed me and I have found lost Guards and Hunters, people I had mourned. Yet now I can rejoice that you're alive. It was never my intention for you to be in this place, although I see you have made a wonderful home. As Enoch rightly says, if you go to the surface to help save the Prison, you will no longer be hidden, but you have my word that when this ends, you will all be free. I have much to learn about you and your existence, but all I ask of you now is that you help us." His voice filled with determination. "We *will* defeat Nyteria, and bring back freedom to the Prison!" he bellowed.

The cheers were even louder now and the energy in the closed space was electric. "How long will it take to get them ready, Eswith?" Val asked.

"An hour, maybe a little more."

"They have Sam now Enoch. How are we going to stall Nathan whilst we get them ready?"

"We need a distraction." Enoch said matter-of-factly.

"I'll be that distraction; they won't hurt me," Val said.

"I will come with you." Val turned to see the Warden had joined them. "I can make this right for you, Enoch. You were a brave and loyal Guard. I am happy with the knowledge that you are the one who will come and save us."

Enoch bowed his head in respect. "It was a lifetime ago."

Val interrupted. "No pressure, but get vaccinating the Guards and whoever else we have. I just need to get

Sam's location from Jason." She left them and headed back to her friends. Jason was diligently tapping on his keyboard and Fran was by his side. "Got any news for me?" she asked.

"Yes, here's the place they took him. If you look at the map you'll see that it's five corridors south of the teleportation room." He pointed to the flashing cursor.

"This is where we need to teleport." Zac showed her on the map.

"There is no *we* this time, buddy. I'm going with the Warden and they need your help here."

"This is not a clever move. You will need me."

"Zac, they need every last piece of information about the Prison. They need you. I'm just going to get captured, that's not hard. Please stay here and help them."

Zac looked distressed. "You know what they will do to you if you go back."

"Yes, Sam showed me, but I'm prepared to take the risk. Are you prepared to let me?"

He nodded, not in agreement, just in resignation that he wasn't going to win.

"Ok then, me and the Warden are going in."

Jason handed her a tiny ear piece. "Take care and put this in your ear; nothing like good old fashion technology." She took it, he was right. Maybe the old stuff would work better in a place controlled by advanced technology.

They embraced and Val left them. As she was leaving the room, she spotted Wendy waiting for her. "Hey, you ok? You look tired." Val could see that the experience was starting to wear her down.

She took both of Val's hands. "I've had another vision."

"Stop! If it's bad news I don't want to know. I'll run with fate."

"It wasn't about the battle; it was about you and Sam." She smiled.

"What did you see?" Val was now very interested.

"You were choosing a wedding dress. There were so many, all different colours and designs." Now Val could see why her friend was grinning.

"Well, let's look at the positive side, if I was looking at dresses it means we'll make it through." She kissed Wendy on the cheek. "I'm not quite ready to walk down the aisle at eighteen, but it's nice to know it may happen one day. Now I have to go and sacrifice myself for my future husband."

"Stay safe until I arrive," Wendy said pulling Sam's silver wand out.

"You took that from Lailah's body!" Val was impressed. "See you soon."

She left her friend and joined the Warden who was busy greeting his lost Guards and Hunters. For the first time she saw a human side to him. They were all showing him the utmost respect. "Warden, it's time we left." She broke up the reunion.

"Yes, let us go." He patted a young man on the arm and Boden walked with them down to the door. Val said her goodbyes once more and then they were out in the open, ready to teleport.

"Take this." The Warden handed her his bracelet.

"You need it to keep your power up." She pushed it back at him.

"I'm an old man and what power I have has no use for me at this time. I have always underestimated you,

Earth girl. You are power in its purest form. Let's go and free our Prison."

Val put the bracelet on next to her own. *Our Prison* he'd said, it whizzed through her mind. The rest of her family were stuck on Earth, possibly being interrogated by MI5. Her mum and dad had lost everything, Jason his dad, and Fran her sister. What was it all for? She loved Sam, but this had to stop. "I have one request before we leave."

"Anything."

"When this is over and we have won, I want to go home with my parents and friends to a world that doesn't know who Val Saunders the disappearing freak is. I want to live a normal life."

"I can make that happen." They shook hands to seal the agreement and left the monochrome landscape of the Space.

*

Their arrival was instantly detected, but that was the aim of the game for Val; Zac had given them the perfect location. She was struck by a soldier from behind and fell to her knees. The Warden was a tougher prospect and it took four to bring him down, however, they were both subdued in seconds. She knew better than to retaliate, she wanted them to believe she had been affected by the virus. If they knew she had her powers they would be able to take them away, and the aim of this exercise was to stay alive as long as possible in order to get the others back.

The soldier relayed to his superior. "We have them; seems the female has made the right decision."

Val could hear the message going into his headset. "Nathan orders that they should be delivered to him without harm or he will personally punish those responsible." The soldier passed the message on. Val and the Warden's hands were bound behind their backs; they were then raised roughly to their feet and set marching. Val intentionally dragged her feet, slowing them down, to the annoyance of her captors. She was willing to try anything to gain the hour she needed for the people from the Space to be vaccinated. Every second counted.

"Hello, can you hear me?" a voice whispered into her ear. She coughed. "Two coughs for yes." She coughed twice quickly. The soldier pushed her again in disgust at her weak and feeble coughing fit. "I have you on a one-to one headset to keep the noise down. You're moving into the coordinates where we lost Sam. Vaccinations are going well here and Zac is collecting all the Hunters together. Boden and Hadwyn are making the Guards ready. Stay strong, Val, we're coming." She coughed again. Glancing across at the Warden she nodded her head discreetly. He responded with the same action and they continued to march.

*

Val knew they had arrived at the centre of operations. The air was dense with fear and obedience. Every person in the area was on edge. Nathan seemed to inspire gut-wrenching terror in everyone. She'd been scared of Excariot, but this was a deeper feeling. She had felt it on Nyteria. It was like life had no value to him, and everyone knew it.

Nathan appeared - his skin a vibrant blue. Now Val could see him in the light of the Prison she was almost mesmerised by his colour. It glowed, palpitating as he walked. His jaw was squared, his hair blue to match his skin perfectly. He walked towards her and she felt her insides start to shake. "Welcome to my Prison, I'm pleased you came." He greeted his newest acquisitions. "You have taken the Warden from me twice and that's two times too many. Do you understand what I'm saying to you?" His voice was firm but not yet raised. Val was forced by two soldiers to kneel down in front of him. She kept her eyes on the clean white floor. "Take the Warden back to where the Guards can see him and make sure everyone knows he is back in our power. We need to make an example of this girl, something they won't forget in a hurry."

Val felt them pulling the Warden away from her. She calculated they had been at least half an hour so far. As long as his example of her didn't last less than the half hour they needed, she might just make it through this.

"Come with me." Nathan pulled her to her feet. His grip was firm, but not tight enough to hurt her. She rose and followed him through a large group of his soldiers and out onto a balcony. She recognised where she was now. The Warden had brought her out here before. It overlooked a large part of the Prison that stretched out in front of her and she could see row after row of standing Guards. They were eerily still and had clearly been brought out to see the spectacle.

Val wondered if he would torture her in front of them. That would have a lasting effect on everyone who witnessed it. He moved her out to the edge. Val looked down and realised just how high up they were. She still hated heights, and shivered uneasily. The crowd started to move backwards and spread out a little. Something was coming out from below the balcony, but she couldn't yet see what it was. She knew it was bad judging from the muffled gasps coming from below.

Slowly a procession came into view. There were eight people wearing dark green cloaks. Their heads covered. Val saw that they were tied together by something that looked like a neon cable. It sparked and buzzed between each one. The soldiers proceeded to line them up in clear view of the balcony. "Reveal my power!" Nathan called to his soldiers. They pulled back the hoods. There stood five men, two women and Sam. Val wanted to call out his name, but he was going to see her soon enough. They looked like they hadn't been hurt, but this wasn't a good situation. The Guards were fidgeting in agitation. "Have you never seen the faces of your gods?" Nathan asked the crowd. "The ones that took you from your homes and made you their slaves?" No one spoke. "Do you not want retribution for the homes that they destroyed? To stop you longing to see your loved ones again?" His voice echoed around them all.

"Val, that's your name isn't it, not number thirteen?" He pulled her closer to the edge so that everyone could see her. As soon as he saw her, Sam started to struggle, but the weapon of a soldier colliding with his head soon ended that. Blood ran down the side of his face. "See these people, Val. They took you from your home, from your mother and sent you to the future." Val was shocked. How did he know that? "They made you a weapon of destruction with no thought for your family or your planet. Is that a lie?" he asked her.

Val could see the Guards looking at her, waiting for her to speak. Sam's eyes met hers. "No." She hung her head. It wasn't a lie and that hurt.

"Did they take away your life and treat you like a reject, something imperfect, something that they were stuck with?" Then he pointed at the Judges. "And then you caught one of their most wanted criminals for them: Excariot. Is that not the truth?"

She couldn't understand where all this information was coming from. "Yes." Answering him was so painful. He was right and what he was saying was the truth and it grated in her throat.

"Is it true that you just created the largest portal in the history of the Prison, bringing several hundred aliens to their knees? May I also add to that you escaped me twice, and took the Warden to freedom and still returned to save them after everything they have taken from you?"

Tears had started to form in her eyes. "Yes," she cried. This was crazy. He was turning her against her own people. Listening to what he was saying she wasn't sure what to think anymore.

"This girl, this human, or reject as you have chosen to call her, is a true god." He looked out at them all, waiting for their full attention. "I will take her to be mine!"

"NO!" A cry came from Sam and he was brutally silenced again.

"When you see her at my side you will see her as a symbol of my dominance over you, and you will remember everything that has been taken from you by these creatures of power." He pointed at the Judges. "They will be sent to the Interspace for you to see that they have no power over you anymore."

Val's head was spinning so much she felt she might pass out. Before she had a chance to look back at Sam, Nathan pulled her away from the balcony. She could only pray now that the others were on their way, because if they didn't succeed, she was going to be Mr Blue's girlfriend far too soon.

CHAPTER 20

The Union

"Can you hear me?" A soft voice echoed in Val's ear. She gave two sharp coughs. "We're on our way. We have over a hundred and fifty Guards ready plus enough airborn Vaccine to treat most of the affected Guards within twelve hours."

Nathan had sat Val down on a bench to await his next orders. Soldiers were stationed round the perimeter of the room. "Not the right people." She said clearly. "What?" The soldier turned and walked towards her.

"I said, there are a lot of you guys on this planet, thousands I'd guess. Am I right?" she asked him.

His gaze grew suspicious. "What's the reason for your question?"

"Well, you have to cover all of us and that must take thousands of you surely?" she gave a weak shrug as if she was genuinely interested in what he had to say.

"We have enough. Anyway, once you remove your power to resist, you need little force. The Guards were our only real threat, so the power of the Prison has gone. Now one soldier with power could rule this place, the rest of them are a joke." He turned away.

"But you still have the High Judges as prisoners, they still have their powers."

"Not for long. Now shut up." He moved further away to prevent her from questioning him further.

Jason spoke after a few moments of silence. "So, you're saying we don't have the right people?"

The soldier was now a few metres away from her and she was able to whisper carefully. "Listen to me. I want you to come, but this is a battle we can't win with the amount of Guards in the Space. They have the High Judges and Sam's alive for now, but we need people to get the Vaccine onto the surface." The soldier turned to look at her. She stopped speaking, waiting until he lost interest. "Tell Eswith to send Zac and his Hunters, they'll stand a better chance of being undetected. Send them to all the highly populated points where our Guards are being held. We can't do this without the support of all our Guards, we're not strong enough." She went quiet again, waiting for a moment. "I've just seen the prisoners and they're all Guards. He sees most of the others as unimportant. Tell Zac to get the Extractors' help."

"Makes sense. I'll speak to Enoch now. Are you ok, Val? I heard what he was saying to you."

"Been better."

"SHUT UP!" the soldier shouted at her.

"But I'm lonely I want someone to talk to…" She fell silent as Nathan returned.

"You will come with me." He pointed at her and she knew if she was going to stay alive until the Vaccine had had a chance to work on the surface, she would need to do as she was told. She stood, her hands still tied behind her back. "We need to get you something different to wear. Untie her arms. She won't be a problem, she knows better." A soldier hurried to release her.

It felt good having her hands free again. He led her out of the room and they walked down corridors that she was becoming familiar with. She plucked up the courage to ask a question. "So, what's your plan?"

"Freedom." He took her hand and Val noticed his skin felt human. "I want my people to have a chance at survival, that's all." Gradually, starting with the hand that was holding hers, his skin was changing colour, matching her own skin tone, slowly travelling up his arm and then all over his body, until he looked human. His eyes met hers and she was shocked to see they were now the colour of honey.

"But surely war is just causing pain. So, to free one planet you would enslave another?" She kept her voice very calm; she knew that this man could explode.

"Not if the people you enslave are the cause of your pain. Tell me, Val, when you caught Excariot, what had he done that made you want to imprison him?"

She thought for a moment as he moved her along. "He killed my real father, threatened my family and he was a bad person, he wanted to take over the world. That tends to make you enemy number one."

"But what of his love for Lailah? Wouldn't you risk everything for someone you loved?"

She hated that he made sense. "Yes, I would, but I would do my best not to hurt anyone else."

"Who have I hurt Val?"

"The Warden looks pretty black and blue to me."

"He resisted. We told them to hand themselves over, we gave them the option, but they insisted on fighting. That was the Warden's decision."

A waiting soldier opened a door for them. Spread around the room in front of her were several rails of dresses, not just any dresses. Val immediately knew that these were the dresses that Wendy had seen in her vision.

"I will leave you here. There is no exit and if you teleport out I'll kill the Judge they call Sam. I know you came back for him."

"I'm not going anywhere. Don't hurt anyone, please," she supplicated. "I'll do anything you want."

"Choose one of these dresses and then we will talk again." He turned to leave. "Look your best or I won't be happy." His skin turned blue once more as the door closed on her designer Prison.

"Jason can you hear me?" She waited in silence, unsure if this room would have a signal.

"Hello mate. You ok?"

"You need to get Boden or Hadwyn for me now!" she ordered.

"Will do. Fran, get the boys. Enoch agreed with your plan and Zac and the others have left for the surface with the vaccine."

"Good, I just need to keep this going. Jason, he wants me to wear a dress. Scarily my uniform now looks good."

"They're here. Can I put you on speaker?"

"Yes, we're alone."

"Ok, go for it."

"Help me Boden, Nathan wants me to put on a dress, which means no uniform, which means no weapons." She was pulling at the dresses as despair washed over her. "What is it with men and dresses? Boden, I remember when you showed me your tattoo; you made your uniform invisible? Can I do that and put the dress on top?"

Boden responded, his voice soft and familiar. "Yes you can, it's the same as your helmet and your weapon:

it has to come from inside you. Your suit is made to respond to your requests. Just focus on it becoming invisible."

Val closed her eyes and she imagined herself naked. Cautiously she peeked from one of her eyes. "Ok, I have a naked leg and left arm."

"Val, imagine me shooting you," Hadwyn added from the background.

She laughed out loud, "You're not here!"

"How do you know that? You can hear me and I'm invisible when I want to be."

Val span around, her uniform again covering her whole body. "That's not helping!"

"Ignore him Val, he's here alright, driving us all mad. Just try again. See yourself being washed over by a feeling of freedom from restraint."

She closed her eyes again and the feeling came from her head this time, thoughts flooding out of the cool breeze she had felt when she had left Shane in the Space. Then came the scent of lilies. A tear formed in her eye. She breathed it in for as long as it lasted, then with a sense of inner calm she opened her eyes. Looking down, all she could see was her superman pants and matching bra. "All good here."

"Well done! Stay alive until we can get there," Boden said.

"Yes, we shall stun them all into submission when we arrive." Hadwyn added his brutish take on the situation.

"Need to choose a dress. Is Wendy there?"

"I am."

"What dress did you see me wearing in your vision?"

"It was pink." Wendy's voice was a little shaky. "I'm so sorry."

"*You* should be pink!" Val complained.

"I'm sorry I got the vision wrong."

"Hey, you did your best. But seriously - pink?"

"Yes. It was on the third row."

Val scanned the hideous collection. "I do believe Nathan's been watching that gypsy wedding program." She found the offensive object of Wendy's vision. "I'll never forget this day as long as I live." She pulled it off the rail. It was a deep magenta with more lace netting than Katie Price's entire wardrobe. "Seriously, the things I do for this Prison," she groaned as she climbed into it.

There was a knocking at the door. "Yes," she replied. The door opened and in walked a woman. She seemed petrified. Val felt for her. "Hello," she greeted her as the door shut again.

"I am here to prepare you. That's a beautiful dress." The woman admired Val's magenta meringue.

"Who are you?" Val wanted to know more about her before she let down her guard.

"I am a Ranswar. My name is not important. We serve those who rule and now we will serve the Nyterians." she moved around Val and started to bunch her hair in her hands.

She thought it wise not to mention that she had recently had the Ranswar Princess bitten by a killer alien dog: bad way to start their relationship. "I want to know your name. It matters to me and you don't serve anyone here."

"My name is Dahntey."

"Well Dahntey, it's nice to meet you." Val wouldn't speak to the others now. She wanted to believe this woman was who she said she was, but she couldn't be sure this wasn't a trick.

The woman worked diligently, twisting and hooking Val's mass of hair. She could only imagine that she now looked like every five year old girl's dream doll. She smiled for a moment as she imagined being the scary plastic doll standing on her great auntie's loo covering the roll of toilet paper.

"You seem happy to be going into a union with Nathan," the woman commented, picking up on her smile.

"Sorry... union?" Val's grin disappeared abruptly.

"Yes, you are to be united with Nathan."

"What - like married?"

"I don't know what this married is, but he sees you as a symbol of good fortune and great magical power. It's normal on Nyteria for people of power to be united."

"What else do you know about Nyteria?" she asked.

"Not much. I met a girl from there once. They used to have a leader who believed in talking and all that achieved was more talking. Now they have someone much different. And look, he has taken over the Prison in no time, so he must be powerful. You are a very lucky person to be united with someone so dominant." She tucked a few loose hairs away. "It's time for you to go now." Val watched as she moved gracefully to the door and knocked to be released. The soldier let her out and beckoned Val to follow.

She was curious to see what Nathan's next move would be. He had her dressed like Barbie and would parade her around as an example to the Prison, obviously had poor dress sense. Val would not let herself imagine what the union would mean. She knew from Nathan's warning that he was going to use Sam as a weapon against her, which meant he might not kill him for now. If he felt the need to threaten her, then he clearly still saw her as a threat. She just needed to keep that feeling going, without pushing him too far.

She stood in the corridor, invisible suit under her dress, hair up, waiting for him to arrive. As he approached, he changed from his shade to hers. "You look spectacular!" He seemed very pleased with her ridiculous appearance.

"Why do you change colour for me?" she asked him as once again he took her hand. He seemed to want physical contact with her, which she hated to her core.

"I want you to like the way I look." He smiled as if they were a normal couple off on a stroll around the local park.

"Why would I like you?" It came out before she could stop her stupid tongue from running away.

His grip on her hand grew tighter, she moaned and he released it again. "You will learn to like me, it isn't an option," he said through gritted teeth.

"Then I will," she said, "but I want something from you." She felt it was risky, but she had to ask.

His smile had returned at her submission. "What do you want?"

"I would like to see the Warden one more time." She waited for him to answer. He seemed to be thinking about her request.

"Strange, I thought you would want to see the Judge you love so much that you would risk your life to save him. You have confused me a little. However you may see the Warden one last time. You will be leaving the Prison shortly, so I will make this happen for you now." He nodded as if agreeing with himself.

Val felt her knees go weak. She would be leaving the Prison. She hadn't planned on leaving. "When will I be leaving? I thought you wanted to keep me at your side as a shining example of your power?" she asked in a sweet tone.

"And I will. The Prison will be an almost dead planet once we move everything to Nyteria. The Guards will come with us to help rebuild our new home."

Val suddenly felt sicker than she had before. "But why take the planet? How will you move all the prisoners? They can't be left here. Don't you need the energy?"

"Yes I do. So many questions." He patted her hand as they entered a new area. "The energy will be sent to us by the portals we have built. We have been creating transporters for a very long time. You seem concerned about leaving the Prison. Why?"

She realised that she was showing her vulnerability to him and putting their plans at risk. He would never get all the Guards off the Prison before the Vaccine started to work. "Just interested in my future."

"Good, because so am I." He led her across the room and there, in a clear perspex-like cell, sat the Warden. "You may have a moment with him. I don't need to remind you of what I will do if you cross me."

"I know." She looked at the floor and after a moment he left them alone. "Can you still hear me, Jason?" she asked, smiling at the Warden.

"Yes, I heard it all. Val, you can't let him take you off the surface. Zac says they're nearly done."

"I'll do my best, but you'll have to just focus on the plan."

"Stay safe," he told her.

"What's happening?" the Warden stood, bumping into the sides of his restrictive cell.

"As you can see, I have a new uniform." She gave him a twirl. "Seems like I'm going to be united with Nathan and shipped off to Nyteria. Then he's going to bring the Guards to Nyteria to work as slaves until his planet is back up to full power, leaving someone here in charge of teleporting the energy to the surface. Any ideas on how to stall him for the next ten hours would be good, because what he doesn't know is that Zac and the other Hunters have deposited the vaccine all over the surface."

"When are you going to be united? There are strict rules that say a Guard cannot be united with anyone other than their designated Ranswar."

Val was confused. Hadn't he heard the good news she had just given him. "Are you serious? I'm a girl like all the Ranswars, if you hadn't noticed." Val pointed at her dress. "And the vaccine…"

"Listen to me! We have never had a female Guard, Val, but if he unites himself with you there will be repercussions."

"Seriously, like a slap on his crazy wrist? I don't feel like this is helping me in any way."

"Val, this galaxy has a Prison planet for a reason. On Earth, you have Prisons in small boxes of bricks and mortar, where you contain a few. The Ballany Galaxy has us. We needed a whole planet for our prisoners. There are powers overseeing us, even bigger than the High Judges. There is always a force to rule a force."

"So why haven't they stepped in? Why is it in your Galaxy no one steps in until all hell has broken loose? The Prison gets overrun and no one moves, but Val Saunders gets hitched and the Angel of Darkness gets on his high horse."

"Val, no one can stop Nathan attacking, and as long as one of the Judges is alive and the Prison is still running they won't step in. He's not stupid. I'm talking to you about a loop-hole. You must trust me when I say you really don't want these powers to get involved - ever. I have a feeling Nathan doesn't know this rule and it could work in our favour. You must get a union as soon as possible. Make sure he makes this error and you will be free." He seemed almost uplifted at the prospect.

"So let me get this straight. I get united to Nathan and because he's not my designated Ranswar he will be punished by something or someone?"

"Yes." He sat back down.

"Will they appear before us at the altar? Anything I should be looking out for?"

"Did you ever hear of the Returners? They are the ones who return your humans to Earth when they have stripped their memories. Everyone stays clear of them. They work alone. Well, the last time I saw a Guard make a union with someone who wasn't a Ranswar they were brought in to deal with him. He hasn't been seen again. The punishment can take many different forms. It just depends on who and where they are when it takes place."

"So what about Excariot and Lailah?" Val asked.

"Your father caught them on Gingua and they were brought back to the planet for punishment, but Excariot escaped."

"And my father and Wyetta?"

The Warden went quiet, he shuffled his feet. For someone so big, at that moment he seemed very small. "He was never united with your mother, but I would have reprimanded him on his return. I'm sorry, Val, but rules are rules and this one is going to work in your favour. Make him perform the union with you as soon as you can and the planet will be free. Soldiers need a leader and the one mistake Nathan has made is making his soldiers follow him through fear. It has the opposite affect to hope. They will surrender if he's removed. If this doesn't happen, then when the Guards are back up to strength, they can defeat the Nyterians." His face looked old, tired and bruised.

"Doesn't it sound wrong to you that people can't be with the ones they love?"

"Val, it's the way it is and always has been. I didn't make the rules, I just follow them, and this one could save us all."

She took a deep breath. "Then I guess that's what I'll have to do. Jason, don't tell my Mum I'm getting married."

"Ok." The voice in her ear complied.

CHAPTER 21

Rule Breaker

Nathan sent a soldier to collect her; her time with the Warden was up. She had said her goodbyes, knowing what was now expected of her. She just had to get married and everything would be fine. "This way." The soldier guided her into a room.

Nathan was sitting in a chair waiting for her. The seat was strange, it looked a little like a tête-à-tête chair she had seen at a museum once. It had a wooden back in the shape of an S. Nathan invited her to sit facing him.

She pushed her hands down on the wood. "It looks like mahogany," she said.

"Yes, a friend gave it to me as a gift. He said that one day I would sit in it with someone I hoped to love and they would face me and this would be our special place."

Val didn't know whether to laugh out loud or cry. Was he seriously trying to woo her with a chair? "It's a hard wood and needs to be treated correctly for it to bend." She smiled sweetly. The quicker he began the ritual to unite them the better, though she couldn't seem too eager because that could cause him to be suspicious of her intentions. She was aware too, that every minute that passed, was one closer to the Guards getting their powers back.

"We have a ritual on Nyteria." He placed his hand on hers and changed his colour to a paler version of her skin.

"Really?" Val continued to smile even though her stomach was churning.

"Yes, but it has never been performed with a human, so I don't know how you will feel about it."

"I think I'll be fine," Val responded quickly, possibly too quickly as he seemed taken aback by her forthrightness.

"Well, when we celebrate a union on my planet we have to connect."

Val knew about this, she'd done it before with Zac. She was ready. "Yes?"

"This is to find out if we're compatible. Now I know that we are going to be united, I just want to follow tradition."

"Fine, let's do it." She said turning to face him, putting out her wrist to show her bracelet.

His expression became questioning. "What is this?"

"For our connection. I did it with my Hunter. It's fine."

Nathan pushed her hand back. "No. We connect our souls."

"What?" Val was confused. Souls? That was something very different to what she had been expecting. "Do I have a choice?"

"You said it was alright to go ahead." His voice became stern.

Val couldn't back down. This union could save everyone. Sam and the Space would be free. "Yes, sorry, it's just that the word *soul* means a great deal on Earth."

"It won't hurt, I promise." He looked to the soldiers who were still in the room. "Please leave us. We'll be fine."

Their body language made Val feel like they saw her as a threat and Nathan had to repeat his order before they would leave.

Val was starting to feel very nervous. She didn't like being left alone with Nathan, but she had her invisible uniform, plus her bracelets. She would be able to fight if it was necessary.

"Val, I need you to relax." He leaned worryingly close. "I want to look inside your head."

She was really scared now. "What for?" She touched her exaggerated hair.

"For answers to questions that would take too long to ask." He reached out his hand and placed it gently on her cheek, touching her scar with his fingers. He was surprisingly warm. He held her face and gazed into her eyes. It was unnerving having him this close. Then he started to change. His eyes were the first thing she noticed. They went from their usual golden to a deep green. Next, his hair started to move and turn mousy brown, the style short, but not shaven. Then his face shifted shape and his skin assumed a tanned hue. She realised she was shaking.

"This is who you want," he announced, clearly proud of his altered appearance.

Val's mouth was slightly open; she couldn't allow herself the luxury of gawping. "Is it?" she asked.

He took away his hand. "Well, it's what your head told me. Val, I know this must feel strange, but I want you to like me. I just want the best for my people and the Guards."

Val couldn't take her eyes off his face. In her head a bell was starting to ring. "You look like someone I know, that's what you just saw, someone I know." She shook her head as if to wake up.

He snapped at her. "You love this person! It's the truth without barriers."

"No, he's just my friend," she replied, annoyed by his implication.

Nathan pointed at himself. "This face I have was in your soul's heart and when you look at it, you are filling with emotion. You need to face the truth."

"I do not love Jason," Val blurted.

"What?" a voice spoke in her ear.

"Nathan, I'm sorry, I can't do this right now. Please let me go," she pleaded.

"No! I have more to show you." He was getting angry with her. His eyes flashed a warning at her.

She mustn't argue. She was trapped. "Yes, of course." She tried to relax a little. Annoying him now wasn't a good idea. The clock was ticking in her favour.

He took her hand again and placed it on his heart, holding it there. "Just relax. Take a deep breath." Val followed instructions like a child at the doctor's. She took a huge breath, and as she inhaled, she felt her heart slow down. The room started to spin and all she could see was the man in front of her. Nathan seemed to stand and she followed. He held her close. "Look into my heart; it is a reflection of yours," he whispered softly into her ear.

She closed her eyes, feeling almost drunk on what he was saying and suddenly she was standing in the Arcsdale shopping centre. She was waiting for coffee. She had a list running through her head, mocha, hot chocolate and something else. Then she felt a hand on her shoulder and she turned. Her eyes moved across his broad chest, up into his eyes, her heart was pounding, her throat was tight and she wanted to speak, but nothing was coming out.

He took her hand and placed it onto his chest the same way Nathan had and held it on his heart. She wanted to fall, deeply and overwhelmingly in love with this person. He made her complete. He reached up, pushing her chin towards his face and kissed her. Val was in trouble. Somewhere in her mind she could hear a quiet voice. "Fight it, Val, it's just an illusion. This is what you wanted before; not what you want now." He moved back and she wanted to follow him to the ends of the Earth. He took his hand away and she started to grieve instantly. Her eyes opened and there in the seat opposite sat someone she felt she couldn't live without. Whatever Nathan had done to her, she wanted to cry out loud and plead that he never leave her again. But deep down, somewhere inside her, she knew this was a trick.

He stood up and she followed. This was it. They were going to be united. She could feel it and she was blissfully happy. She couldn't wait. "Stop being an idiot," her brain told her.

"Val, if you can hear me, please cough." Jason's voice was like sweet music in her ears. She didn't cough, she was fine. Fit as a fiddle and now she was getting married to the man of her dreams, Nathan Akar. Val Akar, it sounded terrible, but who cared. They moved out of the room. The soldiers seemed unaffected by Nathan's new appearance, which Val found odd. He reached out his hand and she grabbed it, eager just to touch him. He took her down the hall and they made their way to the docking bay.

There was a ship waiting, just like Val had seen in the movies. The docking entrance was open and soldiers were walking calmly around it. She was nearly skipping as they reached it. "When are we going to get this union on the road?" She smiled at him.

"Soon, very soon."

Yes, those were just the words she longed to hear. They would have three children, one red, one blue and one pink. She felt amazing. She just wanted to kiss him from morning till night. "Val, what's going on?" That funny voice in her ear spoke again. It made her hair stand on end, all the way down her neck.

Nathan came to a halt as a strange looking man, covered in a shimmering gold cloak came down the ramp towards them. "Is this her?" he asked, his deep blue skin now looked odd against Nathan's bronzed tan.

"Yes, we have performed the connection. You may continue." Nathan took both Val's hands and she almost swooned. He was all she would ever want again.

"Bring in the High Judges." He gestured to a soldier.

Val's eyes never moved from her beloved Nathan's face. The Judges were brought in and lined up before them. Val glanced over at them. She spotted Sam and wondered why he looked so worried. Why would he be bothered by this wonderful moment? It was her moment of glory; he was so selfish. "Val, he's the one you love," her brain insisted. "NO!" she knocked at her head with the hand.

"What's wrong?" Nathan asked her nervously.

"Nothing." She let her gaze return to him.

"Jason?" Sam called.

She turned, annoyed with this man, Sam. "He's not Jason," she hissed. "He's Nathan Akar and I will be his, now shut up!"

"Please carry on," Nathan said, pleased with her reaction. They moved into position, facing someone Val could only imagine was some sort of intergalactic priest. "Can the Prison see this?" he asked one of his soldiers, who nodded.

The priest started to speak words that Val couldn't understand. She thought weddings were boring at the best of times, but this was bordering on the ridiculous. Boring and in a foreign language. Nathan replied to some of the words with more weird words of his own, and then the priest turned to Val. "At last," she sighed rudely.

"You can't do this!" Sam implored pain in his voice.

Val retaliated. "Shut him up!" she bawled. A soldier was quite happy to follow orders and Sam was struck and brought to his knees. He looked up, tears forming in his eyes. Val's inner voice tried again. "Look at him. You love him."

"Please answer the question." The priest repeated in English.

"Say it again?" She had completely forgotten what he had asked her.

"Do you wish to be connected and forever belong as Nathan Akar's soul possession?"

"STOP!" a voice hollered from the back of the bay. Val was really starting to get annoyed. She wanted to get to the kissing part. There was a young sandy-haired man walking towards then, his expression was black as thunder. She could tell through her strange emotional roller coaster that he wasn't happy.

"Friend, why have you interrupted us?" Nathan demanded, clearly annoyed.

"Because it's a trap. If you perform this union you will break one of the most sacred rules of the Prison. She is a

Guard, and to my knowledge my friend, you're not a Ranswar." He had arrived at the almost happy couple and now Val wanted to punch his lights out.

"I'm human, now let's get it done." She really wanted to be married to Nathan.

"Is this true?" Nathan walked over to one of the Judges. No one answered him. In the blink of an eye he changed; his skin was red and his eyes black. "I SAID IS THIS TRUE!!?" he bellowed into a female Judge's face.

"Yes." She responded, trying hard to keep her composure.

He pointed at Val. "Take her away from my sight," he yelled at two soldiers.

"But we're getting united. What have I done wrong? I love you," she cried.

"Excariot, I owe you my life." He took the hand of the man who had interrupted them.

"Just returning the favour." He slapped Nathan on the back. "Watch her, she's dangerous."

"I won't be fooled again." He said as they dragged her from the room screaming abuse.

As the soldiers pulled her down the corridor a voice in her ear spoke. "Did I hear that correctly, Val? Did he say Excariot?"

CHAPTER 22

All Hung Over

Waking up in a glass cylinder-shaped cell, Val started to come down from what felt like the worst sugar high of her life. Her head ached and all she craved was a glass of water. Her mouth felt like she had licked a carpet repeatedly and as she tried to revive her tongue, she could hear Jason trying to talk to her, but she just couldn't face him at the minute. With everything that had happened, just at that moment, she would rather never face any of them again.

Surely Sam would never forgive her? She had clearly chosen Jason as the man of her dreams or her "soul" partner as Nathan had told her. She let out a moan. Why had it turned out that way? She knew how she felt about Sam, and it felt like love. The thought of losing him was intensely painful, so why, why had it been Jason? Ok, so she had had feelings for him before, but he had Fran, and she had moved on. Maybe it was losing Shane that had made her feel love towards him. Yes, that was the answer. Or was it? She fidgeted on the floor of her cell in her stupid pink wedding dress and started pulling at her hair.

In all honesty, what had just happened was the least of her worries. If she remembered correctly, Nathan had called the young man who had interrupted her union

Excariot. She had sent Excariot to Prison and he didn't look like that. So who was it? Another son he had named after himself? He did come across as narcissistic. They had thanked each other on saving each other's lives. What was that all about? And why Jason? She moaned again, her head dropping onto the Perspex-like cell wall.

"Val, I can hear you moaning. Just talk to me please?" Jason pleaded again.

How long was she going to be able to ignore him? At the end of the day they were all still in danger and her probably more than anyone. "What do you want?" she mumbled.

"Thank you. Where are you?" His voice was full of relief.

"In a cell again. Seems like I'm destined to be locked up."

"Are you hurt?"

She didn't want him to care so much. "Physically no, but mentally, I'm scarred for life. If another alien inflicts hallucinations on me, I'll deserve to be locked-up after I finish with them."

"Do you want to talk to me?"

He was the last person she wanted to talk to. She never wanted to see his face again. There wasn't a galaxy far enough away for her to hide from him. "Not really, not unless you have good news."

"Look mate, I know you've been drugged or whatever. I know it was out of your control. I could hear that by the way you were talking, Val, you're my friend. Don't worry about it, it wasn't your fault."

Why did he have to be so damn nice, and why wasn't Fran screaming in her ear about how she had promised she was over him? "Yeah, that's it. Where's Fran?"

"She's with your Mum, helping get more people vaccinated to go to the surface when the other Guards get their power back. They think more numbers will help at the right moment."

Val was pleased Fran hadn't been witness to the disaster of her wedding. "How long have I been out?"

"At my last check, nine hours."

"Great, I'll be remembered as the Guard who slept through the war. So how long do we have until all the Guards are back with us?"

"Eswith says about an hour. Val, no one heard what happened, but me. It'll be our secret."

Secret. Yes, that's what she would tell Sam. He saw the whole thing front row. That's if, after her snooze, he was still alive. "Yes, that would be good. Thank you."

"Good," Jason replied.

"I'm so sorry. I haven't asked how you're doing?" She had forgotten that he was the one who was truly suffering pain right now, not her.

"Fine, trying to stay focused." His voice gave away his pain.

"So, what's the plan, Batman?" She lifted the tone of her response.

"Well, Princess Peach, let's talk about the E word. I haven't told the others yet; I didn't want to worry them. Plus I wanted to hear your view on it. Was it really him?"

"Didn't look like him; I reckon the name Excariot might be as common as John in outer space though." She heard Jason laugh, that made her feel better.

"I'm going to get the others now I know you're ok. By the way, Hadwyn, crazy man, glad his gun only stuns!"

"That's my Hadwyn. Speak to you soon."

"Bye." There was a moment of silence, he was gone. "I miss Shane too," she whispered banging her head gently on the side of her cell trying to knock the emotions out of her body.

She stared out at the lowly lit walls, seeing that she had been locked in a room by herself. There were no soldiers with her, just the cell in the centre of the room. Still, what could she do? She had been warned not to teleport by Nathan and she couldn't risk crossing him now as he would surely kill Sam. So, was she just supposed to sit here and wait? She didn't have to wait long to find out. A door opened in the wall and in walked the sandy haired young man who had called himself Excariot.

"Hello again, Val," he grinned as he circled her cell. She felt like the main attraction in a very small zoo.

She didn't bother standing. "Do I know you?" she asked.

He laughed at her, drumming on her cell wall with his fingers. "Did I mean so little to you?" he asked, turning his lip down like a sulking child. "I'm disappointed. After all we've been through."

Val knew it was him now, no one else could get on her nerves this much, but she was in a cell, so she felt no need to jump up and look for a fight. "So, is this the new and improved cloned version of Excariot? I hear clones have no powers and in general are galactic floor cleaners. Not that there's anything wrong with that job," she replied.

Excariot banged his fist on the glass unexpectedly. Val jumped. "This is the body of a young man I knew, and yes I'm as powerful as ever. Now my friend Nathan is here, you are the last thing in the world I should be worrying about, but I still find myself returning to you like the proverbial old penny."

"So what's your story, you and Nathan?" she asked in the hope she could glean a little information that might help the others.

"Nathan Akar was the leader on a planet called Gingua. Have you heard of it?"

She had, the Warden had said that very name only a few hours earlier. "Not jumping into my head," she lied.

"I escaped to Gingua with Lailah. Then your father came for us. Nathan was generous enough to let one of his soldiers take my place. You see, male Nyterians have a special ability, to take on the form of someone else, which having learned, has served me well in the past. So, when your father brought Lailah and the soldier here, he transformed and it looked like I escaped, but I never really returned." He kept walking and Val stayed still, even though it was unnerving when he was behind her. "I was free to search for a way to free Lailah. Luckily, one of the last things I did on the Prison was hear all about this planet, Earth it was called; a place that could hold prisoners. You can imagine how elated I was now that I knew where to go to seek my revenge, that I could bring Lailah back to life in the body of a human."

"Elated, yes," she muttered.

"Nathan helped me get to Earth to make plans for Lailah's escape and I gave him information on the weaknesses of the Nyterian government. The rest is, or was, history. When Nathan came here, he asked around about the female Guard who was great enough to free the Warden and found out that you had captured the infamous Excariot Crow, and he once again kindly released me. Now I have a new body and a new life. I get to run the Prison when Nathan returns to Nyteria. You see, Val, I know the rules. As long as the Prison is still being run and one Judge survives, and Nathan doesn't get united with a Guard, there is nothing that can stop us. So you see, I win."

"Well, you should be pleased to know that Lailah, Eva and your son are all dead. I killed them!" Val tried to shock him.

"Really?" he scoffed, "You expect me to believe you actually killed them? Not possible. You are a Guard through and through."

"Daniel killed Shane, so I returned the favour."

Excariot's expression changed. Val thought that maybe he would believe her now. "About time. I killed his wife, so it's only fitting that my son kill her husband. I'm now proud of the child I never wanted."

"You killed Elizabeth?" Val felt weak, like he had stolen her strength, taking what she had left.

"One in a long list, my friend," he grinned. "Now, I'm going to look around my new home, and start making the required changes to the Guards' DNA. Did you know we could do that?"

"No."

"Yes, in the same way we rid them of their powers, we can give them back. Now they will only work under my orders. They will be like puppets. I did love Punch and Judy. Those were good days on Earth." He looked wistfully into the distance.

"You're a nutter and I will get out of here, out of this ridiculous dress, and make sure you pay for what you're doing." Val pulled herself to her feet.

"I'll look forward to that. The rest are no competition." He tapped her cell for good luck and walked away, leaving her once more in silence.

*

She stared down at her pinkness. She was trapped and, knowing that if they could extract the Warden's DNA, there was no reason why Excariot couldn't insert his own, was a living nightmare. There would be a Prison full of Excariot's. The question was: would that counteract the vaccine Zac had delivered? Or would the vaccine over-ride the change?

"Jason, can you hear me?" she waited for an answer.

"Hello Val it's me, Eswith. Jason has taken a break. How are you doing? Not long now."

"We could have a problem. Excariot's back and it seems he has another virus to change the compliance of the Guards. I don't know when he's going to administer it or if they have already done that."

"Right, we need to get someone on the surface and fast, to take some samples. Stay where you are. I will contact you as soon as I have news."

"Not much chance of me leaving." Val tapped the wall. The door opened at the same moment, causing her to jump. She waited for someone else to enter to tell her she was next in-line for the extraction chamber, but there was no-one there. She looked around her. There were only two people she knew who could enter a room without being detected.

"Val." She heard one of the voices she was hoping for.

"Hadwyn, what are you doing here?" she whispered through pursed lips in case she was being watched.

"I was bored," he replied, his voice full of childish play.

"I can't leave this cell or Nathan will kill Sam," she whispered.

"We know. Boden has gone in search of them."

"So, just me and you then. And you came here because?" Val asked.

"Just had to see if that dress looked as awful as it sounded," he said. "So, if we can't get her out without risking the Judges, what can we do Wendy?"

"Hadwyn, I'm Val," she shook her head.

"I know." A female voice answered. It was Wendy. "We need to swap places," she said.

Val wanted to cheer and whoop, yet she had to contain herself. "Hello, can't tell you how nice it is to have someone normal here." She tried to keep her face emotionless.

"Can you do this?" Hadwyn enquired ignoring Val's comment.

"I think so. It's a traditional trading spell. Sam taught me this one, clearly he saw what was coming better than me. I have to get through the glass, which will take me a bit longer."

"Wendy, you're taking a very big risk trading with me, I don't know what's coming; anything could happen." Val was worried for her friend.

"We need you out of here more than we need me right now, so I'm willing to take that risk. Just give me a moment."

"Take your time," Val said. "I'm not going anywhere." She heard a large slapping sound, like a clapping of hands, followed by what sounded like a rubbing of palms. "Mutare locum, mutare loca, in me et eam." Wendy started to chant. "Mutare locum, mutare loca, in me et eam." Val desperately wanted to know what she was saying, but was far too scared to interrupt.

Hadwyn whispered, his voice tinged with concern, "Val, she's shaking."

"Get ready." Val closed her eyes tight. Whatever happened, it normally hurt or made you sick. Then the drawing feeling started.

"Put your helmet on," Hadwyn advised. "I will make you invisible." Val did as she was told and then her heart seemed to stop; she knew she was alive, but couldn't feel her body, there was no breathing, no heartbeat. She peeked a little and her eyes blurred, everything was moving in slow motion. She could feel herself moving through the wall of her cell. Then everything came back into focus. She was out of the cell and Wendy was inside and looking pretty in pink.

"They're going to see it's not me if anyone checks?" Val said.

"Give me a second." Wendy placed her hands over her face. "All that is seen, all that has been, in my reflection, now give Val protection." She pulled her hands away.

"Oh dear God," Val gasped as Wendy's reflection mutated to match hers.

"Don't worry, it's just an illusion."

"Good, I don't think I can cope with two," Hadwyn groaned.

Wendy smiled. "Ok, go set the Prison free. They'll never know it's me in here."

Val saluted her. "See me soon."

CHAPTER 23

The Beginning of the End

Hadwyn was now visible to her, although he had assured her no one else could see them.

"I can't keep this up for long, so let's mingle," he said as they reached a group of Guards. They rammed their way to the centre of the group as the Guards looked around in confusion, wondering who had pushed them. "We're going visible now."

She allowed her helmet to retract. The Guard next to her was familiar; it was the young man she had met only a few days ago. His expression became panicked, "cover your face, quickly, they all know what you look like," he insisted.

Val's helmet covered her face once more. Hadwyn was behind her and was eyeing the Guard. "Are you ok?"

"Yes, he was just telling me to cover my face."

Hadwyn looked at his Dellatrax. "We only have thirty minutes before the vaccine takes affect and the reinforcement from the Space arrive. We need to let the Guards know what's going to happen."

"Is there a way to send a message to all the Dellatrax at once?" Val asked.

"Yes," the Guard behind her interrupted. "There is a way. In the Warden's office he has a device that only he can use to communicate with all the Guards and Hunters if there is an emergency. I delivered a message once that merited distribution."

"Good, then let's go get it." Val said. "Keep your chin up, we'll all be free soon." She patted the Guard on the shoulder and he offered her a weary smile. Hadwyn and Val started to move through the Guards. Recognising their uniforms, the Guards moved to conceal their path. "Jason? Eswith? Anyone?" Val asked.

Jason was back on the job. "Hello mate. Have our guests arrived?"

"If you mean crazy gunman and Wendy, yes. We're on our way to the Warden's office, so any help you can give us is welcome."

"I'll check the maps. Everyone has started teleporting to the surface. We can keep most contained in the rooms that have been protected by Sam over the years. We'll need your go ahead to start the assault as you'll be the only ones who can get the message to the Prison Guards that we're coming."

"No pressure then?"

"Just a minute, Eswith wants to speak to you."

"Hello Val. We have run some tests and the atmosphere hasn't changed since you arrived. If there is something that they are going to release into the air, you will have to stop them."

"Right, so we need to get to the Warden's office and send a signal to all Guards, and stop Excariot's plan to make the Guards into drones. Is that everything?"

"For now it is. Please stay safe."

"Just one last question: any news on Boden?"

"We lost contact when he entered the sector that's holding the High Judges. We can only hope all is well," Eswith replied.

Hadwyn paused momentarily. "He's fine, I would know if there was something wrong."

"How?" Val wondered whether they had something in their uniform, something that gave a signal when the other was dead.

"He's my brother, I would just know." He surged on, leading the way as they moved into a new corridor. He knew where he was going.

*

Hadwyn moved swiftly, but with caution. Val watched how he timed each turn to perfection and seemed to know what side to stand on. He was amazing and she felt a little like a rock around his neck as she did her best to keep close behind him.

He raised his hand. "His office is around the corner, but there are people outside." He flashed a second look around the corner. "Four soldiers and the man who came to visit you in your cell before we arrived."

"Excariot. Great. What are they doing outside?" she asked.

"Excariot?" Hadwyn's face filled with anger.

"The very same, new body."

He looked again. "Looks like they can't get in. I would like to bet that the Warden has that office locked. Without his bracelet they won't be able to get in."

Val smiled and pulled back her sleeve to reveal the very bracelet he was talking about. "Like this one?" She grinned widely.

"Yes." He looked again. "Excariot has gone to get the Warden's assistant for sure. I can deal with the soldiers, but you need to get in there and shut the door behind you, and you won't have long."

"What about you?" Val's smile was gone in a breath.

"Val, the mission is what counts. Do what you have to do." He drew his gun.

Val was concerned. "What if you need my help?"

Hadwyn laughed. "Seriously?" He pushed her and turned to run. "Do your job." Then he was sprinting around the corner, firing at the soldiers and chasing them along the corridor.

Val followed a few seconds later. Reaching the door, she shoved her arm against it and as Hadwyn had predicted, it opened. She turned, slamming it shut quickly. "Hello, Jason?"

"I'm here. I can see you're in the office and Hadwyn is still moving down the corridor."

She looked around the outer office. It surely wouldn't be here. "I need Enoch."

"He's helping teleport Guards. I'll try to connect you direct. He has one of your ear pieces."

"Hurry." She said retracting her helmet. She needed to stop seeing her heart rate, it just made her feel worse. 'Come on, Val. If you were the Warden, where would you put something you use to communicate with everyone? She moved into the Warden's office. His desk was just a flat glass screen, holding nothing. Where was the device?

"Val can you hear me?" Enoch's voice was a welcome interruption.

"Loud and clear. I need you to tell me how the Warden communicates with all the Guards at once through their Dellatrax. What does he use?"

"I'm not sure. I can only surmise he uses a device similar to the Dellatrax. I'm sorry."

"Don't worry, I'll keep looking." Val was by the wall, checking the shelves. Her hand passed over bare glass.

Then she heard a click and a recess opened in the shelf triggered by the proximity of the Wardens bracelet. She reached into the opening and felt a box. She pulled it out quickly, but as she did so she heard the external door opening. Excariot must be back with the Assistant. She looked desperately for somewhere to hide. There was only one place: under the desk. 'You came all the way to another galaxy to hide under a desk!' she thought. Luckily for her the Warden had big legs and so she fittted easily, hiding away just as Excariot entered the office.

"Where are the star charts?!" he bellowed at the poor woman who was with him.

"I...I don't know. I told you, I've never heard of any star charts," she whimpered.

"You lie." Val felt the woman being shoved against the desk. She wanted to go and kick his butt back into a cell, but personal revenge would have to wait. Thousands of people were relying on her to do her duty.

"It's the truth. The only person who dealt with charts is now a prisoner."

"Who?"

Val spotted his feet coming around the desk. She held her breath and gripped the box she had just acquired.

"The Judge, Sam." The woman replied through her tears.

"Have him brought to me," he ordered, sitting down in the Warden's chair. Val flattened herself against the back of the desk, hoping he wouldn't stretch his legs out. She was so frightened she thought she was going to be sick. He pulled up the chair and she tensed, but to her relief there was still room for them both.

"Val, I can see another person in the office with you, so I can only guess you're hiding. You have ten minutes before the Guard's return to normal. When that happens, if they don't know what's going on, we may lose before we've started. We need to get that information out."

Excariot coughed and shifted position. Val could see his arms moving over the Wardens desk and a glimmer of light appeared. Then came what sounded like touch-tones. She took the opportunity to look at the box she was holding. It was made of what looked like smoked glass. She ran her fingers gently over the top. The last thing she needed was for it to make any noise. She heard the door opening. This was it. Sam would be here and she would fight to save him. She tensed up, getting ready to pull out her sword.

"Who are you?" Excariot enquired.

"I am an old friend," a man replied.

"Of whom? This body? Because I have never seen you before," His response was curt with annoyance.

"It's time you came with me," the man said.

Excariot laughed. "Do you know who I am?"

"Indeed."

"Then you will know that you should show me more respect if you wish to live."

"Well Excariot Crow, I'm Slyig oldest of the old ones, and I don't feel like showing you anything of the sort."

Val's ears pricked up, Slyig, oldest of the old. What was going to happen now? "Slyig, such a pleasure to see you, although I do prefer to think of you as Flo. How did you get here?" His tone had now changed; some of the arrogance had gone. Val watched as he reached into a pocket on his trousers and pulled out a handgun, keeping it hidden under the desk. It now pointed at Val's face. She held her breath.

"A book of tricks brought me here. And now you will pay for four hundred years, but first, Delta and I have a use for you, so I will take you with me now."

"I don't think so." In that moment time seemed to slow down. Excariot went to shoot Flo, but couldn't because Val had grabbed the weapon. It was an act of desperation, but she wanted Flo to get Excariot off the planet. She pushed on the end of the weapon, forcing it hard down as Excariot tried to raise it. Val heard another weapon go off and Excariot's body fell limp, his head hitting the table with a thud. Val quickly prised his fingers off the weapon and pulled it away, holding it in her lap.

Excariot's body was lifted from the chair. And then they were gone. Val took a deep and much needed breath. "One down, one to go," she muttered.

"Have you found it, Val?" Jason was in her ear again, sounding tense. "They're about to get their powers back."

"Just one second." She fumbled with the box. The top slid open and out dropped a watch, like the Guards' Dellatrax only Red. She didn't have time to give it to the Warden so she was going to have to try and do this herself. Tentatively she put it on. Nothing happened. She looked at the screen, but it remained dark. "Please do something," she pleaded with it. As she spoke the screen lit up, along with the Warden's bracelet. "This is a message for all Guards. Your powers are restored. We'll be launching an assault in the next few minutes. You should support the assault, but only engage Nyterian soldiers. NOT, I repeat, not anyone who has wheels or metal limbs. They're on our side." Val placed her head onto her knees and took a moment to hope that somehow she'd got it right.

Then the pain began, it started in her tattoo then ran the full length of her arm, hitting where the Warden's watch rested with a sharp pain, like poison running into her veins. She tried to get it off, but it was too late. Her body jolted so hard it hit both sides of the underside of the table. She shook violently, her hearing gone, nothing but static running through her head. Her body jolted once more, this time enough to throw the table over and leave her suspended in the air.

The door to the office opened and in walked the Assistant with Sam. "Dear me," the woman exclaimed finding not Excariot, but a girl suspended in mid-air.

"Get out of my way." Sam moved forward. Val was unconscious and had clearly entered into what he recognised as a transformation. But how? This only happened to higher beings. What had she done? He looked all over her body for a symbol. There on her arm, through her uniform he could see the tattoo was changing, burning bright, right in front of his eyes. "I need to help her."

"But Excariot was here, he wanted some charts, Sam," the Assistant dithered.

"Well, he's not here now. I don't know what's happened, but let's hope she's going to be ok." He looked out the window of the office to see Guards beginning to move purposefully. "She may well have just saved us all."

CHAPTER 24

Information Download

Sam reached out to touch Val's body, but a bolt of light shot out of her and struck him. He was thrown back several feet and had to grab the upturned desk to keep on his feet. "This is crazy." The Guards were back to normal and pandemonium had broken out. Shots were being fired and he knew Val would be needed. Then he spotted the watch on her wrist. He knew it was the Warden's and that with his bracelet and the watch together she had caused her very own transformation.

"Get out." He ordered the Assistant who made a hasty retreat. "Val Saunders, I'm sorry for what I'm going to do, but it's the only way." He checked her tattoo had stopped changing then pulled out his sword. Taking aim he touched her sharply, directly over her heart. Her stillness was broken and suddenly her body was jolting. There was a noise like cracking bones and her eyes snapped open. Val let out a scream, as though the pain was overwhelming her. "Val, come back to me." Sam shouted at her. "Please, we need you. Now."

She stopped screaming. Her eyes closed and she breathed, deep and slow. Then her body tilted as her feet lowered to the floor. She turned to Sam and the corner of her mouth lifted. "Hello, I missed you," she said. "Where have you been?"

Sam grabbed her, holding her close. "It doesn't matter." He kissed her cheek. "The Prison is under attack and we need to move."

"It's ok, I know what I have to do," she said calmly.

"Glad someone does," Sam replied as they headed out into the battle. They approached the melee. Soldiers were running, Guards were attacking and their friends from the Space were causing havoc among the Nyterians, spinning across the walls to launch attacks from unexpected directions. Val gazed around in wonder, why wouldn't they want a Guard who could ride the ceiling she thought to herself as Sam fought off the soldiers that dared to cross his path. Extending her sword she struck two soldiers down with ease. "Sam, I need to get to Nathan."

"I thought we were heading in the opposite direction?" he replied, confusion in his response.

"I can stop all this. Help me get to him. Listen to me Guards; you must help me get to Nathan." Her watch buzzed as three Guards quickly surrounded her. Together they moved with speed along the corridors. "Jason do you know where Nathan is?" she asked

"Not sure, but we have another problem. Wendy's on the move."

Val remembered that Wendy looked like her. "Jason, she'll be with Nathan. He's going to try and use me as a bargaining chip. Where is she?"

"Four corridors to your left and she's just gone static. Be careful, Val."

"I will. Tell Belinda she'll be fine. Four corridors to the left," she shouted her orders. The groups moved together as wheeled fighters made short work of the Nyterians. It seemed like the biggest bar brawl in the galaxy. Val was moving at speed when Sam grabbed her. They all stopped, "What's wrong?"

"Look up." Sam pointed to a screen that had appeared in mid-air in the middle of the main Prison hall. On it was Nathan. He had Wendy by the throat.

Nathan glared out at them from the screen. "Listen to me. Stop fighting now or I will let your precious freak unleash her powers on you. She will teleport you all to the Interspace. Anyone want to test and see if she can do it?"

"Stop now! Let him think you're surrendering," Val ordered. There was a moment of buzzed conversation and the Guards came to a standstill. "Sam, get me closer to him." Her helmet flipped over her face. The Guards closed around her and Sam.

"Let's go," Sam ordered.

"Val, you have one corridor and you're there," Jason said into her ear.

"What's your plan?" Sam asked her.

"When I put on the Warden's watch it seems that I downloaded all the rules and regulations of the Prison. I'm like a walking encyclopaedia."

"So you're going to throw the rule book at him? That doesn't seem like a good plan. He has Wendy."

"Just trust me." Val signalled for the Guards to wait. They were close to the balcony on which Nathan had held her only hours earlier. There were soldiers hanging onto the doors. "You there Hadwyn? You have my permission to let loose." He shimmered three feet in front of Val and took out the soldiers with ease.

"How did you know where Hadwyn was?" Sam asked.

"He's my brother." She moved past Sam and towards the door. Hadwyn pulled it open and there they found another group of soldiers protecting Nathan and his hostage.

"Stop!" he yelled at them. "I have the power in my hands." Val could see Wendy was scared, but holding up.

"Are you sure about that?" she asked through her helmet.

"Don't take another step, Magrafe."

"Really? Do you? Helmet off." It retracted revealing her face. Nathan stepped backwards. Clearly shocked by what he saw.

"How? This is a trick!" he bellowed as his followers looked on.

"Nope, she's the trick. I'm the real deal, look." She lit a blue flame on her hand.

Nathan threw Wendy at Sam and reached out to grab Val. Hadwyn moved in to protect her, but Val held up her hand.

"We are going to release Excariot's virus if you don't stop this right now." Nathan threatened.

"Do you know something?" she smiled at him.

"What?" he spat at her "That I will have what I want?"

"I agree," she grabbed his hands. "You should have what you want. I agree to be connected and forever belong as Nathan Akar's soul possession." His face filled with fear. "You see, when you start a union with a Guard, unless the Guard refuses, the union can still be finalised." She pushed forward and kissed Nathan on the lips. He struggled to push her off. "I do," she said softly, stepping away from him with a smile.

He fell backwards looking terrified at what she had done. No one dared to stand near him. He looked frantically for support. "It's not true! You're just trying to scare me!" he screamed.

"Shame, I saw a great future for us." Val saw a dark figure appear behind Nathan, coming towards him. It walked in mid-air over the watching soldiers and Guards. Everyone shrank back. A palpable shiver of fear ran through the room. "Think we broke the rules lover," Val said.

"No, I don't want a union with you." Nathan screamed, launching himself at her. A small hand came between them and Val saw her Collector holding him in place.

"Nice to see you Val. I see you have someone for me." She raised him high up in the air. Unable to escape, he yelled and kicked at the atmosphere, his skin turning through all the shades of the rainbow.

The dark figure continued its slow approach.

The room fell into deep silence, broken only by Nathan's ragged breathing. Then a familiar voice delivered the sentence. Zac was standing at Val's side, reading solemnly from his watch.

"Nathan Akar, you have broken protocol. You will now be sentenced for all your crimes. As one of the most dangerous dictators in the galaxy, with no thought for the life of others, and for breaking an inviolable rule, you are sentenced to life imprisonment on Alchany. Your designated number is 301329."

They watched as a humanoid figure wearing a full black metal uniform, stepped through the air towards Nathan. Its eyes were as black as the metal of its uniform. Val could feel her skin crawling. There was no waiting, no jury. A dark hand grabbed his neck and Nathan screamed in anguish. She looked at the creature and its dark shadow of a face looked back at her. She felt her soul freezing. This was a truly horrible creature, exactly as the

Warden had described. She closed her eyes, breaking contact. When she looked back, Nathan was writhing and flailing in the creature's grip. Slowly, Nathan and his captor faded and eventually disappeared.

For a moment no one moved; no one spoke. Hadwyn broke the tension by slapping her on the back. "Congratulations."

"Thank you," she replied, "now I think it's time to get rid of some unwanted visitors." She made her way to the edge of the balcony. Leaning over, she called out to the now subdued crowd, no one sure what their next move should be. "My advice to you Nyterians," she shouted over the stunned crowd, "would be to head home, take your ships and never return. You have exactly one hour. Or we can help you all face trial, after all, you're in a Prison, and it's our PRISON!" She raised her fist into the air and her fellow Guards broke into a chorus of joyous triumph.

*

Val gave further orders and the Guards moved the Nyterians out to the docking bay where she had almost been married. They all worked together and she was relieved to eventually see the Warden come to join them.

He greeted her with a warm smile. "I see you have been busy with all my toys." He pointed at her wrists.

"I'm so sorry, I had to." She blushed, pulling off his watch and bracelet and handing them over.

"Do not apologise to me, ever. You and your friends have saved our home. We will forever be indebted to you, Val Saunders from the planet Earth. We will make preparations for the people of the Space to be welcome on the surface and we will work to integrate them back into our society."

"Thank you," she said.

"Do you remember what you asked me for? Does that still stand?" he asked her.

"Yes. I want you to please send my family and friends home as soon as possible."

"What about you?" he asked, but he didn't get an answer. The High Judges arrived and arranged themselves in a row in front of the Warden, Val and the others.

"Warden, I'm pleased to see you old friend." A female Judge removed her hood. "But I'm sorry to say I'm the bringer of sad news."

"What would that be at such a time when we should be rejoicing?" he asked.

"Nathan Akar's partner is to be extracted immediately. The law states very clearly that if a criminal has a partner they will also be held accountable for his crimes. She also united with one who wasn't a Ranswar." Her eyes were sad.

Sam reacted first. "Are you mad? Val has just risked her life to save our Prison, and we did it."

The Warden cut in. "Sam, I will deal with this."

"Sam stop, she's right," added Val, having somehow downloaded all the rules, she knew about this one. "I knew what I was doing. I knew the risk."

"Be quiet!" the Warden said, pain filling his sharp response. Sam and Zac stepped forward, moving in close to her.

"Selene, Val saved you and me and just about everyone still alive."

The woman seemed grieved at what she had to do as much as them. "I'm truly sorry."

Sam moved in front of Val. "I wish to defend her."

"Sam, you are a wise Judge, but your heart rules your head when it concerns this individual and so your judgment will not be taken into consideration."

"I understand," the Warden interrupted. "I will take her for extraction now myself." He took Val's arm and with his bracelet she felt his strength returning. He coaxed her away from the others. "She will be dealt with." He relayed his words of compliance as they started to move. Val looked back at Sam who had broken into a heated argument with the High Judges. Wendy was crying and Boden had a firm hold on Hadwyn's arm. Zac followed them. "Just keep moving," the Warden instructed.

As she was paraded in front of the Prison, the Guards bowed their heads low in respect. Val thought it ironic: one day the sinner, the next, she was a saint going to the bonfire like Joan of Arc, just as Wendy had predicted.

"Warden, please re-think. Maybe a position as a Mechanic? Surely you can't do this." Zac pleaded as they made it around the corner.

"Zac, you're a good Hunter and her friend, I would no more extract this girl than do it to myself." The Warden led them into his office.

They stood together like bemused children. "You must extract me; it's the law. I can't stay here. Just keep your word and get my family to safety." She couldn't believe how matter of fact this felt. "I can give you what you asked for, but you will go back to Earth too, and no one will ever know." He looked around him; then made his way over to a shelf and pulled out a crystal box. He placed it on the upturned desk. "If you go now, your family and friends will be safe. No one will remember you Val. You are no longer a Guard of this planet. I release you from your duty."

"Can you promise the Space will be safe and you will not be in trouble?" she asked.

"Yes."

"Then as I have been released from my duty, I will go. One condition, no one comes looking for me, no one tries to make me work for you again - ever. You keep Sam safe." Her voice was failing as tears started to fill her eyes.

"I promise." He placed his bracelet on the box and it opened. Inside was a ball of fuzzy light. Val actually thought how beautiful it looked through her tears.

"Bye Zac." Val kissed him on the cheek. "I hope your next Guard is a little less problematic."

"There will never be another Guard as useless as you." He tried to smile.

The Warden leaned down and spoke to the ball of light. "Let this Guard be free. Let no one remember her but her loved ones and family. Take her home to her parents and allow her and her friends to be united once more." The ball jumped into the air spinning over their heads. "This is not what I would have wanted. You have been brave and we owe you a debt of gratitude, not this. The ball started to spin around her and Zac. She grabbed his hand sure he wouldn't be taken to Earth if she was no longer his Guard.

"You are sending me home to my Mum and Dad. And Sam will definitely be safe, you really promise?" She asked as the ball's speed now made it look like a solid line of light.

He nodded. "I promise. Be well and thank you." The Warden was now only visible in flashes and glimmers.

She held on to Zac's hand, but she could feel him pulling away from her as the light started to lift her off the ground. Everything she had done was wasted. Or was it? She had saved the planet, captured alien criminals and made some good friends - and lost some. Her body was whipped up and she knew she had left; she could no longer feel Zac's hand in hers. She just let the energy take her away. She wanted to cry, but the light lifted the tears from her face and drew them away. Just think: home, a Hawaiian burger, no more aliens, and no more Sam. Well, it wouldn't have been permitted anyway; he wasn't a Ranswar. She almost laughed at the irony, then she landed hard on the ground.

CHAPTER 25

Home Sweet?

Sam teleported into the Warden's office. "Where is she!" he demanded.

The Warden was sitting at his chair, head hung low. "She's gone," he replied.

"No! You can't have extracted her after all she did for us. Why? If it wasn't for her you would all be in cages still."

"Don't you think I know that, Sam?" He lifted his head.

"Where is she? Please tell me," Sam pleaded.

The Warden knew he could trust Sam. "She's safe. I sent her home, to forget and be forgotten and to finally be with her parents in peace." As he spoke a small light appeared in the room, still spinning but slowing it came to a halt in front of the Warden. He lifted the box and the light floated back in. Then he closed the lid once more.

"I need to find her." Sam's voice was full of pain.

"If you do, you will put her at risk and you know it."

He turned to leave. "You should know that she's been transformed."

"Are you sure?" The Warden stood up, looking and sounding shocked. "How do you know?"

Sam didn't look back. "I saw it happen, I saw the symbol."

The Warden groaned. "Then she's truly at risk now."

"I know." Sam walked away. He made his way down the corridor towards the main teleportation room where a group of Collectors were ushering the Nyterian's home. He knew who he wanted and who would help him.

She was there near her portal. He walked towards her and dropped to his knees at her feet. "I won't live without her." He sobbed.

The Collector placed her small hand on his face and wiped away a tear. "No we won't."

*

Val opened her eyes. She was lying on the ground and her back hurt no end; it hadn't been the easiest of journeys. But now everyone would be safe, no media circus, no Delta, no Excariot and no unwanted job. She lifted herself up onto her elbow. They could have at least dropped her off somewhere closer to home. There were leaves and foliage all over her. Where was she? She stood up, brushing herself down.

She was surprised to find she was still wearing her stupid uniform; she looked forward to putting this one away in her cupboard for Halloween. Then she could get out her favourite Spiderman t-shirt and jeans. Oh how she had missed her jeans, and better not even mention the Converse. Then Sam popped into her head; she pushed him out. He would be better off without her. She tried to rationalise that one for a whole thirty seconds and then gave up. She would miss him until the sun went out, but she had to be brave. This was for the others, and at least she hadn't been extracted. She knew Sam would make sure the people from the Space were safe.

She was wandering down a path when reality started to dawn on her. Surely the Warden hadn't dropped her off at Manningtree? It would take her hours to get home, and she didn't have any cash for a taxi. Then she heard a scream coming from the distance and her awareness kicked into overdrive. She moved though the bushes and forged forward. If her mum had arrived in a bush then she would freak out.

Val burst into the opening to find Jason, and Fran who had clearly screamed at a deadly leaf, Wendy, Belinda, and Zac. "What on Earth's going on? Why are you here?" She pointed at Zac who looked as shocked as them.

"I do not know. We were separated and I arrived here. What about you?" he asked Jason and the others.

"We were in the Space, then something like a ball of light surrounded us and that's the last I remember."

Wendy nodded in agreement, "Same here. I'm so pleased you're ok. I was so scared and Sam was going mad."

Fran interrupted. "There was a mouse, a real one." She pointed sheepishly at the ground, justifying her scream. "Can someone tell me where we are?" she asked.

"It seems we're back at Manningtree for some reason," Belinda observed.

"It turned out that I had to pay for my new husband's crimes. I was sentenced to extraction, but the Warden helped me to come home to my friends and family. Good news is I got the sack, and no one will remember Val Saunders off the TV. We just need to find my Mum and Dad now," Val replied.

"We left the truck here, so we have a ride at least," Jason reminded them, to everyone's pleasure.

A joyful voice from the distance called out to them. "Welcome!" A woman waved.

"Who's that?" Jason asked pointing over Val's shoulder.

She span towards the voice. "Oh no, this can't be happening," she said as the cloaked woman made her way towards them.

"What? What can't be happening, Val?" Fran asked, tension in her voice.

"That's my mother... Wyetta."

The End

Special acknowledgement goes to:

Miss Nichola Boulton, Deputy Head, Market Rasen C-of-E Primary School -

for your advice and support in everything I have asked of you.

Competition winners:

Jade Paul, Conner Janney, Matthew Eckersley, Jade Pennell

Laura Reynolds and Molly Bradley

Who together created the Novelia!

Adele Badiali, Michelle Potter, Kerry Lambie and Jason Davey,

for reading all of those pages.

Once again a massive thanks to Waterstones staff all over the country for your support.

Matt Timson for bringing Val to life.

Frankie Holah, for allowing me to take part in the amazing Sunshine Week.

Facebook, Youtube and Twitter fans, plus the 10,000 children I have met –

I thank you all for reading the books and listening to my talks.

Jackie, for your unwavering belief in me,

and Chris, as always, for the magic xx

Lightning Source UK Ltd.
Milton Keynes UK
UKOW050446050512

192084UK00001B/2/P